Marisa Mackle was born in Armagh, Northern Ireland. She is single and divides her time between Ireland and Spain. Her books *Mr Right for the Night* and *So long Mr Wrong!* were both international bestsellers. Marisa was an air hostess before becoming a full-time writer.

The Mile
High Guy

Marisa Mackle

DODDER

First published in Ireland and Great Britain
by Dodder Books Ltd, 2004.

Dodder Books Limited
9 Airfield Court
Dublin 4.

A CIP catalogue for this book is available from the
British Library.

ISBN 0954491319

Cover by Slick Fish.
Cover photo by Jim FitzPatick.
Typeset by Palimpsest Book Production Limited,
Polmont, Stirlingshire.

Printed and bound in Great Britain
by Cox and Wyman
Ltd, Reading, Berks.

Acknowledgements:

Thanks to:
God, for everything.
Sheila Collins for being the best grandmother in the world.
Eamonn and Daphne Mackle for being wonderful parents.
My sisters Tara and Naomi and my friends, Leah, Noelle, Catherine, Karen, Fiona, Niav, Rachel, Barbara and Angela, Leisa and especially Roxanne Parker.
Sine Quinn and Marjorie Parker for all their hard work and Alison O'Reilly for the PR.
Dave Lawlor, Sile McArdle, Stephen Rae, David Diebold and Frank Coughlan of the *Evening Herald* and Fionnuala McCarthy of *Woman's Way*.
Jim FitzPatrick for the cover photo and Tatianna for the coffee, for making me laugh and feeding my darling cats.
Fellow writers Tina Reilly, Suzanne Higgins, Catherine Barry, Maeve Binchy, Julie Parsons, Cathy Kelly, Claire Dowling, Shari Low, Deirdre Purcell,

Mary Stanley, Marita Conlon McKenna, Dawn Cairns, Jacinta McDevitt, Sarah Webb, Catherine Dunne, Martina Devlin, Miriam Lee, Collette Caddle, Gemma O' Connor, Niamh O' Connor, Annie Sparrow, Cauvery Madhaven, Melissa Hill, Anne-Marie O'Connor, Mary Hosty and Tracy Culleton for all the support and the laughs!

As always, enormous thanks to St Jude and St Anthony.

And to my readers, thanks so much for buying the books. I still nearly keel over in shock when I see anyone reading them! Keep in touch at

www.marisamackle.com

This book is dedicated to my incredible grandmother, Sheila Collins, with all my love.

Chapter One

From now on I stay single . . . or stick to Mr Average.

No more good-looking men.

No.

The plainer the better.

Plain men are always grateful.

At least I think they are.

I always used to date gorgeous men until I met Tim. And Tim is not exactly good-looking. He's what I would call 'pleasant'. At least my mother would describe him as pleasant. Which is probably why I'm neither in love nor in lust with him. And probably why I don't find him sexy. Because I don't want to have sex with somebody whom everybody approves of. There isn't anything exciting about that.

My friends think he's a dote. But a 'dote' will never drive me wild in bed, will he?

A dote will make me a nice cup of tea. And buy me tissues when I've the 'flu. And that's all very well. But what happens when I get better? Eh? And want someone to swing naked from the curtains. What happens then?

My mother loves men who talk about plants. That's why she likes Tim. He loves plants too, although thankfully he doesn't talk to them. Not as far as I'm aware anyway. And he also works in a bank. Maybe another reason why Mum likes him. She reckons he's stable. And he is. Stable and safe. But dare I say, also a bit dull.

My dad likes him too.

Well, I think he does.

Then again Dad doesn't say very much, so it's hard to know. My sister Ruth thinks Tim's just all right. And she's pretty vocal about that. But considering her own terrible taste in men, her opinion doesn't really count.

One friend tells me I'm lucky to have Tim. But she is the same girl who is thankful for any roof over her head, a job with a pension, and a caravan in Wexford where she goes on her annual summer holiday. Alone. So as you can see, although she's a very nice, very grateful kind of a girl, she doesn't exactly walk on the wild side. And to be honest she's the last person I'd seek relationship advice from.

You see, I want an exciting man. Someone who's not afraid to push out the boundaries of life. A free spirit. And someone who talks about . . . well things I wouldn't really like anybody else to hear. Especially not my mother.

Anyway I shouldn't be giving out about Tim. I have no real reason to. There is nothing *wrong* with him really. In fact I think he would be almost handsome if he lost his beer belly and got rid of the brown and green jumpers. But Tim is Tim. And at least he's shaved off that awful beard.

He did that for me.

It's the nicest thing anybody has ever done for me.

Anyway I'm older now.

And wiser.

I don't really care about looks these days. And people driving me wild in bed. It's so superficial and messy. And who cares about things like getting flowers every week anyway? As Tim always says, 'you should never trust a man who buys flowers. It means they're hiding something'. Hmm. Interesting that.

I went out with a guy from New York once.

A guy called Geoff.

A hotshot ad exec, who worked on Madison Avenue.

Who sent flowers every week.

And cheated on me probably twice a week.

I was a silly girl.

A twit really.

Always swapping my flights with the rest of the cabin crew.

Yes, I am a flight attendant. Or an air hostess, if you prefer. Or cabin crew member. As long as you don't call me 'trolley dolley' or a 'tart with a cart' I'm not fussy. Sorry, did I forget to tell you how I earned an oul' crust? Well, now you know. In fact I've probably served you before and you probably didn't even look up as I carefully poured you a glass of sparkling water and added two cubes of ice and a slice of lemon. But sure, you probably didn't think I was very friendly anyway. You probably thought my cheeriness was all put on. But actually I'm pretty friendly all the time. To most people. And unless you've ever crossed me, I probably think you're very nice too. Because I usually go around thinking everybody is really nice. Especially after a few drinks. Then I think everybody is absolutely wonderful and I want to give people a hug and get their email address so I can write to them when I'm sober.

Of course, when I'm sober the last thing I feel like doing is emailing people I casually spoke to at parties. In fact I'm always mortified the morning after a party when I open my bag and find people's email addresses and mobile numbers on the back of bus tickets and cigarette cartons.

And of course I never have the contact details of the guy I thought was the best looking man at the party. No. In fact I can never think where *he* got to at the end of the night. I usually vaguely remember telling some gorgeous man not to go anywhere without me. Which of course is exactly what he does . . . but never mind that . . . I'm learning all the time . . . putting it all down to experience . . .

The next time I spot the man of my dreams,

however, I won't be drinking (well, not that much anyway) and I'll look very well . . . and hopefully I'll be slimmer than I am now 'cos I'm on a kind of a diet. Then again, when am I ever not?

Now. Where was I?

Oh yes. New York and Geoff.

I walked to New York and back. With a teapot in my hand. Hundreds of times. I sang 'tea/coffee'. Thousands of times. And occasionally stopped drunks from opening the airplane doors.

All in the name of love.

Or stupidity really.

You see, one day I decided to surprise my man in New York.

Yes, it definitely was quite a 'surprise' for him. When I let myself into his apartment, a blonde was er . . . reclining on his bed.

Can you imagine the shock? Geoff said he could explain. I told him not to bother. But looking back, maybe I should have let him explain. Just to hear what on earth he could have come up with. I know he worked in advertising, but Jesus he'd need to have been a bloody genius to come with a plausible excuse for that.

But at the time I was too distraught to have to sit there listening to some cock 'n' bull story while the blonde got dressed. So I ran all the way to Fifth Avenue, with tears streaming down my cheeks. Actually no, I didn't run. I just walked very fast because that's what everybody does in New York.

And I was crying a little bit, maybe, but because I was wearing my fake Gucci sunglasses that I'd bought in Canal Street for ten dollars, I just looked kind of normal.

Of course it was my own fault. I'd let him treat me like a doormat. *I* was the one who had decided to do constant transatlantic flights just to see him twice a week. He'd never had to persuade me. He was Mary and I was his little lamb. Following him around everywhere. Pathetic, I know. But people often look back in horror at the way they let others treat them. I, unfortunately, am no exception to this miserable rule.

Of course Geoff never came to Ireland to visit me.

Not once.

Although he said that he'd love to visit one day.

His great-great-grandfather was from Co. Roscommon, and he once told me it would be kinda cool to look up some of the old relatives one day.

But he never got round to it.

Looking back, it's easy to see where I went wrong. I ran after him too much. Naturally I should have played it cool. But I didn't. I should have stuck to early morning flights. Instead of going to New York all the time. Chasing Geoff. But I hate doing the really early flights. They're so bloody unsociable. I'm talking 5.45 am check-ins. Sinfully early flights. To places like Frankfurt and Munich.

Also, those flights can be pretty boring. Because you work mainly with married women who need to be back before lunch to collect their kids. And you sit in the galley talking about washing machines and the rising cost of babysitting.

But the good thing about the early flights is that no alcohol is served, and the passengers are nearly always asleep. Sleeping passengers, like babies, are always my favourite.

The JIFFS are my least favourite passengers. They're the people who fly once a year to the sun and tend to start their holiday in the airport bar. On their way home they board in shorts, Hawaiian shirts and flip-flops, still on their holiday high. Landing in cold, wet Dublin however, reality hits as the plane door opens and they squeal 'Jaysus, it's fucking freezing.' Oh the JIFFS! Will they never learn? Still, overnight flights are not as bad as the morning flights, when you rise at, say, 4.00 am. It's awful getting up at that hour. Especially at the weekends. It's so horrible having breakfast when you know your friends are munching on curry chips somewhere after a brilliant night out.

On Sundays, for some reason, I always seem to get stuck on the red-eye flight to Brussels. Before you start wondering why anybody would want to fly to Brussels at that hour, let me explain that these passengers are usually transferring at Brussels to head off to more exotic locations. Just in case you thought for a moment that our politicians might be working overtime!

Now, I'm losing track again. Sorry, I've a tendency to do that. Okay. Oh yes. Back to average men. I read somewhere once that it's better if you go out with someone who likes you a little bit more than you like them. Good advice. My boyfriends have always liked me a little more. At the start anyway. You know how it is. People always make a huge effort at the beginning of a promising relationship, don't they?

But then, after a while, and after a few romantic dinners too many, I for one, get lazy, and start putting on weight. And then I don't really want to go out and meet people any more. Because none of my clothes fit. Then, for some reason, I seem to rekindle my love affair with the DVD player and the local chipper and forget to renew my gym membership.

Then I start phoning 'said' boyfriend on the mobile with requests. The usual ones:

'Would you ever pick me up a pack of fags, a magnum and a copy of *OK!* on your way over? Chinese? Oh, OK great. Order me the curry vegetables and egg fried rice. And a couple of spring rolls.'

After a while then I don't bother putting on make-up or anything, just open the door in my pyjamas, remind 'said' boyfriend not to trip over the cat on the way in, and give him a half-hearted kiss.

This is usually about a week or so before the 'I

don't think this is working out' speech. You'd think I'd have learnt my lesson by now. But do I ever see the speech coming? *Never*. Call me naïve but it's always a complete shock. You see I've always thought once you become 'comfortable' with a man, he should see you as you really are.

It makes sense doesn't it?

But apparently this isn't really the case at all.

So after a couple of weeks moping about, I retrieve the weighing scales, cut my hair, buy a new wardrobe, lock away the videos, join a night class and start all over again.

Then I'm out one night; dancing and back to my old fun self, surrounded by men, when I usually spot my ex staring over. And I ignore him because I've got over him now. And have spent so long convincing myself that I'm 'better off' that I actually believe it.

Of course said ex-boyfriend often approaches me, and tries to explain how he has made a 'terrible' mistake. But I'm having none of it. My grandmother always told me that 'nothing is deader than dead love' and I believe her. Who am I to raise the deceased?

So if you're an ex of mine reading this, now you know why I won't be taking you back.

Ever.

But it's a vicious circle. Once I'm looking okay again, more often than not, some new hunk appears on the scene proclaiming his undying love for me.

And of course, I'm strong. At first I am anyway. And tell him I'm happy being single, 'thank you very much.'

But then, unfortunately I succumb. It's very hard to ignore someone who is telling you you're the most beautiful girl in the world. Even if you know they're only trying to lure you into the sack . . . and then it's back to the humdrum of action films, Sunday walks, office parties and Friday nights making small talk with people (his colleagues) you don't know. And before you know it, the weight is back on, the roots are showing again and the 'It's not you, it's me' speech is on the tip of his tongue. Even though it *is* me. In their eyes anyway.

And suddenly I'm back on the market again.

Like a commodity without a price tag.

But I'm glad to report that for nearly three years now I've been single. Well single apart from the fact that I'm supposed to be going out with Tim. I am happy and sane. And although I do not enjoy the 'highs' of falling in love, at least I do not have to suffer the 'lows' of rejection, waiting for the phone to ring, the constant suspicion etc.

I enjoy my girlie nights out, sipping wine, listening to my friends moan on and on about their men. Of course, I know that even while they complain, they secretly think they're better off than I am. After all, I spend Friday and Saturday nights selling cheap tins of beer to gangs of drunken teenagers going to Ibiza. And I'm not getting any younger either. But

I don't mind. At least I don't have to suffer soirées with in-laws I can't stand (God my own folks are bad enough!) or fight about whose house I'm going to eat my Christmas dinner in.

At this very minute, while I'm filling you in on my love life, I am sitting in the back galley of an airbus 330 having my break. I'm on my way home from New York.

But a break on an airplane unfortunately is not like a break anywhere else so I'm not expecting much peace. Let me try to explain. If you worked in a shop, you would normally go out to have lunch. At least, what I mean is, you wouldn't have to sit at your checkout desk munching a sandwich. Likewise, if you worked in an office you could go out or visit the canteen. But on an aircraft you cannot simply pop outside. So you draw the little curtain and hope the passengers will respect your privacy for a little while. After all, the other crew members are covering your breaks.

But life is unfair and before long, some old guy whips back the curtain and throws a used napkin on my tray. I think he thinks he's doing me a favour. Like saving me from having to pick it up off the floor later on. Another woman barks that one of the toilets is overflowing. I politely ask her to inform another crew member as I am on my break. Unfortunately though, she has already succeeded in putting me off my cheese and pickle sandwich.

Soon my break is over. My insides feel funny. It's

weird having a meal at four in the morning. I never know whether to have dinner or breakfast so I usually have a little of both: an omelette and a bit of ice cream. Or crackers, cheese, cornflakes and chocolates.

Then I put on my lipstick, which makes me look like I'm smiling even when I'm not. I got it in Duane Reades last week for 99 cents. Worth every single cent.

The best thing about this lifestyle though is the shopping. Everything is discounted in the States. If it's not discounted you don't buy. Simple as that. I have tons of little knick-knacks. All bought because something was knocked off the original price.

Around 30 bottles of half full nail varnish removers currently lurk at the bottom of my wardrobe. And boxes and boxes of pills: which will keep me slim, my hair glowing, my feet clean, my sinus cleared, my teeth white, my mood fresh, my cycle regular and my conscience calm. Well you just never know when all these little gems will come in handy, do you?

After all, one day I'm not going to be flying any more and where will I be able to snap up bumper bottles of hand cream and anti-hair frizz serum then?

Anyway, enough muttering, it's time to get back out now and serve another hundred teas and coffees. Agh. I hate this bit because people are beginning to wake up and the sun is streaming through the window even though it's only about 5.30 am. The smell of feet is insufferable. Why do transatlantic passengers remove their shoes and worse – how can they *contemplate* walking into a tiny toilet cubicle in their bare feet? Everybody is now looking for iced water – especially those who have consumed alcohol solidly for the past few hours.

Some passengers, when they find out the drink is free, ram it down their throats like it is going out of fashion. But there's a price for everything. And the price for a hangover on board an aircraft is the dearest of all. Funny how these passengers are not as jovial now as they were getting on the plane back at JFK, huh?

Babies are waking up and beginning to scream. Kids are yelling, 'How much LONNNNGER Daddy?' Adults are searching for aspirin and sick bags and I cannot wait for this plane to land.

I'm going to try and sleep for a few hours when I get home. Hopefully I won't meet my parents on the short journey from the front door to my bedroom. Not that I've anything against my parents, but after a sleepless night, cooped up in a stuffy metal machine with a couple of hundred passengers, I hate meaningless questions like, 'How was New York?'

I'm now making tea like a zombie. Not concentrating, I pour half the boiling water on my hand. No harm though; water on airplanes is never really hot enough to do serious damage but I do notice my Sunshimmer fake tan is streaking badly.

Debbie is at my shoulder. Debbie and myself
trained together and get along pretty well. I haven't
seen much of her tonight though because she's been
up in first class serving the Champagne Charlies.

'Just think,' she whispers. 'We've the next three
days off. I can't wait.'

She disappears again and I stare after her, slightly
bemused.

It's funny the way the cabin crew always seem
so delighted with all the time off. I disagree with
that theory. I don't think we've any more time off
than anyone else. Because the first day after a
transatlantic trip all you do is sleep. And when you
do wake up, your body clock is all over the place
and you don't know whether it's morning or night.
That to me is torture, not time off.

Anyway I'm not complaining – of course I'm not
– after all what other job gives you a few days in
LA when the most stressful decision will be whether
you have a pedicure before or after lunch? And if
it ever gets too much I'll leave. Why stick at a job
you don't enjoy and spend your time moaning about
it? Life's not long enough for that.

We're at Shannon Airport now where some of
our passengers are disembarking. I'm standing at
the plane door, the icy Atlantic wind is biting my
tan coloured tights, and I'm forcing myself to smile.
My teeth are chattering and I'm trying to remember to say 'Good-bye' instead of 'Hello'. A few
passengers then embark; mainly businessmen going

to work in the capital. They look so clean and fresh and I feel dirty and grubby in comparison. I can't wait to go home and have a shower.

Debbie comes to the door to relieve me. She says I can go up to first class and read the morning papers. It's a tempting offer but I decline. I think if I sit down now I'll never want to get up again. And besides I don't read newspapers – they're too depressing. Full of job losses, rising property prices, and gory stories about freaks living somewhere in Middle America. But Debbie says I should take a break anyway so I do.

It's a pleasure walking into the first class cabin. It always amazes me how calm it is up here while a few seats away, behind the curtain, chaos prevails. A couple of passengers are reading, others are simply snoozing in their luxury reclining leather seats. One well-dressed woman, dripping in heavy gold, is quietly flicking through *Vogue* and another elderly man in a charcoal suit is staring out the window. There's nobody yelling for decaf tea, iced water, sick bags or landing cards. I relish the peace. It's nearly always a joy working in first class as these passengers – whose tickets cost thousands of euro – rarely ask for anything.

I make a strong black coffee. It's real coffee up in first class, not the instant rubbish served down the back. I still refuse to sit down because to get up again would be hell. I look at my watch and will the hands to move. A tap on my shoulder makes me jump.

I swing around. The tall man opposite apologises. He's smiling though. And he's cute. Very cute actually. So he's instantly forgiven.

'I didn't mean to frighten you but I was just wondering, if it's not too much trouble, I'd give anything for a cup of that coffee. It smells divine.'

He has the most endearing smile I've ever seen. The type of man I bet other women love. Imagine being married to someone like that. Waking up to that face every morning. He's like something from a Ralph Lauren commercial. I can't believe he's Irish.

'Sure.' I smile back but am so tired I'm wondering if I'm dreaming. This guy with his twinkling greenish grey eyes has to be the best-looking thing I've seen all night. In fact he's probably the best-looking man I've ever seen in my life. But then I remember that I don't like good-looking men any more so I'm going to stop admiring him. Anyway I'm genuinely pleased to have something to do.

When you're this tired it's best to stay busy and keep talking. I ask my first class passenger if he slept well. He answers that he must have been asleep since take-off.

Lucky sod.

As I'm waiting for the coffee to brew, I ask if he was in New York on business or pleasure.

'Business,' he answers with a smile, 'Kind of.'

I'd like to ask him what kind of business but I don't. People who interrogate others with 'What do you do for a living?' leave me somewhat cold and anyway we are not at a cocktail party here. He is my customer. Sort of.

The senior hostess arrives into the galley and peers at my handsome male passenger. He seems sorry that we've been interrupted. The coffee is made now anyway so it's not like I have any excuses left to talk to him. I head back to the door where Debbie is now shivering.

'Well?' she smiles quizzically.

'Well what?' I answer. I'm so whacked I badly need two matchsticks to keep my eyes open. 'You don't suppose the captain will be able to get away early? I'm dying of exhaustion and my contact lenses are clinging to my eyes.'

'Did you see anything nice in first class?' Debbie raises an eyebrow.

'Yeah,' I nod. 'I saw plenty of soft reclining seats with luxurious blankets and pillows that I'd give anything to rest my head on.'

Debbie is shaking her head. 'Do you mean to tell me you went up to first class and didn't see Adam Kirrane?'

'Adam who?'

'Good God girl, have you no life? Adam Kirrane is a God, an absolute God. He is the star of *DreamBoat*, that new American soap. Don't you watch it? I cannot *believe* you missed him.'

'I only have RTE and TV3 and that Irish language programme,' I tell her.

'He's the hottest thing in the US at the moment,' Debbie gushes.

'He's American?'

'Irish, but he works in America and is always in magazines and the papers.'

'What does he look like?'

'God, where do I start . . . er, tall . . . '

'With dark hair wearing a white shirt? The guy with the tan?'

'So you *did* see him.'

'I was talking to him,' I laugh as Debbie's eyes widen.

'You have GOT to be joking!'

'I'm serious,' I shrug, 'I just thought he was some guy.'

'I've been working non-stop in first class and Adam Kirrane has been fast asleep for most of the night with a blanket pulled around his head. I let you go up for five minutes and you have a whole conversation with him?'

I laugh. Debbie would get excited if Westlife were on board. She knows everything about everyone on television. I don't get it. She's the type of girl who, if the plane is delayed, pops into the toilet with her mobile phone to ring her mum. I used to think she was telling her mum not to bother collecting her. But no, she's telling her to video *Coronation Street*. Unbelievable!

Debbie goes back to her station but at this stage the wind is behind the plane so we're probably going to land early and I know there isn't a chance in hell she'll be able to talk to Adam now. Poor girl. I hope she doesn't ask for his autograph or something. I run down the back throwing uneaten muffins into a large plastic bag and collecting money in white envelopes from all the generous Irish people to put into another bag for UNICEF. Then I'm yanking headphones off people even though the film hasn't ended yet. But what can I do? The landing gears are going down and there are people still standing up, wondering is there time to go to the toilet. I can't believe it. They've had five or six hours to use the loo and they think NOW is a good time?

Looking out the window I can see Ireland's Eye in the ocean so we must be very close. Somebody grabs my skirt and wonders if the duty free bar is still open. I look at him like he's completely mad, then run for my seat and strap myself in.

Thump. We land. I am beaming at the passengers now and they are all saying what lovely girls we are. Americans love the Irish air hostesses. They say we're the nicest girls in the world, still smiling after all this time. I don't know about everybody else but the reason *I* am smiling is because it is nearly time to go home and I have managed to survive yet another transatlantic flight.

I stand at the plane door wishing everybody a

safe onward journey and I'm really glad I don't
have red hair or my name isn't Eileen O'Hara.
Americans love red hair and Irish names. But
because my name is Katie and I have dyed-blonde
hair, that makes me a lot less interesting in their
eyes.

Once the last passenger has got off, I do a quick
security check to make sure nobody has left
anything 'suspicious' on board. But what I'm really
doing is checking to see if anyone has left an interesting magazine like *Marie Claire, People* or *Vanity
Fair*. My luck is down. Somebody has left a copy
of *The Enquirer* but it is soaking wet. It looks like
tea but I don't like to take a chance so I leave it. I
also leave all the torn copies of *USA Today* that
are flung around the floor among the empty plastic teacups and filthy tissues. Now I'm ready to go
home.

I meet Debbie at the carousel and we wait for
our luggage. The reason we all carry such large suit-
cases is because we need them for all the 'essential'
shopping we do in the States. Debbie is staring at
me a bit weirdly. I smile back at her as if she just
looks like that all the time. She leans towards me
and whispers something into my ear. I think she
calls me a bitch so I don't answer. I'm sure I've
heard it wrong. I mean Debbie is a friend of mine
so why would she be calling me names? But when
she repeats herself, I turn to her in surprised shock.
She grabs my hand and slaps something into it.

It's a blue boarding pass, which means it's a first class boarding pass. I wonder if this is her idea of a little joke. I know it's been a long night but she hasn't been drinking so there's no excuse really. I take a closer look at the crumpled blue boarding pass. And I notice there's a mobile number scribbled on it. I then take a look at the printed name on the card. It reads Mr A Kirrane. And I freeze. Because suddenly I'm enlightened. And Debbie whispers in my ear again. 'He told me to give it to you,' she hisses. 'Bitch.'

Chapter Two

I'd like to tell you that TV stars give me their number all the time. And that it's no big deal. But you'd know I was lying. Because I'm really just an ordinary girl with a pretty ordinary life. Although I'm always kind of hoping this might change and that one day I will in fact have a *great* life.

But a TV star giving me his boarding pass with his phone number on it is definitely a first. I've been approached by a few nutcases on flights all right, but that's not exactly what you'd call flattering. Because you know those guys are just chancers who ask everybody out. However nobody remotely famous has ever approached me before, so this is really pretty exciting.

Although I'm slightly ashamed to admit it, as soon as I get home I quickly google Adam's name on the Internet. Just to be sure the guy is authentic. Then when I see all the hits he has on his fan site, well I'm more than a little impressed. Wow! I mean this guy isn't just big in the States, he's massive. There are a zillion sites dedicated to him.

And he has given his phone number to me. Imagine. Little old me. Katie, the air hostess.

I'm not going to ring him however. No. No *way*. Never. Well . . . not straight away anyway. Not for at least a day or two. Oh I know you probably think I'm mad, but I do have my pride and don't want him thinking he's some big star and I'm just another air head. He probably hands out his number ten times a day. Yes, indeed. It's probably a little game he plays to massage his massive ego. Well I'm not playing so I throw his number in the bin. Actually I don't. But I do put it in the drawer of my desk where I can't see it. Just so I won't be at all tempted.

I decide then to take off my uniform before going to bed. This might not sound like too much hard work but believe me after a transatlantic flight, anything that requires even the slightest bit of energy, such as removing a jacket, blouse, skirt, tights and a scarf, is sheer torture.

I shouldn't really tell you this in case you think I'm a slob, but I'd sometimes sleep in my uniform in school in order to have more time to sleep on in the morning. And now, sometimes, when I come in from work I just fall on the bed fully-clothed and conk out.

I'm just about to let my hair loose from the awful bun they make me wear at work, when my mum bursts through the door.

'Oh hello love, you look completely wrecked,'

she smiles while squinting at me. 'And your roots need to be done. They're dreadful.'

'Get the hell out of my room,' I say. 'And stop insulting me for once in your life.'

Well actually, I don't quite say that. No of course not. You see, although my gut instinct is to shout at her, I'm aware that I still live at home rent-free. Therefore although my mother has a habit of insulting me on a regular basis, I'm not really allowed to insult her back. Maybe you don't understand. Perhaps your mum is one of those mums you see on American TV and on gravy ads, standing at an oven wearing an apron and a huge smile. If she is, you're lucky. I often wish I'd a mum like that. One who'd told me I was a great kid. But unfortunately when God was giving out cheerful mums, I must have been at the very end of the queue. In fact I can't have been anywhere near the queue. I probably couldn't find it.

I don't pay rent but I do pay for my keep here by doing nearly all the ironing and constantly buying booze for my folks in the duty-free. My mother sometimes comes on trips away with me and stays in my hotel. She especially loves New York and stays in the other bed in my room. She has a happy knack of waking me at three in the morning by putting on the kettle. I hear it whistling in the corner of the room and every time I wake up with fright.

She always looks astonished to see me sitting up in bed and says, 'I didn't wake you, did, I? It's just that it's now eight in the morning back in Ireland.'

That's another thing about my mum. She has a very annoying habit of pointing out the time difference wherever we are. Even if we're only in France. Dad's convinced my mum is going to be flying somewhere one day, only to meet herself coming back.

Poor Dad. He's just such a quiet man. I often wonder how himself and Mum got together. I mean, she really does talk non-stop, only pausing every now and then to say, 'Isn't that right George?'

And Dad just nods. He nods more than Noddy ever did. But I think he does it just to keep the peace. He's all for an easy life. That's my opinion anyway. After all, he can't really agree with her on everything, can he? I mean doesn't he have opinions of his own? I often wonder what Mum sees in Dad and vice versa. I wonder how they ever got together. Isn't love odd?

Okay, I know you're probably thinking I've no right to complain. After all, my parents raised me and they're still kind of stuck with me, God love them. But my living arrangements are not entirely my choice. I would definitely move out immediately if there was any possible way I could get a mortgage. But the last time I went to a building society the smug man in the suit, sitting behind the desk, had a right old laugh at me when I showed him my payslip. I remember leaving his little office, positively fuming. I remember thinking that one day, when I'm worth a million euro (after the screen play

I'm writing is picked up by Hollywood) I'll never invest my money with that particular building society.

But in the meantime I haven't even written my script yet, never mind tried to sell it, and I know I'm never going to be very wealthy working as an air hostess. So what else can I do? Well, I could try and marry a rich man. But he'd need to be good-looking too.

Of course every other Irish woman is also looking for this particular guy, so my chances of winning the top prize are pretty slim, aren't they? And even if I did marry such a creature I doubt he'd let me just travel the world on his credit card. He'd probably want me to start having babies right away, and I'd just like to wait a few more years before even contemplating that.

And as I said, the other thing I want to do is write a screenplay. Seriously. Wouldn't it just be so fab to be a scriptwriter and live somewhere like LA where the sun shone all the time and people always told you to 'have a nice day' even if you just bought a cup of coffee?

Well, that's the big plan. I'm hoping to write some kind of Irish tragedy with lots of violence and alcohol abuse thrown in. I reckon the Americans will love that and I can get a hunk like Brad Pitt to star in it with any luck, and then I'll be kind of famous and very rich. That'll suit me because I don't want to be like mega-famous with people hassling me on the streets. And stalkers sending me threatening letters. But it would be nice to have a lot of money and not have to set my alarm at three in the morning any more.

A cool little laptop would be handy too so I could write in bed and take it around with me when I'm on holidays. Actually, I get really excited thinking about my new life as a scriptwriter. I must get cracking on the script soon. Oh you didn't really think I'd started it already, did you? Oh God no, I'm not that organised. I'm terrible for talking about things but never really getting around to it. I'm like Mum who is always talking about losing a half stone but never quite managing it.

I love talking about my script though. Just as much as Mum likes buying slimming magazines and clothes that she thinks she's going to fit into one day. Dad thinks we're as bad as each other. He says I'll never write a script and Mum will never lose weight. But I will, I will, I will. I just need to sort some things out. Like tidying my room properly instead of just shoving everything into the wardrobe. I really need to sort everything out. And put stuff in files and clear a proper space for writing. Maybe I'll ask Dad to build me a writing shed where I can have some peace. Then again, maybe not.

My head hits the pillow. I'm so exhausted now I'm afraid if I go to sleep I'll never wake up. Within minutes I'm dreaming of film deals, shopping in Beverly Hills and whizzing down Rodeo Drive in a convertible with a certain Mr Adam Kirrane.

Chapter Three

'It's Tim on the phone.' Mum's voice frightens the
life out of me. 'Will I tell him to call back?'

'Yes,' I mumble grumpily. I can't believe my
mother woke me just to tell me about something
as unimportant as the fact that Tim phoned. I feel
like I'm hungover now even though I haven't been
drinking and my mouth feels like the bottom of a
wheelie bin. Why did Tim phone my mum anyway?
He must have tried my mobile, which is switched
off of course. Surely to God he realises that when
my mobile is off, I'm fast asleep and obviously do
not wish to be disturbed.

But the main reason why I'm *particularly*
annoyed is, because in my dream, Adam was about
to kiss me and now I'll never know whether I let
him or not. Dammit. I close my eyes again and try
to get back into my dream but can't so I decide to
get up.

I sit up in bed and wonder what I will do with
myself today. The curtains are drawn so I've no
idea what the weather's like. In fact I don't have

the slightest clue what time it is either. Flying really does mess up your sleeping pattern. I don't even know whether it's day or night. Stretching myself like a cat in the sun, I contemplate my options. If it's still morning I think I'll go and have some break-fast but if it's evening, I'll have some lasagne and a nice glass of wine. Or a bottle. Why not? I could murder a good bottle of Chablis just now.

I pull back the bedclothes, so thrilled that I actu-ally have a couple of days off to look forward to. My uniform is flung on the floor so I'd better take it to the dry cleaner and get that boring task out of the way. Then maybe I'll have some time for me and get cracking on my script. Hmmm. Maybe not though. I'm too tired to have to think about some-thing as depressing as that just now.

I wander down to the kitchen to see if I can look up any more info on Adam on the computer. I kind of like him a bit more now because of my dream. And there's a lovely photo of him on his website. It's probably airbrushed but who am I to complain? I wonder has Dad fixed the printer so I can print Adam's mug out and stick it on my bedroom wall?

As luck would have it my Dad is glued to the PC looking up something trivial as usual. He's always going on about the Internet being so wonder-ful with all the information on it. Then again, the local library has always had lots of information in it and he never used to go there. How much infor-mation does one person need anyway? Oh well, I shouldn't criticise anybody for surfing the net. I mean it's not like I don't spend hours looking up my horoscope, and wait till I tell you about the time I joined that online dating agency . . . then again, maybe I'll wait until I know you a bit better.

'Hi Dad,' I call breezily.

'Hi Katie, good trip?'

He doesn't turn around.

'Great,' I tell his back.

I don't say anything else because I know he doesn't want to hear about bargains in New York or passengers who wreck my head or God forbid – the screenplay that I'm supposed to be writing. Dad just thinks that's the biggest joke going.

I grab a coffee and pop some bread in the toaster when I realise it's not even lunchtime yet. Then I sit down to read the *Irish Independent*. When I open it up my heart does a mini somersault. There, in the middle of page five, is a huge photo of Adam. And he seems to be smiling back at me with eyes that just seem to say 'got ya'. I just keep staring and say nothing, although part of me would love to show his picture to Dad and say 'Dad, see that man? He gave me his phone number and he's like, really famous in the States.'

But I've spent my whole life trying to earn Dad's respect so it wouldn't make any sense to start back-tracking now. Dad has about as much interest in celebs as I have in politics.

'Tim phoned,' Dad says suddenly.

Great. So Tim was on to my father too. Oh dear
he really is like part of the family now. Maybe he
should just move in permanently with us. After all
it'd save him a small fortune in telephone bills. I
sip my coffee and wonder why I'm so reluctant to
ring Tim. After all we've been together almost three
years. On and off. More off than on to be perfectly
honest.

When I first met Tim he was really rather attractive, although he isn't any more. Not really,
although, as I said before, shaving off the beard
was a major step in the right direction.

I do find though that men are often more attractive when they're single and taking care of themselves. But then when they get a girlfriend they feel
they can give up exercising. Just like that. And start
ordering take-aways the whole time. Mind you, if
Tim were going out with a girl who could cook
(unlike me) well then maybe he wouldn't have put
on so much weight recently. So it's partly my fault.

I, like most women I know, have a love-hate relationship with the weighing scales. You see, my
weight tends to go up and down. Up more than
down really. And I'm constantly on some kind of
diet. I've tried them all. Even the cabbage soup diet,
which I really didn't enjoy and didn't lose any
weight on either. I wouldn't really recommend it.
Calorie counting is a pain too. There's nothing more
tedious than writing down every single morsel that
passes your lips. By the time evening comes around

you realise you've written so much that you might as well keep eating.

Some people swear by the Atkins diet but since I'm a veggie that's a no-go area for me. Unless I want to stuff myself with cheese, eggs and nothing else all day. Could you imagine it? Diets don't work anyway. It's a well-known fact. Yeah, you can lose a half a stone in a week but you'll put it all on the following week. Much the same way as you can cram for an exam but remember nothing once you leave the exam hall. The best diet is the no-food diet I find. It genuinely works. But it's very boring and doctors definitely don't recommend it.

However it does make sense, doesn't it? The no-food diet. Think about it. If you don't eat, you simply don't put on weight. Ask any successful model who'll probably agree. As my dad always points out, there are no fat people in Ethiopia so you can't exactly go around blaming genes, metabolism, big bones or whatever.

The main reason I remain trim enough, is that I know I have to do the safety demonstration every day with at least fifty passengers staring at my tummy as I raise my arms to put on my life jacket.

There's nothing like a live daily audience to put you off stuffing your face from morning to night. Anyway I'm not dieting today, I tell myself as I smother a piece of toast in butter.

I sip my coffee and stare at Adam's photo again. As I'm doing so, I just know that I'm going to phone him. I won't have the strength not to. My willpower isn't strong enough. Well maybe I won't quite phone him but I'll text him anyway. Aren't texts just the best invention? Because of them, you could go through life speaking to almost nobody at all. Wouldn't it be great if you could just get passengers to text you when they wanted something? Instead of pressing that annoying call bell all the time?

Incidentally did you know when passengers in the main cabin press the call bell, the annoying BLING cannot be heard up in first class? Oh the joy of being able to fly in complete luxury! If I had the money I would only ever fly first class. I bet 'my Adam' has never known the horrors of flying all the way to LA with some annoying little brat kicking his chair for over eleven hours!

One day I hope I'm rich and famous and that I'll be able to sit in first class while some handsome steward pours me coffee. Or something stronger. Maybe when I write my script and Hollywood comes knocking on my door, my life will change dramatically.

Hopefully the dream will work out. I'm planning on writing something about the Great Irish Famine so that it'll appeal to the Americans. Maybe I'll become the female version of Frank McCourt and people all over the world will know my name. Wouldn't that be cool?

I'm imagining it now. I'm in Sak's Fifth Avenue,

carrying an armful of designer gear to the desk. I plonk down all the clothes at the cash register, and I'm so rich I haven't even bothered checking the price tags. The assistant is looking at me curiously because she thinks my face is very familiar but still she isn't one hundred per cent sure. I hand over my credit card and she glances at the name nervously. Then she recognises my name and her face breaks into an excited smile. 'Oh my God,' she screeches, as nearby shoppers stop in their tracks wondering what all the fuss is about. 'It *is* you. I knew it. I just love all your films. Listen, could I have your autograph? Wait, could I possibly get my photo taken with . . . ?'

'Katie, the phone's ringing.' The sound of Dad's voice startles me. How could he? He's just killed my daydream. Reluctantly I get up.

'Hello?' I answer.

'Hello baby.'

Oh no. It's Tim. And he's calling me baby again even though I've asked him to stop. A zillion times. But Tim's memory isn't the best.

'Hi,' I mutter unenthusiastically.

'What are you up to?' he asks. 'Baby.'

'Nothing. And you?'

'Not much. I'm in work. Listen what are we doing tonight?'

Do we *have* to do something?

'Don't mind. You decide.'

'No. *You* decide.'

'I'm easy.'

'I'm easy too.'

Only I'm not really. I'm never easy where Tim is concerned. Because Tim's suggestions are never that great. He always says things like 'I'll call over and then we'll take it from there'. But we never do take it from there. Because when he calls over, Mum puts on the kettle and basically we do nothing. Because Mum always ropes him into a conversation about old Irish castles, or plants, or George Bush or traffic or whatever.

Please don't think I'm a moany old cow. I might sound like one but come on – surely you've gone out with someone like Tim too. A well-meaning chap with good intentions that never really lead to anything.

'How was New York?' he asks.

See? I told you he was just like Mum. If he'd met her when she'd been my age, they'd be married by now. Or at least engaged. They'd have been perfect for each other. Instead she married my dad whom she constantly refers to as 'Oh silent one'. Not that he takes a blind bit of notice though.

Eventually we agree to go and see some action film out in Liffey Valley Shopping Centre. It's what we usually do really. Tim doesn't like pubbing or clubbing. He doesn't like pubs because he says they're just full of drunks talking shite. And he hates clubs because the music is too loud and they make him feel old.

We used to get invited to a lot of dinner parties, but after a while I refused to go because people kept asking us when we were getting married. They seemed to think that was funny. At first I used to smile shyly but now I just can't be bothered. Anyway, the other reason why I hate dinner parties is because I don't cook very well, so we always have to invite couples to restaurants as a return. And Tim complains that it costs him an arm and a leg. It's not that he's mean or anything but he is saving for a house. And you can't save for a house in Dublin *and* take random couples for expensive meals every second weekend. Especially the type of couples who go mad on the drink when someone else is paying. And unfortunately for Tim, most of our friends are that type.

If I were in love, I'd start getting ready now for our big, ahem, night out. But because I'm not, I just hang around the kitchen eating more buttered toast out of boredom and wait for Dad to get off the computer so that I can look up more info on Adam. Oh God, I know I said earlier that I wasn't going to ring him or anything, but you really should see him!

I can't *not* contact a guy who looks as divine as Adam Kirrane. I'd only torture myself for the rest of my life wondering what might have been.

How can I describe Adam to you? Well, he's a bit like Ben Affleck with a smaller jaw. And he's probably more down to earth. And he hasn't gone out with J-Lo as far as I know. Hmm. I wonder whom he has dated. I mean, I wonder has he dated anybody famous? How could I compete with somebody famous?

I bet he has a string of girls after him. Of course he has. In fact I bet the only reason he gave me his number is because he's sick of being accosted by groupies. Well, at least I'm not like that. I don't care who he is. I'd like him even if he was the gardener. Yes, really. Even if he hadn't a bean I'd probably still find him very attractive.

And if you believe that, you'll believe anything!

Chapter Four

We're sitting in the cinema and I wish they'd turn on the lights so I could see which Revels I'm eating. My favourites are the orange ones but I keep biting into the coffee ones by mistake and it's so annoying. The film is unbelievably boring but I can't say anything because Tim would take it as a personal insult. As if he personally wrote the script. Or starred in the film or something. He's a bit funny like that.

There doesn't seem to be a storyline or anything. Just lots of special effects and martial arts stunts. Basically it's the type of film most girls wouldn't go to see in a fit.

I'm really tired now and my contact lenses are irritating me. I close my eyes hoping that it will make them less dry. And soon I'm dreaming. Yes, I'm dreaming I'm at the premiere of a film. It must be in LA because it's warm and balmy and all the women are wearing off-the-shoulder dresses and they're all tanned and very thin. I myself am wearing a lovely silky red Versace dress that I've been given for free and I'm gliding down the red carpet, my arm linked to Adam's. I spot Halle Berry, Kate Hudson and Tom Hanks and I give them a courtesy nod, but I don't have time to speak as the photographers are all calling out my name. I'm not sure why I'm this famous but I give them all a smile because basically I know they're just trying to make a living and I would never punch a photographer or stick up my middle finger. Or grab their camera and smash it on the ground. No. I would never do anything like that. Not like some celebrities.

'You're not eating all those Revels, are you?' an eager autograph-hunter asks as he thrusts a pen in my hand.

'Excuse me?'

'Here, come on, don't eat all those Revels or you'll get fat, hahaha.'

I'm about to call security, as I don't much like this guy's attitude.

'Wake up. God Katie, I can't believe you've fallen asleep again.'

It's not a fan after all. It's Tim.

'Sorry,' I mumble. I'm so tired. I really am. Not just because I was up all last night serving passengers. No. I'm tired of my life. And Tim. And my parents. Suddenly I realise I'm tired of just plodding along without much purpose in life. Tired of flying to places and coming home again and then doing the same thing the next day all over again. Wouldn't it be great to have some excitement in my life? Wouldn't it be nice to have fun? For once? I swiftly make up my mind that as soon as I get home I'm going to ring Adam Kirrane. Maybe he'll end up breaking my heart but I'm prepared to take that chance. At least it's better than dying of boredom!

'That was brilliant,' Tim says as we queue to leave the cinema complex. 'Absolutely class.'

I just nod in agreement because, as I said earlier, Tim takes it personally if you don't like the films he chooses.

'Do you want to go for something to eat?' he asks me.

I shake my head.

Tim wants something to eat though. He says he's famished even though he demolished half my packet of Revels earlier. We head for Eddie Rockets. His choice, not mine. I'm not a bit hungry. As we sit by the window I stare at the jukebox in the corner and wonder what my life would be like if I was the girlfriend of a really famous guy. A guy like Adam. Wouldn't it be a dream? For a start, I know if I was with Adam we wouldn't be sitting here eating garlic mushrooms and chips. No. I'd probably be in The Ivy over in London. Or Browne's in Dublin. Or anywhere but here.

Back in the car, Tim asks if I want to stay the night in his place. To be honest that's the last thing I feel like doing. I tell him I'm too wrecked but agree to meet him again tomorrow. He leans over and gives me a kiss. His breath reeks of garlic. I wonder whether I should just break up with him now and save us both a lot of heartache in the long run. But I'm much too much of a coward to suggest breaking up so I smile, get out of the car and bid him goodnight.

I'm in my bedroom about two minutes when I have my mobile phone out and I'm punching the digits of Adam's number. My heart is racing but I don't care. This is what I want. I'm craving excitement. I'm thinking although I'm a big girl now, I still feel like fourteen. And I'm thinking how much easier it is now that people have mobiles.

Remember when you'd ring some guy and their mother would answer the phone with a chilly 'Who is this?'

God, that was a bit horrible, wasn't it?

Thankfully I'm not a teenager anymore.

'Hello?'

Yikes, that was quick. I was kind of hoping Adam would have the phone switched off so I could just leave a message. Don't you just hate when people answer their phones?

'Adam?'

'Yep? Who's this?'

His voice is deep and sexy. No wonder millions of women turn on the telly each week to hear his voice.

'It's Katie.'

I'm not going to tell him where I work. Or how he might know me. No. I'm not going to make it easy for him. For all I know he asks several women out every week. Or every day.

I wait for him to say something and try to convince myself I'm not at all nervous. The palm of my hand feels clammy.

'Katie, the air hostess,' he says and I can visualise him smiling. He sounds like he's smiling anyway and suddenly I'm glad I met him in first class on a plane and not in some nightclub locked out of my head.

'That's right.' I'm smiling back but he doesn't know that of course.

'I wasn't sure I'd hear from you,' he says but his voice is warm.

'Why's that?'

'Oh, I'd say I'm not the first passenger to ask you out.' He laughs.

I laugh too.

He's not *completely* wrong of course. I once had a stunningly beautiful Brazilian man leave his phone number on his tray for me. He was going to be in Dublin for one night. But one night with a Brazilian wasn't exactly what I was looking for so I declined his invitation for dinner. And whatever else he had in mind.

Then, there was that other time, when four very drunk teenage guys on their way to Gran Canaria, kept asking for more beer. When I made it clear I didn't want to serve them any more, one of them told me I was by far the most beautiful air hostess on the flight and asked if he could go out with me sometime.

I was flattered because he was a bit of a cutie, albeit a drunken cutie. But the flattery vanished as soon as I remembered I was the only air hostess on the flight; the other three crew members being stewards.

'There's been a few but nobody like you,' I answer truthfully.

'So, do you want to meet up?' Adam asks as my heart does a quick somersault.

I pause as if I'm thinking about it and then speak. 'Sure,' I try to sound as normal as possible. As if TV stars ask me out all the time. 'Er . . . when?'

'Tonight?'

'Tonight?' I look at my watch. It's a quarter to twelve. Time for bed. He's a bit cheeky now, isn't it? Asking me out at such little notice. Does he think I'm desperate?

'I'm about to go to bed,' I tell him.

'Sounds promising.'

'I can meet you another time,' I offer, simply ignoring his somewhat suggestive remark. If he thinks I'm the type of girl to go chasing strange men in the middle of the night, he has another thing coming.

'I can't meet you tomorrow night because I'm going to an award ceremony in London,' Adam explains.

Well, that's too bad then, I think. I notice he doesn't offer to whisk me over and be his guest for the night. But maybe I'm jumping the gun too much.

'I'm back Friday,' he says.

'That's a pity. I'm going to Boston on Friday.' I tell him. 'Sorry.'

'What are you doing there?'

'I work as an air hostess, remember?

'How long will you be in Boston?'

'Just a night. Hey, how about I write up my entire timetable and fax it to you?' I laugh.

'Where are you staying?'

'In the Back Bay area, just off Newbury Street.'

'I know it well. I love that area. I might come and visit you.'

'You're joking.'

'I never joke. I don't have a sense of humour,' he laughs.

'Well come if you want,' I say, not taking him at all seriously. After all, I've been seeing Tim for years and he's never once managed to accompany me on any of my trips so I'm hardly expecting someone I barely know to follow me out. Especially someone as famous as Adam Kirrane. But I decide to humour him anyway and give him the name of my hotel.

'I'll be in touch, Gorgeous,' he says.

'Right so, thanks for ringing,' I say before I remember it was *me* who rang *him*.

'No probs,' he says and cuts off.

I look in the mirror, my phone still in my hand. I look the same as ever. I don't look like I've just been speaking on the phone to a big TV star.

Nobody in the whole world knows I've just had a conversation with Adam Kirrane. It's a nice feeling. And it's my secret.

Chapter Five

'Katie. I didn't wake you, did I?'

'Well you *did* actually Debbie, what time is it?'

'Time you were up. Did you ring your man?'

'What man?'

'Get away out of that? Adam Kirrane. Did you ring him?'

'No.' I lie. And I feel terrible for lying to somebody as nice as Debbie but I really don't want anyone to know about last night's phone call. For a number of reasons. You see if I end up dating a high profile guy like Adam and it doesn't work out, people will forever be asking why. And if it does work out, I don't want Adam to think I'm gossiping about him at work. So I need to be careful. Anyway, as far as I know, I might never speak to Adam again. After all, I refused to go out with him last night. And I know he says he's going to follow me to Boston but sure, that'll be the day.

'Do you want to go into town?'

'I don't mind. I've no money but what's new? If I hang around the house all day I'll just end up watching TV and eating though, so I might as well.'

'I'll meet you outside The Bailey at one so.'

'Er Debbie . . . do you mind if I meet you some-where else?'

The thought of standing outside The Bailey on my own fills me with dread. It's where all the beau-tiful and wannabe beautiful people hang out.

'Okay. Outside Brown Thomas?'

'How about just inside Brown Thomas? The menswear department.'

'Sure. See you then.'

I think about taking the car into town but then decide against it. The traffic in Dublin is appalling now. So I decide to get the bus instead. At least, this way, I won't have to drive round and round Stephen's Green looking for a car parking space when I get into town.

I meet Debbie in Brown Thomas. When I spot her she's picking up ties pretending to look at them. She's visibly relieved to see me. After all, there's only so much interest you can pretend to have in ties when you're manless.

'My bus was late,' I give her a hug.

'Your bus is always late,' she laughs. 'You should really get another one.'

'Haha. Anyway I'm here now, so are we going for lunch or what?' I ask.

'Sure, but let's go upstairs first and have a look at some clothes we can't afford. Just to put us in a really good mood.'

We head upstairs for a look. After a while though, I'm beginning to feel slightly depressed. How many charter flights to Athens would I have to do before I could afford a single Armani suit? I spot a few immaculately dressed women wandering about, pausing to hold various garments against themselves in the mirror. I wonder if they have fabulously wealthy husbands. Or are they mistresses even? Or did they simply win the lottery? I know they're not high-powered executives because if they were, they'd be at work, wouldn't they?

I love speculating about other people's lives. My imagination goes into overdrive as I think about the exciting lives other people must lead. I sometimes look at little girls' faces on flights and they look back at me, probably thinking I must have the best job in the world. And I look at other people in office jobs with every weekend off and think how nice their lives must be. Sometimes I just wonder what constitutes a *really* exciting life. Maybe we're all just lost souls looking for something that simply doesn't exist?

Debbie is looking a bit bored at this stage. She's fingering the racks of clothes but not really paying close attention. She has a glazed look in her eye. I know that look. 'Come on,' she says. 'Let's go and get ourselves a drink.'

Alarm bells sound loudly. If she thinks I'm falling for that, she has another thing coming. I've known Debbie for the last few years and I have never ever known her to go for just the one drink.

'Let's get something to eat first,' I suggest. I've a strong feeling I need to line my stomach.

We eat in a salad bar in The Powerscourt Centre before heading downstairs to Ba Mizu where we order two quarter-bottles of wine. The glasses they give us are so huge. Mmm. I wonder why they do that?

Anyway I like this bar, despite the large glasses and its dark interior. It's dark in a pleasant way. I like dark bars, especially late at night, when the old make-up starts to wear off and my eyes become a bit bloodshot.

The wine tastes good. Almost too good. There's something very satisfying about sitting in a bar drinking wine in the middle of the day while the rest of the world is at work. It's a bit like mitching school, isn't it? I also love drinking on planes. Because it's a bit like drinking at the office. Of course I don't drink while I'm at work. No. Well, *obviously* not. Even though that's the very time I could *do* with a stiff drink. But when I'm going on holidays I love sipping wine while somebody else serves the passengers. I don't want to drink too much now though. I'm afraid if I do, I'll end up telling Debbie about my phone call to Adam. Alcohol's desperate like that, isn't it? One drink too many and all innermost thoughts are anybody's.

Don't you just hate revealing secrets under the influence of alcohol? It's easy to do at the time but it's horrible waking up and remembering that you've said lots of things you shouldn't have. And I especially don't like not remembering how I got home, or whom I snogged. And I hate finding unfamiliar phone numbers in my bag without knowing how the hell they got there. Of course the worst thing is remembering half way through the day that the person I snogged is someone that I work with. Someone I don't even like. Or somebody with a girlfriend.

'Would you ever get that into you?' Debbie urges. She's almost finished her glass of wine and I've just started sipping mine.

I know any minute she's going to nod at my glass and go, 'Same again?' and I'm afraid I'm not going to have the willpower to say no. I sip slowly but that doesn't stop her from ordering two more quarter bottles. She never even asked if I wanted another drink. I'm embarrassed. After all, it's my round. But she says I can buy the next two. *The next two?* Oh, God, I just *knew* this was going to happen.

After Ba Mizu we head to Davy Byrne's. My choice. I really like the atmosphere there and there's always a few decent-looking men hanging around. We grab a seat down the back and order another two glasses of wine.

'We should really drink two glasses of water as well to limit the damage,' I suggest.

'Yes we should,' Debbie agrees but then we forget all about the water and head off to Cocoon for another few. In Cocoon, they show fashion videos all day on large screens. Debbie and I sit back and stare at various male models modelling tight briefs and try not to laugh.

I'm pretty merry now and basically laughing at anything. I'm kind of tempted to tell Debbie about Adam but luckily I don't. She confides in me that she slept with one of the married pilots on her last overnight in Kerry and I am *so* shocked. She makes me swear not to tell anyone though.

Then I feel really bad because she has told me something so personal and I'm not even prepared to tell her about a silly phone call to Adam. A phone call that might or might not lead to anything.

She asks me if I still have Adam's number and I tell her I have. She tells me she thinks he is the most beautiful man in the world and would kill to go out with him.

'Suppose he is just after one thing though?' I ask her.

'He could have it,' she gives a dirty laugh. 'Over and over again.'

'Do you not think a man like that would be impossible to trust though?'

'*All* men are impossible to trust.' Debbie is adamant about that and shakes her head as if to confirm her point.

At this stage I feel people looking over at us and I'm conscious that we're probably being very loud, so I suggest we try somewhere else. We step outside and I'm immediately struck by how bright it is. The

sun is dazzling and we've probably had too much
to drink. I hope we don't meet anyone we know.
After all, it's not Christmas or either of our birth-
days. And as far as I know, Ireland hasn't won a
match today, so we're going to look pretty sad stum-
bling around Grafton Street in this state. I suggest
we get a taxi back to Debbie's flat where we can
get something to eat and open another bottle of
wine. She seems to think that's a good idea and
suggests ringing a few more people so they can join
us. I'm not so sure about that last part.

We stumble out of the taxi at Debbie's Rathmines
flat where her flatmate looks slightly bemused to
see us in such high spirits. Her name is Fiona and
she works as a customer service agent in town and
thinks our job is really glamorous even though
we've already told her all the horror airline stories.

But I suppose if I was stuck in an office all day
dealing with customer complaints, I'd think we were
lucky too. Isn't it amazing though that some people
still think we spend our lives on beaches and shops
and stuff?

Debbie puts on Eminem's latest CD. She turns
up the music and then draws the curtains. It's raining outside and suddenly I'm glad we came home
when we did. Debbie finds a disco ball and places
it in the middle of the floor so we can dance around
it.

Fiona declines to join us on our makeshift dance
floor. She also suggests turning down the music, as

she doesn't want the neighbours complaining yet again. She insists she doesn't want to miss her evening PR class, even though Debbie tries to persuade her not to go. But Fiona has been here and done that a few times now and still thinks she should go to her PR class. She disappears with her umbrella into the dark miserable evening and the two of us are left alone bopping to Eminem.

'She's not as much fun as she used to be,' Debbie laments once Fiona has disappeared down the front steps. 'She's always working or studying. But there's more to life.'

'Mmm.'

'What's the point in life if you don't have fun?'

'Well I suppose it *is* only Wednesday,' I point out.

'Is it really?'

'Yep.'

'I still think there's more to life though. Will we open a bottle of wine?'

'Why not? And let's turn off Eminem. He's always in a bad mood.'

Debbie takes Eminem out of the CD player and sticks on Christina Aguilera.

After a few songs I need to go to the bathroom. Clumsily I try to find the bathroom and open the hot press door instead. I must be mad. What on earth am I doing drinking midweek when I've a million things to do? I should really be writing my script. After all, nobody else is ever going to write it for me. However I'm only young once, I reason with myself, eventually finding the right door.

When I come back into the kitchen Debbie is on the phone telling someone to fuck off. I actually think it's quite funny until I realise it's my phone. Then horror sets in rapidly.

'What are you doing?' I shriek.

'Don't worry, it was just a crank call,' Debbie laughs. 'The guy said his name was Adam Kirrane. Yeah *right*. Funny guy. How many people did you tell about him Katie?'

I'm shocked. I can't believe Adam just rang and Debbie told him to fuck off. How could she *do* that to me?

'How do you know it wasn't Adam himself?' I splutter.

Debbie nearly cracks up laughing. 'How do I know haha? Sure you told me yourself you didn't ring him so how on earth would he have your mobile number? It *must* have been Tim. Hang on; Tim's not that funny, is he? Maybe it *was* someone else.'

I feel nauseous. I cannot believe that Adam is at some big award ceremony in London tonight and that he actually took time out of his busy schedule to ring me, and was insulted by my best friend.

Debbie is still chuckling. She thinks it's hysterical that someone has rung pretending to be Adam Kirrane. She thinks it might be a guy called Shane, who is Tim's friend and is quite good-looking and kind of funny. I know Debbie's kind of fancied him

for a while. My phone rings again. This time it's
not Adam, it's Tim.

'Hello,' I say.

'Where are you?'

'Debbie's.'

'What are you doing there?'

'Just hanging out.'

'You drinking?'

'I've just had a glass of wine.'

He doesn't believe I've had just one glass but I
don't care. He wants to come over. I don't think
this is a good idea. Debbie thinks this is a great
idea however. She grabs my phone and tells him to
come over and bring his friend Shane.

I groan. I *know* this isn't a good idea but of
course Tim agrees to come over straight away. He
hates when I'm out drinking without him. I know
he's just coming over to take me home. And spoil
our little party.

The two lads arrive about an hour later and
Debbie opens another bottle of wine. Tim isn't cross
with me for some strange reason. Maybe he knows
I'm going off him and therefore is being extra atten-
tive. Men are funny like that. They often start loving
you the very minute you decide to stop loving them.

Shane seems delighted with the attention Debbie
is lavishing on him. She's making it really obvious
she fancies him and they've already started dancing. I don't get it. I mean I know she's tipsy but
he's supposed to be sober! Debbie gets away with

throwing herself at men. She just does it so effort-lessly. If I do it, they always run a mile. It's so unfair!

Suddenly I hear Shane denying he ever rang pretending he was Adam Kirrane. Tim wonders what the fuss is all about. I shoot Debbie a warning look and thankfully she shuts up. The *last* thing I want is for Tim to find out about Adam.

After a while Tim reckons we should go home. I don't want to leave though. I've just got going. I feel like I'm a child at a birthday party and my mother is the first parent to arrive to take me home. I point this out but Tim suggests we should leave Debbie and Shane alone.

Reluctantly I agree, although I'm pretty annoyed about Tim dictating to me. However I do realise that my head will thank me for not drinking any more, so I say goodbye to Debbie. Tim was right – she seems clearly delighted to see the back of me. Some friend, huh?

As soon as the cold air hits me I realise how drunk I am. It's not a nice feeling. Thank God, tomorrow's a day off. I'll be able to have a nice lie-in. Now I'm sitting in the passenger seat. The car window is open slightly and Tim is caressing my thigh. I'm kind of glad I'm on my way home. At least it has saved me getting a taxi later. Anyway if Tim hadn't arrived with Shane, Debbie and I probably would have hit Leeson Street or something. Perish the thought . . .

Tim parks outside my house and leans over to snog me. I kiss him back passionately because I'm drunk. But in the middle of the kiss I think of Adam and immediately feel ashamed of myself. Because I would hate someone to kiss me while fantasizing about someone else.

'I love you,' Tim tells me when we stop kissing.

'I love you too,' I say back. Just out of habit really. I don't even really realise when I'm saying it.

It takes an age to get my key in the door. Tim waits outside patiently to see I get in safely. Once inside I take the stairs as quickly as I can to avoid having a conversation with my parents. I hear the news on in the sitting room and can't believe it's only nine o'clock. Because we've been drinking all day, it feels like the middle of the night. In my room, I take out my mobile. I know I really shouldn't ring Adam in the state I'm in but I do anyway. I just don't want him to think I'm the type of girl who tells people to fuck off. I ring but don't get through. His phone is switched off. I kick off my shoes and lie down on the bed. I just want a few minutes to relax before removing all my make-up and clothes. Then I'll try ringing him again.

Within five minutes I'm asleep.

With the light still on.

Chapter Six

Dad is playing the piano.

He's playing *The Blue Danube* and has been playing it now for the last six months.

His version is still awful.

Dad retired six months ago. And took up the piano the next day. We've been paying the price ever since. My father, bless him, had all these great plans. He was going to take up hill-walking and cooking, gardening and fishing. And the piano of course. The hill-walking dream ended after his first excursion. The poor man got lost in the Dublin mountains and they had to send out the rescue service to look for him. He was on TV and everything afterwards, but the experience put him off for life.

Dreams of being a whiz in the kitchen were shattered when he tried to make a dessert called an upside-down cake from an old cookbook. The photo on the cookbook was lovely but Dad's version looked nothing like the photo and we all got sick after eating it. Even the dog did. He is no longer my dad's most loyal friend.

When Dad took up fishing he spent a fortune on state-of-the-art equipment and bought brightly coloured baits to lure the fish. Then he took himself off to Connemara to fish with another retired gentleman. Unfortunately though, a great big fish took his expensive, gaudy-looking bait and swam away with it.

I felt sorry for him at the time. All those years when Dad worked in his insurance company, he dreamed of doing fun things one day. Then when he got the time, he still couldn't do any of them. Poor Dad. At least he's still sticking at the piano. Even though it's pretty torturous for the rest of us.

I get out of bed and head down to the kitchen. Dad has his head bent over the piano and is banging it with just two fingers. To annoy him I start singing *The Blue Danube* off-key. I'm sure Strauss is turning in his grave.

'There's an ad in the *Evening Herald* for the flat,' Dad tells me. 'I have to go out and get new net curtains for it, so I was wondering if you wouldn't mind answering the phone. You know what to say, don't you? The flat's on view from six to seven this evening.'

I groan. If there's one thing I absolutely hate doing, it's answering calls from people enquiring about my parents' flat. The ad says 'suit one business person' but people don't tend to read properly. So you get all kinds of enquiries from cohabiting couples, misfit families, and men with

mistresses etc. Not to mention a few ladies, ahem,
of the night who are always pretty vague about
what they do for a living but assure you they'll have
absolutely no trouble paying the rent.

I'll bet they won't!

My parents always expect me to man the phones
when a flat is in the papers. You see they own a
house in Harold's Cross, which has basically been
converted into six small flats and their tenants are
always coming and going. While we're on the
subject, by the way, anybody reading this who thinks
getting 'into property' is a doddle should have a
word with my folks. It's not as easy as it looks.
Especially when you get tenants whose cheques regularly bounce or discover they've locked themselves
out at three in the morning. Then there are the folks
who refuse to open their windows, never mind their
curtains, ensuring that the whole place looks like a
tenement. Anyway, as I said, I always answer the
phone and collect the rent for them, even though
my sister Ruth is never asked to do anything ever
because her answer is always a firm 'no'.

I don't know if I've told you yet but my mum
complains non-stop about Ruth and her boyfriend,
but when they call, she chats to them like old pals.
It's only once they have left that Mum starts moaning about them again. And I'm expected to listen.
Well enough's enough. It's very hard to take, you
know. All the bickering. I mean it's not like I've
anything against my sister. In fact I get along with

her now a lot better than I did as a child. She wasn't very nice back then. A year older than me, she thought that gave her the right to make my life hell and boss me around. And she'd yell at me if I tried to socialise with her saying, 'You've no friends, nobody likes you.'

I kind of looked up to her years ago, because she was a lot trendier and prettier than I was. And she knew boys and stuff. At least she pretended to. She used to tell me about these boys she used to meet behind the church after Mass. They were called Leonardo da Vinci, Winston Churchill and Adolf Hitler. It was only when I got my first history book that I realised the joke was on me.

It's funny because when I was younger I'd always watched programmes like *Little House on the Prairie* and *The Waltons* where families were all really close and sisters shared things with each other. And I couldn't relate to any of it. My sister never ever shared anything with me. Even on her birthday, I was forced to be her 'personal slave' for the day in order to get a few miserable sweets.

As a teenager we fought like mad. She accused me of being a copycat when I got my ears pierced three weeks after she did. As if she was the only girl ever on the planet to go out and do this. She called me Goofy when I got my brace fitted and told Mum not to allow me go to the local disco because of all the disgraceful carry-on. Even though *she* was one of the very girls who did most of the 'carry-on'.

Anyway, I'm not going to spend the day giving out about my sister. In fact I'm going to write my script today because Dad has gone into town now with his bus pass and intends doing useful things like visiting museums and whatever. I don't know how much longer he intends keeping up all this interest in art and stuff, but I'm saying nothing and Mum is glad to have him out of her hair. She was kind of dreading his retirement as she'd heard horror stories from other wives at the bridge club. Some of their retired husbands just sit at home all day watching TV!

No chance of my dad watching TV though. He's always said it was a cod. He claims there's only one thing worse than sitting in a pub talking rubbish; that's watching people you don't know in pubs talking rubbish.

My mum is off playing tennis today with her three friends who do nothing but talk about their offspring, weddings, children and grandchildren. They often ask my mum if there's any sign of me getting married, which she doesn't particularly like. I tell her to take no notice. Tell them to mind their own business, I say.

But Mum won't. She's dying for me to get engaged to Tim. Or anyone at this stage. I've a horrible feeling she has a mother-of-the bride dress picked out and Dad has already written a wedding speech. It's probably gathering dust in the garage along with the gardening tools he never uses.

Anyway it's great to have the house to myself for

once. I sit down at the computer all set to write. I feel very businesslike. Switching on the computer I wait for inspiration to strike.

And wait . . . and wait . . .

Then I stand up.

I need a strong black coffee. Now. After all no serious writer can work without coffee. What was I thinking? As I wait for the kettle to boil I sit back down again. Eventually I start writing SCENE ONE. I feel a rush of blood to the head as my fingers tap the keyboard. The words flow and keep flowing. God, I wish I'd started writing my script a long time ago.

At scene two I'm stuck.

Again.

I stare at the screen blankly and try to concentrate. Something is missing. I really need a cat. No serious writer writes without a sleeping cat nearby.

Right. No more excuses. I seriously am going to write all day today because I don't want to end up like all those people out there who always say they'd like to be a writer, if only they could find the time. Those same people, unsurprisingly, are the very ones who find time to sit in the pub, watch endless TV, gossip for hours and go for long drives in the country. I admit that up until now, I've been one of those people. Not any more though. Today I turn over a new leaf.

I write SCENE TWO. It looks impressive on the computer screen. But what happens next? Suddenly

I'm away again as my imagination takes over. Characters come to life as I write about a violent father and his terrified young son. The father is extremely drunk and he's accusing his son of stealing money from under his bed. The son is cowering in the corner and the father undoes his thick leather belt. The child begs for mercy . . .

Oh God, I'm not enjoying this at all. It's horrible and brings back memories of when I was in school and sometimes the headmaster would cane me. That was before corporal punishment was banned. I feel kind of gloomy and depressed writing this stuff but I reckon the film will be huge, especially in the States. Because Americans love all this kind of stuff, don't they? I mean Frank McCourt's *Angela's Ashes* was a roaring success and that can't have been much fun to write.

I press on. The father is yelling at his son and using a lot of F words and I'm actually beginning to feel downcast. The more I write the gloomier I become. By the time the drunken father starts beating the living daylights out of his son the tears are welling inside my eyes. And when the boy cries out in terror, they start streaming down my cheeks.

Enough. God, I can't stand writing this kind of depressing stuff. I wish I could write something funny instead. Something that would have cinema-goers rolling around in their seats. If I keep writing this morbid stuff, it's going to destroy me. Oh

God, what am I going to do? Isn't there some easier way? How does one become funny?

I'm trying to think of the last really funny film I saw. I can't think of one. Tim finds most films funny, especially if they're crude, for instance that scene in *American Pie* with the apple tart? He squealed like a pig when that scene was shown. When Tim thinks something is hilarious he squeals. I forgot to mention that earlier. He squeals and his whole body starts to shake.

Okay, I know what you're thinking. You're reading this and wondering what the hell I'm dating him for. So let me try and explain. I want you to know why I feel happier with someone like Tim than with somebody who has the potential to break my heart.

You see I was in love once. Seriously in love. With a guy called Paul. He had the most incredible blue eyes and sandy-coloured hair. If he knew he was gorgeous he never showed it. But he was cheeky and confident. Yes, confident, not arrogant. Some men don't seem to know the difference.

Most single people, when asked, will tell you they're not sure if they've ever been in love. I believe they believe that. I think it's very possible they thought they were in love at the time, but looking back, people will rarely admit they were in love with someone who threw it all back in their face. It's just a matter of pride really.

But with Paul it was definitely the real thing. It

was the real thing because I thought about him constantly, even in my dreams. Because I used to fret about what I'd wear in case I bumped into him, sometimes changing my clothes up to ten times before going to college. I knew I was in love because I'd tense up when I met him and not be able to think of anything to say. When I saw him chatting to another girl I'd feel ill and start wondering who she was and why they were talking. I refused to believe that Paul might have any female friends. After all, I was female and couldn't have just been friends with someone like him.

He was the first guy who asked me out that I actually fancied. I wasn't the type of girl who got asked out by lots of gorgeous men. No. The guys who usually asked me would ask anybody out. They weren't fussy – they just wanted to say they were going out with somebody. *Any*body. I'm sure if you rack you're brains, you'll remember being asked out by someone like that. It's not flattering, just depressing.

I remember thinking that good-looking guys were only supposed to fancy good-looking girls. And so it never occurred to me that one would ever ask me out. I wasn't exactly gorgeous in school. People used to call me 'Pudgy'. I blame my mother. You see my mum wasn't the type of mother who would be making nice sandwiches for my lunch or anything. No. God, didn't you just envy the kids in school who arrived with a packed lunch? All nice and neat in a box accompanied by a carton of orange juice. But there was no chance of me getting anything as sophisticated as that. So every morning Dad would throw some money at me to buy something in the school shop. But all they ever sold in the shop was chocolate, crisps and apples. Because I didn't like apples, I just bought crisps and chocolate every single day. No wonder my weight ballooned.

I often think it's funny when they ask in TV commercials 'Remember that flat stomach you had as a teenager?' I think it goes something like that anyway. Well, the point is no, I don't remember. I never remember even being able to see my feet when I was in school.

Anyway, only when I went to college, did I start to look after my figure. I was kind of too broke to be spending money on food anyway. Any money I had was spent on booze. I used to join all these societies just because they held party nights where pints were only a quid; even if they were served in horrible plastic cups. People look back on their student days as being the best days of their lives but I dunno about that. I love the fact that now I can afford to drink beer from a proper glass and not have to drink warm wine in some student flat. Now, that's what I call luxury.

That's why it's the ultimate treat being upgraded to first class when I fly to the States. Because I get to drink wine from a Waterford Crystal glass. Imagine that.

But back to Paul. He was a charmer and he did everything possible to get introduced to me. But because I was a bit of a loner back then, I didn't have a big gang of friends that he could get to know. So he had to work hard to get an introduction.

I became obsessed and would spend half my college days looking for him, wondering what time his lectures were on at. In fact at one stage I'd forgotten why I'd enrolled in university in the first place. Studying was the last thing on my mind.

But if you remember, I confessed earlier that my mother isn't the jolly kind of woman you see in TV commercials. No. At least that's how it seemed to me. She wouldn't let me out after dark because I was supposed to be studying. And so, because of that, Paul and I were never meant to be.

The first time we met properly was in a church. It was coming up to exam time, around the time when I remembered the good Lord and started befriending him again. I went into the campus church, hoping to have a few quiet words with God. The place was full of seemingly like-minded students, all praying frantically. And one of them was Paul. He was sitting at the back of the church wearing jeans and a white T-shirt and his arms were lightly tanned and toned. My heart nearly stopped beating when I saw him and I wondered how I was going to pass him without going scarlet. It's wrong to flirt in a church, I thought at the time.

As I walked to the end of the church I said a

little prayer to St Jude that he wouldn't allow me trip or make a fool of myself. And just as I reached the end of the aisle Paul smiled and said 'hello'. I smiled back, unable to answer and he followed me outside. We chatted on the steps of the church for about four hours before he eventually asked me out for a drink that evening. I had to say no because I knew my mother would go ballistic at the thought of me having some fun. Of course she used the whole 'studying' excuse to lock me up until my exams finished. But there must have been some method in her madness because I passed with flying honours.

I told Paul I was going out with someone else. Because I didn't want to admit I was from a weird family. Yes, sadly I had to lie and when I saw the disappointment in those crazy blue eyes I was gutted. One day, I thought, one day I won't have to ask my mad mother's permission to go for a drink with anyone. And then Paul and I will get married and live happily after. God I was naïve back then.

I was convinced we'd meet again one day. But we never did. He emigrated to America straight after college and that was basically that. I've looked for him since all right. Not actively of course. But anytime I see a man that slightly resembles Paul I wonder if it could be him. On every plane, in every supermarket, and in every bar in every city. It's true what they say about your first love. You never really top it.

Can you believe I'm off daydreaming again? This is ridiculous. I'm supposed to be concentrating on my script, not on past loves.

Maybe I'll just start on the next scene and then come back to this one. Or perhaps I'll just jack in this screenwriting business altogether and write a novel instead. It'd be pretty cool to be a novelist, wouldn't it? I could just sit in bed all day with a laptop eating sweets and thinking up little stories. Then again, how long does it take to write a book and would I really be able to write say, a hundred thousand words? Suddenly I think it's not such a great idea. I mean there are so many books out there, wouldn't my little book look lost on the shelves? And I'd have to think of a completely original plot as well. There are already so many books about middle-aged women whose husbands leave them. And then those women spend the rest of the book losing weight, joining a gym and falling in love with the hunky gym instructor. I'm not sure if I want to write that kind of book to be honest.

OK, sod the novel; I'm going to persist with my script.

'Morning.'

Oh no, it's Dad. He's back early. Please God he won't want to use the computer.

'Morning Dad,' I reply, hoping I look so busy he won't want to disturb me. I notice he's got the *Irish Times* under his arm, which should keep him occupied for a while.

'Are you writing?'

'Yes,' I tell him. 'I'm writing my screenplay. I'm only on the second scene but it's going well. It's about a boy whose father regularly beats him but then he escapes from his violent home and goes to England and works really hard and becomes really wealthy and comes home and builds a mansion for his poor suffering mother.'

I wait for Dad to reply but he doesn't. By the way do you happen to have a father like that? One who simply doesn't reply when you speak? Or is it just me? It's very annoying, isn't it? Sometimes I think I'm talking to myself and have to actually physically turn around to make sure he's still in the room.

Dad's made some real coffee so I decide to join him for one but he's already engrossed in the paper. I try to glance at what he's reading and as I do so my heart does a quick double flip. You won't believe whose picture is taking up a full half-page. Yes, it's the delightful Adam Kirrane. Janey. That's twice in one week I've seen him in the papers.

Everywhere I turn his striking face is looking out at me. There's just no escaping it.

I'm looking for Dad's reaction as he skims through the interview. But I get none. After a few minutes he turns the page. Soap stars hold little interest for someone like my father. Anyway he doesn't really read the newspapers, he just pretends to.

I need to get out of the house. It's suffocating.
Perhaps I'm suffering from writer's block. If I am,
it's a positive sign. It means I'm a real writer,
doesn't it?

I'd like a shower but Mum's already hogged the
bathroom. God, I didn't even hear her come in from
tennis. At times like this I wish I were living else-
where. Sometimes I'm just so thankful I'm an air
hostess and that for a couple of nights a week I get
to have the luxury of my own bathroom.

When I first joined the airline, I wondered what
happened on overnights. I wondered if the cabin
crew had to share rooms. Did you get to choose
whom you'd share with or could you end up sharing with an old cow that snored? So you can imagine my delight when I discovered we had our own
huge hotel bedrooms, all to ourselves.

I'm waiting in my room for my mother to vacate
the bathroom when I hear a beep beep on my mobile
phone. I check who has sent me a message. Adam
Kirrane's name flashes. Oh My God. OHMIGOD.
OK, calm down Katie. Deep breath. I press the
digits excitedly. IN TOWN. WANNA MEET UP?

I stare at the text, my right hand gripping the
mobile. This is just brilliant, isn't it?

This is a fairy tale and I'm bang in the middle
of it. I haven't been this enthusiastic about anything
since I fell in love with Paul all those years back in
UCD.

I'm wondering what I should do. Should I text

him back straight away and say I'd love to hook up? Then again, would it be better to wait a while. Play it cool. As if I'm inundated with requests from TV stars asking me out. Oh God, what are the rules and how do I play them?

I'm really glad I didn't ring back that time now. It's always best not to get too excited. Of course you'll often meet women who say it's only fair to meet men half way. That they shouldn't be expected to do all the chasing. Isn't it funny though that the well-meaning women who dish out that advice are usually single? Not being flippant or anything but if you were sick you'd go to a doctor, if you wanted justice you'd talk to a lawyer, and in my opinion, if you want advice on how to get a man, it's probably best to ask a woman who already has one!

Anyway, what am I doing hanging out with Dad when I should be in town? One never met a man by hanging out with one's parents! I'm off to Boston tomorrow, by the way, but haven't packed. But there's nothing new about that. Of course I hate packing but unpacking is worse. There's nothing worse than unpacking and Mum always gives out about the stink from my suitcase. I try to explain that it's just the company I keep on my trips. I have to be sociable, I protest. I can't just ignore my colleagues and retreat to my bedroom while they go off smoking, dancing and drinking, can I?

She doesn't accept my excuses but I don't get worked up about it any more. I'm too old for that now. Sorry, I'd actually forgotten to tell you my age earlier. I'm twenty-seven but look younger. So men in bars tell me anyway. My birthday was only six weeks ago but my mother still shouts, 'You're nearly twenty eight!' every time we argue about me not being the perfect daughter. I'm used to it. When I was nineteen she used to yell, 'You're nearly twenty, blah, blah, blah' and so on. I don't quite know what her point is but I refuse to take it to heart. After all, she's my mother. If she can't figure out when exactly she gave birth to me, then what hope has anyone else?

My mobile rings suddenly, making me jump. God, why am I always so surprised when anyone rings my mobile? I always think it must be fairly important when they do. After all, it's just far simpler to send a text, isn't it?

It's a private number. I wonder could Adam be ringing in disguise? I don't like answering private numbers. What have these people got to hide?

Actually it's my friend Patricia from school. She wants to organise a get-together. Drinks maybe. Am I free this evening? Am I free? Not on your nelly. I'm going out with Adam Kirrane this evening. I'd love to tell her this but I don't because (a) she probably wouldn't believe me and (b) even if she did, she probably wouldn't think Adam a suitable date.

Patricia, you see, has made somewhat of a career out of finding a suitable man. She finds lots that are suitable and always seems to be dating someone. But the dates never really lead to anything long-term. I don't know why. She's a pretty girl and nine months older than me. She doesn't smoke or drink, drives everywhere and her apartment is so neat and tidy. She even stacks her books in alphabetical order. Personally I think she'd make any man a great wife but obviously they don't feel the same way. I wonder what she's doing wrong. Maybe she's like a really bad kisser or something.

Anyway I know I'm single too (if you don't count Tim) but that's my choice – kind of. I mean I genuinely can't see myself married before I'm in my mid-thirties. I've this fear that I'll marry someone and then a few months later meet someone who might have been THE ONE. And just think how sorry I'd be then. So I've been holding out for someone special. I just didn't want to make do with the first man who happened to come along. And well . . . now that I've a date tonight with Adam Kirrane . . . I think it was probably worth the wait.

On the subject of Adam, I'd better get off the phone to Patricia and ring him. 'Yes, it's just that time of the month Pat, you know yourself, I feel dreadful, absolutely drained, but would love to meet next week for a cappuccino. *Love* it. Really looking forward to it. Bye.'

OK, now that she's off the phone I'd better ring Adam. No, I'll text him instead. If I text him he won't be able to hear my voice shake. I have a horrible phone voice anyway. It sounds high-pitched and childish. You should hear my greeting message on my mobile – I sound hysterical. I'd love to leave a cheerful greeting like 'Hi this is Katie and I can't come to the phone right now but please leave a message'. Then again, would you trust someone who sounds so cheerful when they're home alone talking into their phone?

I stare at the phone. I have to think carefully about the message I'm writing. After all, I don't want to sound too enthusiastic. Then again, I don't want to sound too casual either. In case he changes his mind and asks somebody else out.

Okay, here goes. GR8 2 HR FM U. WUD LUV 2 MEET L8R. WOT TIME?

I press SEND quickly before I can change my mind.

There. Sent. He can't read too much into that message, can he?

I wait five minutes. There isn't a peep from my mobile. Oh God, he isn't going to answer is he? He's probably deleted my message. He's probably laughing at my eager reply. But it wasn't *that* eager was it? I mean, it wasn't rude but it wasn't exactly an 'I scream of desperation' kind of text either. I'm kicking myself. He probably sent a group message. He probably got dozens of replies. I'm kicking myself. Who the hell does he think he is? I'm going to ring Patricia back and tell her I've changed my mind and that in fact, I'd love a sad girlie night out.

Maybe Patricia and I could get drunk and give out hell about men over a bottle of wine. After all,

that's what we normally do and it's so much fun.
Actually it isn't fun. Let's be honest here. It's pathetic.
Suddenly I don't want to be single anymore.

My phone rings just as I'm about to ring Patricia
back.

'Hey gorgeous,' comes the deep voice. I swoon.
My anger immediately evaporates.

'Hi,' I say, delighted.

That was quick wasn't it? He must be keen.
There's no way he could have texted a dozen other
women. I must stop being so suspicious.

'So what do you have in mind for tonight?'

'Nothing I could describe on the phone,' I say
saucily. Christ, when did I become such a wannabe
minx?

'You decide,' he says in that deep, sexy voice that
millions of women religiously tune into hear every
week.

'No, *you* decide,' I insist. Of course I'm only
insisting because I can't think of anywhere exciting enough. After all, I can hardly bring an A-list
star to my local pub, can I? Hang on though, that
wouldn't be a bad idea. Hmm. Why didn't I think
of it before? Come to think of it I would LOVE
to bring Adam to my local. Imagine their faces.
All those people whom I know to see. People that
know me to see too but never bother to say hello.
Then again, a guy like Adam isn't seriously going
to show up at my local pub, is he now? No, he'll
just think I'm using him to show off to my neigh-

bours. Which I wouldn't be. Of course not. Well, not really.

But I guess a TV star like Adam would like to hang out in Lillies or Sin. Not in my local haunt. I reckon he is the type of guy who'd be whisked through the door and escorted up to some VIP area or VVIP area – whatever that means these days.

'I know a little pub in Wicklow,' Adam says suddenly. 'It's a lovely traditional old-school type pub with no loud music or pretence.'

Am I hearing things? Is this really Adam Kirrane speaking? Adam, who flies first class everywhere, is chauffeured around to all the best London parties, presumably, and spends half his life on TV? He doesn't like VIP bars? Well, what do you know? How wrong can you be about someone?

'That sounds great,' I say trying not to squeak like an over excited teenager. 'Er . . . what time will we meet up?'

Of course what I really want to ask is what time he'd like to pick me up at but I don't want to come across all diva like. Also, I think it's unfair to ask someone to be the designated driver for the night. And I don't particularly want him to stay sober all night anyway in case I get locked and end up making a fool of myself.

'Where do you live? I'll pick you up.'

Okay. Relax. Adam *is* offering to pick me up. Fine, no that's fine really. I mean it's not like nobody has ever picked me up before, although TV stars usually don't, I have to admit. However, I'm now thinking I'm maybe a bit too old to be living with my parents. Maybe it's time I moved out, you know?

I give Adam my address.

He says he'll pick me up at 7:30 on the dot.

I make a mental note to remind myself to be ready and looking out the window for Adam's car so I can rush outside. The last thing I want is Mum asking him what he does for a living. She wouldn't approve in a million years. Actors end up in the gutter, according to Mum, along with poets, musicians and everybody else who basically doesn't wear a suit and tie.

I put down the phone and wait for my breathing to return to normal. Oh my God, can you believe THE Adam Kirrane is going to be calling around to my humble home? I wonder should I get a disposable camera? And get someone to snap him leaving my home, so that if he ever breaks my heart at least I could sell the photo to the papers and make a bit of money? Okay, that's just me being silly. I would seriously never sell my story or a photo of the two of us. No. I know some girls do but they're not exactly respectable girls, are they? They're usually cheap-looking things who appear in the tabloids dressed in frilly underwear with their mouth slightly parted under some dubious headline like 'WE DID IT SIXTEEN TIMES'. Sixteen times! Sure where would you get the energy? Those women are usually peroxide blonde and work either in a bar or in glamour modelling, although sometimes, embarrassingly enough, they are air hostesses with some low-budget airline. Not exactly great for the global image of our profession, is it?

But seriously, would you really believe those people do it sixteen times in a row? I mean, do they count? Thank God, tabloids are forbidden in our house anyway. My dad can't stand them. Anyway I don't like reading how so-and-so was an animal in the sack and all that. It's a bit yuck, isn't it? The only reason I read this rubbish is because passengers often leave the daily rags on board the plane. And I flick through them when I'm having my crew lunch. Out of boredom really. Don't believe me?

OK then, I admit it. I love the tabloids! Happy now? I wonder has anybody ever done a 'kiss and tell' on Adam. Hopefully not. After all it's usually footballers and pop stars who get bad things written about them. I haven't seen too many actors caught up in those kind of scandals. I suppose they're too busy learning their lines and going to auditions. I must start reading *The Mirror* again. I love those 3am girls. I reckon they'd be fun on a night out.

Okay, okay, I'd better get moving. I am going out on a date with one of the world's biggest hunks and instead I am imagining a night out with three women. Get real here, time is not on my side. First things first. What the hell am I going to wear? I wander upstairs and open my wardrobe door already knowing I'll find nothing remotely suitable.

I also know I'm going to try on ten different outfits before choosing the same thing I always wear out, which is basically a black polo neck (classy, warm and hides the dirt) and jeans because they are Miss Sixty and flattering. They make me look like I haven't made any effort and that's essential for tonight. I do not, absolutely not, want to look like I've made any kind of effort. I am sure all the girls Adam takes out make an enormous effort. Like wearing lots of make-up and going to the hairdresser. Speaking of hairdressers, I catch a glance at my own wig in the mirror and think I'd better ring Peter Mark now!

An hour later I'm sitting with my head back in the basin and a pain in my neck. Janice, my favourite hairdresser, is asking me if I'm going anywhere nice.

'I'm going on a date,' I tell her.

Janice looks surprised. Well, that's not that surprising really. After all, for the four years I've been coming here the reply has always been 'Oh, you know Janice, just a night out with the girls.'

She raises an eyebrow but I wish she wouldn't look quite so flabbergasted.

'Anyone nice?' she asks.

'Well, I hope he's nice,' I grin. 'Obviously.'

I'd love to tell her. I mean I'd love to announce to the whole salon who I'm really meeting later on but I'm sure nobody would believe me. I feel bad for not telling Janice though considering I probably know more about her fellow than his own mother does. But I mustn't tell anyone yet. You see if it doesn't work out, I don't want people to be asking me all about him for the rest of my days. How annoying would that be?

'Nice and straight?' Janice asks, attacking my head with a comb.

'Yes,' I nod. Janice always asks if I want my hair nice and straight.

'Can I get you a coffee?'

'Oh, please, yes,' I nod enthusiastically. 'Black.'

'And a magazine?'

'A paper please. *The Mirror* if you have it.'

I'm looking forward to reading about what those 3am girls have been up to. What an exciting life they must lead. Schmoozing with A-list stars as part of their job. Wow! I wouldn't like to get on the wrong side of them though. Dear God, no.

Janice disappears and returns with a huge mug of strong coffee, *The Mirror* and the *Evening Herald*. Ah bliss. I just love a trip to the hairdresser, don't you? It's great to be pampered. If I were rich I'd go to the hairdresser every single day.

'Will I put a bit of leave-in conditioner in your hair? It's very dry.'

I don't answer. At first. Instead my eyes are glued to a picture of Adam. It's a huge picture and he looks so stunning. He's smiling, revealing picture-perfect teeth and he's wearing a tux. His necktie is loose and he's sitting on the ground with his legs crossed.

'A bit of leave-in . . . God, he's gorgeous, isn't he?'

'Ye . . . es. I'd like just a little bit of er . . . leave-in conditioner. Not too much though.'

'He's sleeping with your one Jane.'

'Who?'

'Your man. Nick.'

'Nick?'

'Your man.' Janice points her comb at the picture.

I suddenly remember that Adam's screen name is Nick. And that Jane is obviously sleeping with Nick and not Adam. Which is a relief really. If Adam was sleeping with someone called Jane in real life, obviously I wouldn't be too happy.'

'Do you watch the show?' I ask fishing for info.

'Do I watch it?' Janice's eyes widen. 'I wouldn't miss it for the world. I'm a complete addict. My fella hates it though. He hates Nick. I just think he's jealous though.'

'What's Adam, I mean Nick, like?'

'Oh, he's a bastard,' Janice's comb slices through my wet hair. 'But you know a lovable bastard. He gets away with stuff 'cos he's good-looking. You should watch it.'

I agree. I should.

'I wonder if he's like that in real life though?'

Janice looks at me oddly in the mirror; as if she's never considered for a minute what he might be like in real life.

'You wouldn't know, would you?'

'I wonder what it's like to be an actor?' I ask dreamily.

'Oh I dunno, I've never thought about it,' Janice laughs.

I've left the hairdresser now and I'm lying on a sunbed in a tanning salon. People think it's strange that I use sunbeds because I never go mahogany brown. I just get a bit red in the face and acquire a few more freckles but sunbeds make me feel like I've been out in the sun. And I feel warm for the rest of the day. So that's my excuse. Of course I'm not telling people to hit the nearest sunbed as a way to keep warm though, as that would be ridiculous.

While I'm here in the salon I'm wondering should I get a facial. But then I think I'd better not in case my skin breaks out in spots before tonight's big date. It's happened before.

I'd love to buy something new to wear, but sure there's no point, is there? I'll wait till my next trip to New York where I can pick up something in Lord and Taylor. That's my favourite shop in the whole world. Did you know that Lord and Taylor on Fifth Avenue has a whole floor for petite people like me? I love the clothes there and love the way I don't have to get the legs of everything taken up. Little people like me shouldn't be discriminated against.

Yes, I'm small, which I used to find really annoying when I was younger. Because it didn't help me get into bars and clubs. But now I kind of like being small because people think I look younger. I'm not tiny obviously because I had to be five foot three to be an airhostess. I'm exactly that but was terrified going in to be measured for the job. I also had to have an eye test because good eyesight is required (God knows, I've never been able to figure out why!) and I'm as blind as a bat. However, I cheated and kept my contact lenses in throughout the eye test. Well, I was *desperate* to get the job!

I'm off the sunbed now and feeling hot. I wipe my sweat off the machine out of consideration for the next customer, get dressed and head outside. I make my way up to O'Connell Street to get the bus home. I don't drive. I mean I *know* how to drive but I just don't. I can never understand these people who amuse themselves by 'going for a long drive'. Driving in the city terrifies me. So I'm waiting for the bus and suddenly it's getting really dark and I'm having a panic attack in case it rains and my blow-dried hair goes all frizzy.

All I got was a blow dry. Nice and straight. I'll need to get the roots done again next week, which is a pain. I get them done once a fortnight. In fact sometimes I feel I'm only working to pay for my hair.

Oh great, here's a bus. I hop on quickly and go upstairs to get a seat at the top at the very back. The reason I like sitting at the very back is because

I'm hoping nobody will sit beside me. Haven't you ever noticed that people on the top of a bus never go right down to the back? Unless they happen to be annoying kids.

I think it's because people don't like to draw attention to themselves. I mean if you walk down to the back of the bus, and find no free seat, you have to walk away again and everybody stares – very embarrassing.

My phone rings. Oh no. I hate talking on the bus. Adam's number is flashing and I kind of freeze. Oh God, what'll I do? I can't answer and tell him I'm sitting on the 46A. How uncool would that be? Then again, I can't let it ring and ring and annoy the hell out of the other passengers. So I answer tentatively.

'Hello?'

'Katie?'

'YeeSSS,' I answer a bit too enthusiastically. My sister once told me I sound like a funeral undertaker when answering the phone, so now I make a huge phoney effort to be cheerful.

'Where are you?'

'Well I'm out with friends actually. Just having coffee . . . and a bit of a laugh, haha.'

I notice a couple of people on the bus turning around. They either think that (a) I'm completely mental or (b) simply a liar. But I don't care. It's not like I'm ever going to see any of them again.

'Are you in town?'

'Yes, yes I am. That's right.'

'Where are you?'

'Em . . .' I try to think of somewhere trendy. 'Ba Mizu, it's just behind the Powerscourt Townhouse centre. Do you know it? It's very nice, very relaxing.'

'Hey, would you believe I'm just around the corner from there? You don't fancy meeting up now instead of later, do you?'

No I don't. God, no.

'Oh okay, sure.' Oh Jesus, what the hell am I saying? Too late. 'Sure,' I repeat myself as I begin to feel my head spin.

I press the red button on the bus to let the driver know I'm getting out and then make my way downstairs, push past the crammed, irritable commuters and get off the bus. Right. I'm now on Baggot Street and have to hail a taxi to get me back into town to meet Adam. Don't call me a walkover or anything. I mean I *know* how to play hard to get; I just don't have time to play right now.

I stand like an idiot at Baggot Street Bridge with my hand outstretched. God, when is there a bloody taxi when you need one? Thankfully one stops eventually. I look at my watch and wonder what I'm going to tell Adam. I know, I'll tell him I snagged my tights and just popped out to buy a new pair. Then I remember I'm wearing jeans and swiftly change my mind. I'll tell him nothing, I decide. Men like mysterious women. I read that somewhere. From now on I'm going to be mysterious.

Right. The taxi is pulling up outside Ba Mizu. I sneak a quick look in my portable mirror. I look okay, I think, but it's dark so I'm not sure. I take a deep breath, pay Mr Taxi man and get out of the taxi.

'Good luck,' the taxi driver shouts.

Is he trying to tell me something?

I arrive in Ba Mizu but there's no sign of Adam. Phew! That was close. Well thank God for that. A few people look up as they always do when a lone woman walks into a bar. I glare back and they look away. People who stare are just so rude.

I sit at the bar so that Adam will have no problem spotting me when he arrives in. I wonder will I recognise him straight away. Will anyone else recognise him? After all, I don't really want the paparazzi after us, haha. Maybe I should be wearing dark sunglasses!

I order myself a glass of wine.

'Anything else?' asks the girl behind the bar.

'Er . . . no thanks.'

There's no point ordering for Adam, is there? I mean I don't know what he drinks. I wonder is he a Guinness man? It's hard to tell, isn't it? I pay for my drink and hope the girl behind the bar isn't feeling sorry for me. I mean it's not like I've been stood up or anything. Not yet, haha. Actually that's not a very comforting thought. Not nice at all. Being stood up is never great. It happened to me once. But only just the once, thank God.

I think I've time to tell you very quickly. A friend of mine threw a party for me a few years ago. She did it as an excuse to meet my new man. All my friends had been complaining about my mysterious man whom they had never met. Jack, you see, was a private man. *Very* private indeed. I had never been to his house as he lived in Kildare, so it wasn't really convenient. Especially since he lived with his wheelchair-bound sister who wasn't used to visitors – apparently. Because of her, Jack could never stay the full night with me either. I was sharing a flat with friends in town at the time. But Jack's sister worried about him so much. I never actually spoke to her of course, because Jack never got around to giving me his home number. And besides, it never occurred to me to ask for it.

Anyway my friends thought my relationship with Jack was all very suspicious. I mean, he didn't even turn up to the annual cabin crew ball and I was forced to go alone. Jack's sister had supposedly come down with the 'flu on top of everything else. I was more upset than angry. After all, how could I get angry with somebody who was so kind and considerate? He was one in a million and the only sibling in his family willing to look after his poor sister. The rest of them were selfish gits. So he told me anyway. I remember once asking him if he'd consider getting in a carer, but he'd looked at me like it was the most outrageous suggestion he'd ever heard. I felt terrible afterwards and never again complained. Or hassled him to come out with me again on a Saturday night.

Then one night, friends of mine threw a party and invited Jack and myself. At this stage I think they were beginning to question his existence. Not that I blamed them; sometimes I used to question it myself.

Jack and I were great together in the physical sense. He was an expert lover and even had me doing strange things, like spending more on lingerie than I would on a coat. Up until then I'd been a real Marks 'n' Sparks kind of woman. I loved fancy underwear but never saw the point in breaking the bank to deck myself out in frills and lace. If nobody was going to see my expensive undies, then what was the point?

He used to take me to quiet little pubs off the beaten track and loved weekends away. Especially weekends abroad. The further away the better in fact. But he was never keen on meeting me in Dublin for dinner. Or going to a club with myself and my friends. He was definitely more of a take-away, video and then straight-to-bed kind of man, although he always got out of the bed in the middle of the night to drive home to check on his sister, which I privately found intensely annoying.

But something bothered me about Jack. I mean,

one minute he'd be all over me, telling me I turned him on like no other woman, but the minute I showed any real affection or casually tried to mention the future, he completely clammed up.

Now I'm not a lovey dovey freak, but I would have liked *some* reassurance that I was more than simply a convenient bed partner. So one day I just put my foot down, giving him an ultimatum. I said he was either going to meet my friends, or I was breaking it off. It was just an idle threat really, as I'd no intention of dumping Jack, but surprisingly he took it all very seriously and agreed.

I was so delighted. In fact I was proud of myself for taking a stand. If only more women would ask for what they wanted instead of pussyfooting around, life would be a lot less complicated, I told myself smugly.

Of course Jack never showed up. The party started at eight and by half ten everyone was sozzled; a few people had started to dance and party poppers were going off everywhere as I skulked around the kitchen looking for the biggest knife. Well not quite, but I was terribly depressed. Firstly, I felt let down by Jack and then humiliated because I was sure everyone at the party was feeling sorry for me. Poor old Katie and her imagination, eh?

I gave him to eleven and then went upstairs with my mobile phone in one hand and a full bottle of wine in the other. Recipe for disaster or what?

I slowly pressed the digits on my mobile, hoping

against hope that there might be some sort of reasonable explanation for his behaviour. Maybe he'd been involved in a terrible accident. Perhaps his sister had fallen ill or he had lost his mobile phone? Pathetic, I know, but I was clutching at anything!

The phone rang out and then I redialled. Please let him answer, I silently begged.

Someone answered.

It wasn't him.

It was a little girl's voice.

'Hello?' came the soft baby voice.

Oh shit, I thought. I must have the wrong number.

'Hello?'

'I've the wrong number sweetie. Don't worry about it. Bye-bye.'

I put down the phone. Poor kid. Must have thought I was mad.

I rang Jack's mobile again.

'Hello?'

Same baby voice. Funny that. And then the penny dropped.

'Is er . . . your daddy there?' I asked tentatively, my heart racing faster than the speed of light.

'One moment,' the little girl answered as I dropped the phone in shock.

I never quite got over it. And I never found out whether the wheelchair-bound sister was in fact his wife. Or whether he even had a sister at all. Or any more children. Because I never heard from Jack again.

'Can I get you anything else?' the girl behind the bar asks. I'm about to shake my head when I realise that I've drunk all my wine. God, I must stop daydreaming. For a moment there I nearly forgot where I was.

The bar seems to be filling up pretty quickly with an after-work crowd. I don't fancy sitting here with no glass in front of me so I order the same again. I have a horrible, passing thought that Adam might not show up. But I banish it quickly. Not all men are like Jack, I tell myself as the bar girl hands me another glass.

Mind you, it's all very strange. I'm wondering if I'm in the right bar. After all, it's at least twenty minutes since Adam said he was on his way. Maybe he got waylaid on the street. Perhaps he was accosted by autograph hunters or was being trailed by the paparazzi. My imagination is hurtling towards overdrive when my mobile suddenly rings.

'Hey, where are you?'

It's Adam. Oh thank you God. Thank you so much for not letting me be stood up again. I just couldn't have dealt with that twice in a lifetime.

'I'm in Ba Mizu. Sitting at the bar. You can't miss me. I'm the stunning blonde, although you probably won't recognise me out of uniform.' I laugh at my feeble attempt at a joke.

And then I see him. A vision in a crowd of faces

that all look the same. He looks like a star. Then again, he *is* a star. I keep forgetting. And then I notice the heads turn. Men look vaguely ill at ease, women in power suits stare openly. And I'm beginning to realise I'm probably the envy of every person in the room. Adam Kirrane is here. And he's here to see me.

'Hey,' he gives my cheek a quick peck and I hope he doesn't burn his lips because I'm sure my face is red hot. I certainly feel hot anyway. But hot and happy and . . . well, a little tipsy. I haven't had anything to eat all day.

'Hey,' I answer back because I honestly can't think of anything else to say. I feel I have fallen in love for the second time in my life. I'm like a teenager on a first date. Not knowing what to say but realising I've got to say something.

'Are you well?' I ask awkwardly, aware that people are staring over and feeling a bit self-conscious because I'm really not used to this kind of attention. I keep thinking my knickers are showing or something.

'I'm great. A little tired but apart from that I'm flying,' he laughs revealing snow-white teeth. I wonder if they're capped.

'Another wine?' he asks and I nod before I've time to ask myself if I really need another glass on an empty stomach.

I glance around but nobody's looking over any more. Irish people don't like to be caught staring.

We're all very important in this town you see. We have VIPs and VVIPs and then of course people like myself who never get in anywhere. At least not into any members' bars to hobnob with all the 'important' people. But I do get to see a lot of famous people on my flights, which is great really. I've seen U2 and the President and some supermodels, and basically every famous Irish person. Most of them are very nice. But the funny thing is, the bigger the star, the more likely they are to be polite and friendly. It's only the vaguely famous stars that are likely to cause trouble. But anyway I'm rambling again and I know you probably just want me to get back to my date with Adam.

Okay, we're getting on well and I'm not going to tell you word for word what we're saying because it's kind of awkward and the conversation is peppered with the usual first date trivia questions like 'so how many brothers and sisters do you have?'

My stomach is beginning to rumble and suddenly I realise I'm starving. But I don't like to say this to Adam in case he thinks I'm just looking for a fancy meal. As if that was the only reason I showed up.

Out of nowhere, Adam's hand rests on my lap and he says, 'Let's go grab something to eat. I'm starving.'

Oh my God, he is my soulmate. He *must* be. Our minds think alike. It's a sign. And he's got really amazing green eyes and I've never gone out with anybody with green eyes. Maybe that's another sign?

I stand up (rather unsteadily, I have to admit), and Adam holds my coat open. Hmm. I never remember Tim ever holding my coat open for me. Oh God, I promised I wouldn't talk about Tim. Or even think about him.

We leave Ba Mizu and walk to Adam's car. It's a Mercedes SLK and as Adam holds the passenger door open I slide into the leather seat and think what a lucky girl I am. Not that I'm shallow or anything. But I'm getting just a bit sick of Tim's second-hand Nissan Micra. We drive to Browne's on Stephen's Green and I'm more than impressed. Browne's has the reputation for being one of the best restaurants in Dublin. When we arrive, the staff greet Adam like an old friend. I'm wondering how often he comes here. And wonder who else has accompanied him on a date. Maybe the girls' names change every week. Once again Adam takes my coat and then orders a bottle of champagne.

'When's your next flight?' he reaches over and gives my hand a squeeze. The touch of his skin on mine is electrifying.

'Tomorrow morning. I'm going to Boston.'

'Boston? Oh yes, I forgot. I love that city.'

'Me too, but unfortunately we don't stay there very long. Just a night. Pity.'

'A real pity,' Adam agrees. 'If you were staying

any longer I could have popped over to visit you.'

I laugh. Adam is just so, so different to any guy I've ever met. None of them ever suggested 'popping over' to Boston.

'When do you resume your filming schedule?'

'The day after tomorrow,' he says. 'I've had the last few days off but my schedule is pretty hectic for the next couple of weeks. My character gets himself into all kinds of trouble.'

'Like what?' I raise an eyebrow as the waiter pours our champagne.

'Oh you know, I can't be giving the storyline away. It's highly confidential.'

'Ah go on,' I tease and taste some of the champers. 'Tell me are you busy having affairs and breaking women's hearts?'

Adam pretends to look shocked. 'I don't write the scripts. I just read the lines. It's not my fault if the scriptwriters cast me as cad. I'm not like that in real life though,' he gives me a reassuring wink.

'I'm not a huge telly fan,' I tell him. 'But I am working on a script of my own.'

Even as I'm speaking I'm aware of how pretentious I probably sound. Suddenly I'm embarrassed; half wishing I'd never opened my mouth.

Adam looks at me quizzically. 'What kind of script?'

'Well, it's an *Angela's Ashes* type story,' I tell him. 'It's sad, gritty and well, very emotional.'

'I'd love to take a look at it sometime.'

The waiter arrives to take our orders. I'm happy. Deliriously happy in fact. Adam has just told me that he'd like to look at my script. This means that he wants to see me again obviously. I ask the waiter for the vegetarian option. Adam orders the same. I'm astounded. I rarely meet vegetarian men. Funny, I've always thought I'd marry a vegetarian like myself. Another sign, maybe?

I ask him about work and it's obvious he loves what he does.

'Actors don't get paid for acting,' he explains, 'they get paid for all the hanging around.'

'I've never thought about it like that.'

'Most actors love what they do. If you didn't love the life you couldn't do it. It's such an unpredictable profession. Every week I get my script. If it says 'Train pulls in', I never know whether my character is on the train or under it.'

Gosh, I had never imagined it would be like that. I suppose it would be weird if I turned up at the airport every day, not knowing whether I would be on the flight or not. I'm imagining arriving into the cabin crew rest room, and checking in with crew control and them saying 'Sorry love, you're not going to Rome this morning. Bye now'. Can you imagine that? What would I do? I'd have to go home and start typing out my CV again. But if you're an actor on a famous soap, you can't exactly turn up at your local petrol station the following week looking for a job, can you?

I start thinking about all the failed pop stars our country alone has produced over the years. What ever happened to them? All the wannabes. One minute they're on TV and signing autographs. They appear in magazines as the next big thing and then . . . nothing. They just seem to disappear. It shows that you've got to be a tough nut to succeed in the ruthless entertainment industry.

'Do you ever worry about not succeeding?' I ask Adam.

'Never,' he looks me straight in the eye. 'I never stop to wonder "what if?" It wouldn't even occur to me. Life's too short for doubts.'

Our vegetarian dishes arrive and I can't wait to tuck in. The smell of the food is heavenly and there's a lovely relaxed atmosphere in this restaurant. I could fall asleep here, and Adam's right: life is far too short for negative thoughts. I've decided to plough ahead with my script and not worry about rejection. I'll work on it a bit more when I come back from Boston.

A couple walk into the restaurant and something makes me look up with interest. The blonde woman is wearing a jacket just like one that Tim's sister Elaine owns.

The woman turns around slightly as the waiter shows them to their table. As she does, I freeze. Oh Jesus, it bloody *is* Elaine. Oh God, I am so, so dead. What am I going to do?

Adam obviously notices that my face has changed

colour. 'Are you okay?' he enquires. What do I say? Should I tell him the woman who has just walked in is the sister of my boyfriend who isn't actually really my boyfriend? I don't think Adam would understand, do you? I'm not sure I understand myself.

I wonder who the man is. The man with Elaine. He's not her husband obviously. I've met her husband Craig lots of times and it's definitely not him. But I'm not going to read into it of course. Just because you have dinner with somebody, doesn't mean you're screwing them.

Tim's sister is a pretty glamorous woman who spends a fortune on clothes and getting her hair done. Her hair is naturally curly but everyone thinks it's straight because she goes to the hairdresser every second day. She owns a little boutique that does pretty well. And Elaine is a regular in the social diaries, due to the fact that she hangs around with a few minor celebs. Well, the deal is this: she lends them dresses free of charge whenever they turn up to a glamorous do. They, in turn, give her a plug every time they're asked what their favourite shop is. That's the way it works. Mutual back scratching.

I'm wondering if she noticed Adam and myself. I don't think she did but I couldn't be sure. I don't think Elaine likes me. She's a bit funny towards me. It's as if she doesn't think I'm good enough for Tim. Her husband is a lot nicer. He's more laid back and likes to play his golf and isn't into the whole social scene. I can't think for the life of me how he ended up with the boisterous Elaine.

We're polishing off our dinner, and exchanging meaningful glances. At least I think they're meaningful. But maybe he's looking at me and thinking 'Er . . . no way.' I don't know why I always wonder if a guy is going to like me or not. I mean if I were smart I wouldn't think about it too much. But I'm a girl. And girls tend to put everybody else's feelings before their own.

Adam is telling me all about New York and the way everyone over there wants to be famous. It's fascinating. He tells me about various stars he's met including Susan Sarandon and Sarah Jessica Parker, and he tells me he once literally bumped into Cindy Crawford on the street.

'Did she recognise you?' I ask, intrigued.

'Well she smiled at me and said "hi", so I guess maybe she did.'

Wow. Thank God Cindy's married or I might, you know, be getting a little jealous here.

'You know, it's a real pity you're going to Boston tomorrow,' Adam continues. 'If you were in New York we could hook up and I could take you to a club. Actually I could introduce you to the rest of the cast, including the producer. He's cool. His dad is half-Irish, like nearly every American on the East Coast.'

I'm sorry I'm not going too. I mean I love Boston

but meeting Adam in New York would just be incredible. Can you imagine me telling the pilots and cabin crew that I couldn't meet them in Rosie O'Grady's for a drink because I was meeting the cast of *DreamBoat* instead? That would be just too funny.

The cabin crew don't really go clubbing in New York. It's because of the time difference really. I mean when we arrive, it's already evening time for us, yet still the middle of the day in New York. The sun is shining when it should be dark. So by night-time you are usually so exhausted you just want to go to bed. Sometimes I'll just go out anyway and to hell with the consequences. Sure I might be wrecked the next day, but I'll be a long time dead. Whether I go out or not usually depends on the rest of the crew. If they're a boring bunch then I'll just excuse myself and go to my room or go for a swim and a sauna in the hotel. But if any of them are up for a laugh we'll usually just go to Rosie O'Grady's.

Sometimes, we'll just get a load of beer and wine and go to somebody's room for a party, where we'll drink loads and gossip like mad about other crew members or give out about the job and life in general.

Uh oh, I'm at it again. Daydreaming. I give myself a quick reality check. 'Oh I'm sure we'll meet up again,' I say. As casually as that. The champagne has gone straight to my head and I feel on top of the world. So what if Adam is going to New York tomorrow and I'm going to Boston? I love Boston, so I know I'll have a good time there even if I don't have anything in common with the rest of the crew and am forced to amuse myself over there.

If you got bored in Boston, there would be something seriously wrong with you. It has got to be the most beautiful city on earth and it's home of Harvard and Ben Affleck and Matt Damon. But gorgeous Hollywood actors aside, Boston is just the type of place you'd love to bring up kids. So that is why I won't be ringing crew control in order to swap onto the New York flight. You see, I've done all that before. With Geoff. I made a fool out of myself over Geoff. And I sure as hell am not going to do it again. Men never appreciate women who do the running. Believe me, I know all about that.

We order coffee and another bottle of wine. I protest feebly, saying I can't drink any more because of my flight tomorrow.

'I've a flight too,' Adam tries to justify it.

'That's a bit different,' I say. 'I'll be working the damn flight but you'll be in first class fast asleep'.

'I understand,' Adam nods solemnly. 'I'll send the wine straight back'.

I bite my lip pensively. I don't want him to do that either. I really don't want the night to end. If only I didn't have to go to Boston tomorrow. If only Adam didn't have to go back to New York. If only neither of us had to work and we could live happily ever after together. Oh God, I really must be drunk. My mind feels hazy. I must get that coffee into me fast. I must . . .

'Hello, sorry to bother you but, I was just wondering if you were *the* . . . '

I turn around. I'd recognise that voice anywhere. 'Hi Elaine,' I grin.

Well, you should have seen her jaw hit the floor! Elaine just stares at me in utter disbelief. I don't know if it's because I'm with Adam or if it's because I'm out with someone other than her brother, but I have to say I am enjoying this. 'Yes, this is *the* Adam Kirrane,' I continue and Adam holds out a hand. 'And this is er . . . Elaine.'

I don't say why I'm with him, but I know she's just dying to ask. It must be killing her. Then again, she probably wouldn't like me asking her who her 'friend' in the corner is.

'I'm a huge fan of your show,' Elaine gushes and practically breaks Adam's hand she's shaking it so vigorously. She nearly takes my left eye out as she does so. Hasn't she any pride at all?

'I'm just wondering can I give you my card?' she continues, unabashed. 'I've a little shop in town . . . '

She whips a business card from her Burberry handbag and places it on the table. 'I'd love you to pop in and pick yourself out a little pressie of your choice. I'm just branching into menswear and we're *very* exclusive. Just a few hand chosen garments. Anyway, as I said, I know you're probably very busy but we're having a little party before Christmas to celebrate the introduction of our menswear collection.'

'Oh *are* you?' I interrupt. 'Brilliant! I haven't got my invitation yet but I'm sure it's in the post.'

'I was going to give yours to Tim to pass on to you,' she says coolly.

'Oh.'

Oh!

'Yes, well I'd better get back to my colleague.' Elaine says swiftly.

'Of course,' I agree.

Colleague indeed.

'Lovely to meet you Adam,' she says and has the audacity to give him a kiss as if she knows him. The bloody cheek! How dare she embrace my date!

'Who was that?' Adam looks fairly amused as she totters back to her table.

'Oh she's just someone I vaguely know.'

I certainly don't want to talk about her. Elaine is not allowed to ruin my perfect date. I refuse to let her do that even if she is my on/off boyfriend's older sister. I'm wondering when she'll tell Tim, and I'm not sure how on earth I think I'm going to explain our little rendezvous but I'll worry about that later. I knock back my wine and Adam immediately refills my glass. I know I should stop drinking now.

But I don't.

Chapter Seven

Jesus. How did my alarm not go off? I was sure I'd set it last night. How could I have forgotten? Yikes! All I know now is that my dad is yelling at me that the taxi is waiting outside to take me to the airport. I'm not dressed; I've nothing packed and am hungover as hell. Talk about a bloody nightmare! At least my shirt is ironed though. Phew! I ask Dad to tell the taxi man to give me ten minutes as I scramble out of bed like a lunatic throwing God knows what into my case. I pull back my hair into an unflattering bun and slap some foundation onto my face. My contact lenses are forced into my slightly bloodshot eyes and I pull on a pair of brown, unflattering tights. In less than ten minutes I'm sitting in the taxi apologising profusely for the delay, and terrified that fumes of alcohol are emitting from all my pores.

'No worries,' says the taxi driver, to my surprise. I'm lucky. I've got a nice one this morning. Normally they go mad when you're not standing at the door waiting patiently. I'm parched now, my mouth feels like sandpaper. I'm wondering how Adam is feeling. He's probably fine. Men can drink so much more than women. Isn't life so unfair?

Eventually I arrive at the airport. The first thing I do is go to the Ladies to check my appearance. It's not a pretty sight. I look like a drag queen. I get out a tissue and wipe half the chocolate-coloured muck off my face. I apply some bright red lipstick and some dodgy electric-blue eye shadow. There, already I'm beginning to look more alive. Then I head up to the cabin crew restroom and check the roster to see who's flying with me today. My heart sinks. The cabin manager today is a thundering bitch called Clarissa Snakely. I seriously dislike that old witch. She's been flying for about a hundred years and hates anybody young and pretty. She looks fine from the back as she's slim and has dyed jet-black hair, which is always immaculate but Christ, when she turns around, she'd give the most hardened criminal a fright.

Snakely is a woman with a fondness for writing damning reports about new girls. She's always trying to get young recruits fired. Luckily though, she writes so many vicious reports that none of them are ever taken seriously. Nonetheless, I do not fancy flying all the way to Boston with her. Snakely, of course, being a cabin manager, will fly first class with another senior cabin crew member. Some poor unlucky sod will have to work with the pair of them. And I just hope to God it's not me. There's only one thing worse than flying with Snakely, and that's flying with her when you have a hangover.

I go down to the briefing room. I'm last in. I say hello and quietly take my seat. I hate this bit. The whole point of a briefing is that you are informed by the cabin manager on the number of passengers flying. And if there are any special requests to look out for, like special meals, or VIPs or wheelchair passengers or bereaved passengers. That's fine. We all jot down the details meticulously in our little notebooks. Then the cabin manager barks out a few random safety questions. Obviously safety on board is a huge issue – we're not paid just to look pretty you know. And all of us know the drill backwards. But when Snakely starts firing out the questions, it's terrifying. Like being back in school with a bullying teacher. She fires a safety question in my direction. Luckily I'm able to answer immediately but I can't wait for our rigorous drilling to be over with.

Then comes the horrible part. Snakely is looking for a volunteer for the number two position. Now, I normally volunteer to do it because I love working in first class. But today I definitely don't want to do it. I couldn't bear to work a long flight to Boston with that piece of poison so I lower my head and stare at the ground. It works. She asks a fairly new recruit to work up with her so she can train her in. The young girl looks so devastated I feel sorry for her. But I'm still really glad it's not me in her place.

We then head out into the mini bus, which will take us to the aircraft. It's parked next to another airbus, which will be leaving for New York shortly. I cannot believe Adam is going to be on it. I also cannot believe I'm going to be in America tonight. Without him.

Now, I know you're probably wondering what happened between Adam and myself in the end so I'm not going to annoy you by saying nothing. A lady doesn't usually tell but you're different. I feel I owe it to you. Just don't tell anyone else.

We ended up in Lillies of all places. We didn't intend to go of course, but once our meal was paid for and we were hanging out on the street doing nothing, we decided to go to the nightclub. Just for one. Yeah. Famous last words.

We were whisked up to the VVIP lounge where somebody was playing on the piano and several people ventured over to say hello to Adam. Now, if you remember, Adam had previously said he didn't like clubs. But you could have fooled me. He seemed as happy as Larry with this set-up and lapped up the attention bestowed on him. He introduced me to a few people who showed a vague interest. But once they realised I wasn't famous in my own right, their attention waned and I ended up being virtually ignored. Not that I minded too much. I was with Adam. He could have brought anyone along as his date but he chose me and that was all that mattered. I happily sipped my wine (don't tell me you're counting because I'd certainly lost track) and when he kissed me I didn't resist. What I did do though, was resist his invitation back to his hotel room afterwards. I may have been drunk, but I wasn't that hammered. And I am after all, a girl with principles.

To be honest, when I sat in the taxi earlier on, I was congratulating myself on not succumbing. I mean, Adam is fairly irresistible. But Debbie once gave me this great piece of advice. She said 'If you like him, sleep with him but if you really like him, don't'. It's the best advice anyone has ever given to me and I follow it religiously. Even after a few drinks, I might be capable of forgetting my own name, but I always remember not to hop into anyone's bed.

But to be fair Adam didn't pressurise me and called a taxi when the club shut. He also accompanied me home in the taxi just to make sure I was safe. Of course I snogged him passionately in the back seat all the way home but that was as far as things got. Sorry!

I get on board the aircraft and after a quick security check, I start counting the passenger trays down the back. My head is throbbing. Hopefully our passengers today will be considerate and not let their kids scream too much. My pet hate is very loud, very little people.

The flight is practically full, which is a bit of a pain really. Because, as usual, people are arriving

on board who are not sitting together. The reason
for this is because of course they checked in late.
Now, they expect us to inconvenience other passengers on their behalf.

'The girl at the desk said you lot would sort
us out,' one angry looking man tells us. He is
not sitting with his wife and is making a flipping
song and dance about it. Funnily enough, the wife
doesn't look too upset about being separated from
him for the next few hours. I can't say I blame her.
If I were married to this guy I wouldn't want to sit
beside him either.

'The girl at the desk said . . . ' The man begins
again. 'She said you'd look after us.'

'The girl at the desk couldn't have said that, I'm
sure,' I say firmly but politely. I know he's lying.
Passengers love to blame the check-in staff for everything.

'Listen, I can't ask a passenger to move just to
facilitate yourself and your wife but you are more
than welcome to ask them yourself,' I say.

The man throws his eyes to the ceiling and
mutters something about never flying our airline
again. I'm tempted to ask for that in writing. He
storms off as a very large woman approaches me
looking for an extended seat belt.

Okay. We're all seated now and ready for take-
off. My crew seat is facing two men with very long
legs. They specifically asked for seats at the over
wing exits in order to stretch their limbs. But now,

they look rather uncomfortably at the ground, determined not to make eye contact. Oh well, I don't mind. I'm kind of glad not to get roped into another conversation about flying. Some passengers insist on asking all kinds of questions like 'How long are you staying in Boston?' 'When do you get back?' 'What routes do you normally do?' 'Do you like your job?' etc., etc. I know they're probably just being polite, but it becomes irritating. I mean, could you imagine walking into a bank and asking the bank teller if she likes her job and how many hours she normally works? Honestly, it's just ridiculous sometimes.

We take off and I see the man's face in front of me turn a distinct shade of green. I'm a bit nervous. Hopefully he's not going to be sick on my brand new shoes. It's happened before. Believe me, it's no laughing matter.

I see his hand grasp the armrest tightly. His knuckles are snow white. He's obviously terrified. You'd be amazed at the number of grown men who dread flying. It's a fear of not being in control apparently.

As the plane thunders down the runway I try to make eye contact with the terrified looking man. In fact I'm staring so hard, I'm convinced the other passengers will think I fancy him. Eventually he looks up, and I wink at him, mouthing 'It's okay'.

He visibly relaxes. He obviously feels reassured. Often passengers think that if we, the crew, aren't afraid, then we're all going to be safe. They scrutinise our faces for signs of terror. Especially during heavy turbulence. Therefore, even if the plane is rocking, and we fall on the ground, clinging to the nearest armrest, we still have to make sure we look completely relaxed.

Anyway I've done my good deed for today. The man looks better already. I notice the colour in his face is back.

As soon as the seat belt sign goes off, half the passengers stand up to go to the toilet. I head down to the back of the cabin to set up the bar. As soon as I'm finished I push the cart out into the aisle. Now, this is where the fun begins.

'Would you like something from the bar?' I ask the first woman. She's American although she probably claims she's Irish. Most do.

'I'll have a tea.'

'We'll be serving tea and coffee after the meal.'

'I'll have a coffee so. Decaf.'

'I'm afraid I'm not serving tea or coffee just yet'.

Patience, Lord, just give me some patience.

'Are you serving wine?'

'I am indeed.'

'I'll have a red wine with ice,' she says.

I pour her a glass of red and add some ice cubes. Don't ask. You get all kinds of mad requests in this job.

Next passenger.

'I wanna cranberry juice.'

'I'm afraid I don't have cranberry juice,' I explain, and she looks at me scornfully. As if it's my fault.

'You don't? What kind of an airline is this?'

'I have apple juice, orange juice or tomato juice,' I offer helpfully.

'I'll have a Chardonnay,' she sighs. 'Gimme two.'

The woman doesn't thank me but nevertheless I say 'You're welcome'. Just to annoy her. She doesn't notice though. She's wearing headphones and is watching the screen ahead.

The bar service takes forever but that doesn't matter. We've nearly another six hours to kill anyway.

We stack up the meal trays and then drag the heavy double carts into the aisle.

The choice today is chicken or lamb.

'I'll have the beef,' says the woman who was looking for the tea earlier.

'I'm afraid the choice is chicken or lamb today,' I say as cheerfully as I can. My head is beginning to throb again. All that recycled air is no good for a hangover. I wish I could open a window.

'I had beef on my flight over.'

'Yes, well the menu does change now and again.'

'What's the difference between the chicken and lamb?'

'Well the chicken tastes like chicken and the lamb tastes like lamb, I suppose.'

The woman looks at me blankly.

'What do *you* recommend?'

'Well I'm a vegetarian so I wouldn't recommend either.'

'*Right.*'

She looks slightly put out.

And opts for the chicken.

I offer her a glass of red or white wine with her meal but she's still looking for a cup of tea. She doesn't want either.

Too bad.

She'll just have to wait.

About an hour later, the meal service is finished and we're out with the teas and coffees.

'Tea?'

Oh God, I just know that first woman is going to annoy me throughout the flight. She just has that demonic look in her eye.

'Is it decaf?' she barks.

'Yes,' I tell her. It isn't of course, but hell, she's never going to know the difference, is she? Decaf tea, me foot!

At last, it's time for my break. I can't bloody wait. I'm sure you've often wondered what the cabin crew eat on board. A lot of people ask do we eat the passenger meals, but I assure you we do not. Hey we want to live, you know.

I'm joking. Of course I am. But the crew food is seriously great. We get so much of it. Everything from ice cream, yoghurt, sandwiches and cocktail sausages to chocolate bars, vegetable samosas, muffins, as well as a choice of hot meals including vegetarian options, apples, oranges, plums and grapes.

As you can imagine, it's very, very hard to diet when you work transatlantic flights but I can never complain about the choice of food for the crew. It's easily as good, or better than what they get in first class.

In the morning we can have a variety of cereals, omelettes and heated croissants but you're normally so tired when you eat your breakfast, that it never tastes as good as it should.

Anyway I'm sitting down now with my tray and chatting to a girl called Amy, who I've never met before. She's a stunning blonde of about five foot nine with flawless skin. We're chatting about the passengers, as it's hard to switch off the minute you sit down. She's been serving the other aisle and is telling me about a couple who didn't know each other when they sat down, but are now snogging passionately and have even asked for an extra blanket.

'Oh my God!' my eyes widen. 'You must point them out to me after the break. Are they drunk or what?

'I only served them two glasses of wine each,' Amy laughs. 'But they may have got more drink from someone else. Anyway, you know what drinking alcohol on board does to you.'

'I know. It goes to your head twice as fast. Oh

don't talk to me about alcohol today though. My head is raging after last night.'

'Were you out late? You naughty girl. You should never go out drinking the night before a long flight. It's just not worth it.'

'You're telling me?' I groan.

'I did it once and never again.'

'Hmm. If I had a penny for every time I said that I'd be a multimillionaire by now,' I laugh.

'So were you out with the girls from work?' Amy asks.

It's an obvious question. The cabin crew go out together the whole time. It's because we normally don't get weekends off, you see. So if you see a big bunch of very glamorous girls out on a Tuesday night, who are *not* wearing L signs or matching T-shirts, it's probably us. And if we're mostly blonde, slim and look like we're all dressed head to toe in designer clothes, it's *definitely* us. We get all our clothes in the States, remember. And some of it (especially the bags and jewellery) is fake. Sssshhh . . .

'I was on a date,' I say and I'm convinced I'm blushing. I haven't said that word in so long I'd kind of forgotten how naff it sounds. A date. Hmm. I don't really call my nights out with Tim dates, as such. I don't know what they are really. I just see them as nights out. Someone to kill time with. God, isn't that just the most unromantic thought ever?

'A date?' Amy perks up. 'With someone nice?'

'Very nice,' I admit grinning like a Cheshire cat. 'He's gorgeous actually.'

'Oh tell us more,' Amy is delighted. Men are obviously one of her favourite subjects. 'Is he a pilot?'

'Certainly not,' I laugh hoarsely. 'God . . . as if, haha . . .'

I wait for her to join in and burst out laughing too but she doesn't. The girl looks mortally wounded. Her smile has all but vanished. Uh oh, I've definitely hit a raw nerve. Perhaps her old man is a captain or something.

'Not that I don't think pilots are, you know, great.' I start backtracking furiously. 'I mean my friend Debbie, you know Debbie with the black hair? She's been snogging some pilot for a few weeks now and is wild about him.'

Amy doesn't look convinced.

'I take it you're going out with a pilot so?' I decide to get to the point.

Amy looks slightly uncomfortable, yet pretty pleased at the same time.

'Well, it's all very hush-hush . . . ' She lowers her voice.

'I'm intrigued. 'Why?' I ask. 'He's not married or anything?'

'Oh God no, nothing like that.'

'Well, that's something. You know, you're probably right. Sometimes it's best not to let too many people know your business around here. The walls of these planes whisper.'

'So who was your date last night?'

'Not telling,' I tease. 'I'm also keeping hush-hush.'

Two can play this game, I'm thinking to myself.

'Ah go on. Is he someone I might know?'

'It might be,' I say popping a grape into my mouth. I'm going to try and be good on this trip and eat lots of fruit and drink lots of water. I'm going to have a healthy day to make up for last night's binge.

'That's not fair. You tell me the name of your man and I'll tell you the name of mine.'

I don't think that's much of a trade off. After all, why should I tell her something that even the tabloids would love to know in return for the name of some pilot I've probably never heard of?

'It's early days yet so I'd rather not say.' I know I'm being mean but I don't want to jeopardise my chances with Adam. If it gets back to him that I've been gossiping in work about him, he might think I'm just with him 'cos he's famous. Which I'm not. I am absolutely NOT!

'What does he do?'

God for one who looks so sweet and innocent, Amy isn't half pushy when it comes to information hunting, is she?

'He's in the entertainment business.'

'Aren't they all? Bloody clowns the lot of them.'

I turn around in surprise. 'Why? Is your man funny?'

'Fecking hilarious. He's so hilarious in fact that he forgot we were going on a date last night, even though we'd confirmed the arrangements the night before.'

'God, that's a bit much.'

'Yeah, when I rang him this morning he said he was in Kerry and the reception on his mobile phone wasn't great.'

Kerry. Hmm. That's where Debbie is at the moment. With her new man. They're having a get-to-know-you couple of days. I've told Debbie to be careful but you know, that'll be the day!

'What's his name then?' I stand up and re-apply my lipstick.

'Donald.'

Bingo. It *is* Debbie's man. It must be. I knew it. The filthy cad. I'm afraid to turn around now in case my face gives the truth away. If only I could ring Debbie immediately and let her know what's happening.

'How long have you been with him?'

'A few weeks. But as I said it's very . . . '

'Hush-hush . . .' I interrupt. Hmm. Hush hush is one way of putting it all right.

'So what's *your* man's name?' she tugs at my sleeve as the other cabin crew come in for their break.

I give in. Sure if I tell just one person it's not

going to make that much of a difference is it? It's not like I'm sticking an ad on the cabin crew message board or anything. And anyway I'm bursting to tell someone. I've just had the most wonderful date and it's awful having to keep it all to myself.

'You won't tell anyone?' I ask.

She shakes her head. 'Promise.'

'His name is er . . . Tim.'

Oh I know, I know, I'm a chicken. But I just can't tell her. Honestly. I don't want to do anything to jinx my relationship with Adam. And besides he kind of asked me to keep it quiet. He said he likes to keep his private life private, and I've got to respect that.

'What does he do?' Amy asks, obviously trying to place him straight away, so she can stick him in her 'not-a-pilot-so-not-that-interesting-really' box.

'He's not a pilot,' I inform her, not bothering to explain that Tim actually works in a bank.

'Oh.' The light fades from her eyes.

'But guess who we saw last night in the restaurant?'

'Who? Somebody from work?' She resumes a slight interest.

'No actually,' I say very deliberately. 'We saw that TV star Adam whatsisname.'

I watch her face carefully for a reaction.

'Who?'

'Kirrane,' I add nervously and wait for her eyes to pop out of her head.

And so they do. Almost.

'No way.'

'Way.'

'Ooh, I've got a story about him,' she says mysteriously.

'What is it?' My heart gives a sudden lurch.

'Tell you later.'

And she disappears into the aisle.

Chapter Eight

Right. It's duty free time. So I set off into the aisle with my cart of alcohol, cigarettes and perfumes and my little purse and calculator to convert dollars into euros. I hope we sell lots of stuff because we work on a sort of commission, and get vouchers for shops like Brown Thomas and Arnotts every few months in return for all our hard work. I do love going shopping with these vouchers because it doesn't feel like I'm spending real money.

Anyway, I push out my cart and the woman who has been complaining about everything so far is now asleep, so thank God for that. I just couldn't have faced twenty more annoying questions as I'm beginning to feel tired now. The hangover is kind of kicking in. My first customer asks for a Toblerone. No surprises there. We sell so many Toblerones on board, you just wouldn't believe it. Some passengers, God forbid, start eating the chocolate there and then. As if we don't feed them enough already!

The next customer asks to see a horrible old

brooch with a harp on it. I wouldn't wear it in a fit and I've never met anyone who actually would. Well, except for this woman obviously. She's American and has a nice, kindly face but I don't think she should buy this brooch because it's yuck.

She takes it out of the box and switches on her reading light so she can see the brooch better.

'It's beautiful,' she says. 'Isn't it?'

'Yes, it is,' I say solemnly. 'I have one just like it at home.'

Well I *do* have *a* brooch at home so it's not a complete lie. Of course it's a lot prettier than this one. My granny gave it to me and I keep it for sentimental reasons. But you wouldn't catch me wearing it on a night out. God no. Not in a fit. Who wears brooches anyway? I've never seen young people wearing brooches, have you?

A lot of passengers are dithering over watches and various pieces of Celtic mementoes. God I'd love them to just hurry and make their minds up. I'm intrigued about this supposed 'story' Amy has up her sleeve. And to be honest a little worried. I mean what does she know? And *how* does she know it?

I wonder has she actually seen something or heard something? If she's only read something in the tabloids I wouldn't be that worried 'cos Adam himself told me they just make everything up. He says that he's always been linked to people he doesn't know, and he finds it intensely annoying.

'Like who?'

I just had to ask.

'Oh you know Angelina Jolie and Drew Barrymore,' he says and I search his face hard to see if he's joking. I mean *surely* he wouldn't be annoyed being linked to beautiful talented women like them. I think he's lying. If I were linked to say, Brad Pitt and George Clooney and went around giving out about it, people would think I was mental.

'I'm looking for something for my niece.' A customer holds up a horrible bracelet. 'She's the same age as you. Do you think she'd like this?'

Not unless she's blind and/or lying about her age, I think.

'I think it would look stunning on her,' I enthuse.

I hand the bracelet back to her and think that maybe the woman's niece might like it after all. It's not *that* bad. I mean compared to those bracelets the Moroccans try to sell you in Spain, it's actually nice.

Anyway what would Amy know about anything? She probably just picks up bits of gossip from the other crew members. Gossip is just one of the hazards of the job, I'm afraid. For one who knows so much, it's a wonder Amy doesn't know about her own two-timing pilot boyfriend. But sure, that's typical I suppose. The poor girlfriend/wife is usually the last to know about these things.

Of course *I'm* not going to tell Amy. Because I

don't know her that well and anyway, your man would tell all the other pilots I was a troublemaker, and I'd be very unpopular on the overnights.

Oh God, some chubby kid has just started yelling for jellybeans and I don't have any in my cart. I ask his mother if the kid would like something else instead but she shakes her head adamantly. No wonder that kid is spoilt. I have to make my way up to first class and see does Snakely have any jellybeans in her cart. I'm not looking forward to it.

As I make my way up to first class I practically break my neck by tripping over some man's shoes. Why can't people just leave on their shoes during the flight? And if they can't bear to keep their shoes on, then why don't they tuck their shoes in under their seat?

I walk up the cabin very, very fast because if I walk slowly or even normally, I know I'll be inundated with requests for more . . . well, everything.

As I walk through the curtains and into first class, I'm reminded of Adam and I begin to wish I'm on the plane to New York.

There are only about six people up here, including a very famous pop star who is listening to her headphones and drumming her fingers on the seat rest. I wonder if she's listening to her own music. I wonder do pop stars ever listen to their own music to relax. I doubt it somehow. It would be a bit too much like work I suppose. I always wonder at bands like, say, Status Quo who can still stand up and sing *Whatever you want*, after all these years and still look like they're enjoying themselves.

Then again I suppose it couldn't be any worse than saying 'tea', 'coffee', 'milk' and 'sugar' zillions of times a day, while also remembering to smile as if I'm thoroughly enjoying myself.

Snakely is sitting down reading a copy of *Vogue*, which is really supposed to be for the first class passengers. Then again most of our first class passengers happen to be men and prefer to read *The Economist*. When I approach, she wrinkles her nose as if I'm a bad smell.

'Yes?' she shrills.

'I'm just checking the duty free cart for jelly-beans,' I say and to my absolute mortification, I feel myself going red even though I've done nothing wrong.

I open the cart and start rifling through it. I can feel Snakely staring at my shoes, my tights, my hair, everything. I hope to God my hem isn't hanging down or anything. I would hate to give her any excuse to write about me.

'Is that a silver bracelet you're wearing?' she asks.

Aha. She's got me. Isn't she so clever? You're only allowed to wear gold jewellery at work. Some bored person must have thought up that rule years ago and nobody ever bothered to change it.

'Oh sorry about that,' I say slipping it off and putting it into my apron pocket. I've been wearing it since last night and completely forgot to take it off. I wonder if she's going to say anything else. Where are those damn jellybeans? I'm going to kill that bloody kid for putting me to so much trouble. Just 'cos he's too young to have a hangover! I hope the jellybeans (if he ever gets them), make him sick!

I'm sure her eyes have now worked their way up to my neck and are examining my scarf which I'm sure has make-up on it. Oh well, I'll just have to give it a good rinse when I get to my hotel, and hope nobody notices between now and Boston. Oh the thoughts of my hotel bed. I just can't wait to get into it and curl up with my book.

Phew! I've found a packet of those damn jellybeans thanks be to God. A long nail taps me on the arm and I'd swear the force of it has broken my skin.

'Who is your supervisor?' Snakely asks, smiling an evil smile.

'Rowena Little,' I say, rubbing my arm at the same time. 'A lovely lady. She really is wonderful.'

Snakely looks put out. I'm sure she'd prefer me to be terrified of my supervisor obviously, but she isn't going to get that satisfaction from me. And besides, Rowena is sound. I'm one of the lucky ones. Some of the supervisors are hell and spend their time reducing crew members to tears. I've even heard of a couple of the girls being told to lose weight. Imagine that! In this day and age? If some old biddy dared to tell me to lose weight, I'd have my solicitor onto them before the plane's wheels had a chance to touch the runway.

I pick up the jellybeans, and I'm about to head off when Snakely asks me why the buckle on my belt is undone. I look down in horror. How did that happen? She must have undone it with her eyes. The witch must have put a spell on me.

'Oops,' I give an embarrassed laugh. She eyes me coldly and I can see I'm about to get lectured for no reason at all.

'There is no excuse for bad grooming,' the old hag starts off. 'I don't need to point out that . . . '

'Excuse me?'

Myself and Snake-Face turn around simultaneously.

We both smile and I sincerely hope my smile looks a bit more genuine than hers.

The tall middle-aged man in the well-cut suit asks me if there's any chance he could have a glass of water.

'No problem,' I tell him, reaching for a Waterford Crystal glass. I wonder if he can feel the tension in the galley.

I fill his glass and ask him would he like lemon.

'It's fine,' the man says quietly. 'This is great.'

He peers at my name badge. At least I hope it's my name badge he's examining. It's stuck on my left breast so it's kind of hard to tell.

I can sense Snakely is dying to get rid of him so she can continue slating me but our friend is showing no signs of wanting to get back to his seat, and he is a first class passenger, so as far as the airline is concerned he must be treated like a mini-god.

'Not long to go now.' The man leans back against the toilet door. He looks at his watch. 'Just another couple of hours.'

He looks from me to Snakely and I guess he's had a few drinks taken. 'Why are you not working up here?' he looks at me questioningly.

'Oh I'm working down the back today,' I tell him brightly. 'I just came up to get jellybeans for some kid and I got, er, talking to Clarissa.'

'So I see,' the man says in a laid-back tone of voice.

Clarissa looks extremely uncomfortable. How unfortunate for her that her little intimidation game has been cut dead. I'm laughing to myself. Serves her right.

'Well I'd better excuse myself and get these sweets down to the poor little kid. He must think I've gone and jumped out of the plane.'

The man laughs loudly and I'm startled. It wasn't that funny.

He holds out his hand.

'Norman Levins,' he shakes my hand firmly. 'You're a delightful girl and hopefully I'll see you on board one of my flights again very soon. You don't have a comment card by the way?'

'I'll get you one now,' I say reaching over Clarissa to grab one.

'Charlie is a good friend of mine. I'm going to post my comments to him directly. We're actually playing golf next weekend, do you know him?'

'Ch . . . ?'

'Charles Daviston.'

'Oh yes of course,' I smile.

Holy fuck! Charles Daviston is the airline chief executive. Of course I don't know him. Well, I know who he is but like I don't know him to say hello to or to play golf with or anything. But I must say I'm pleased that my pal here in first class knows him. And I know Snakely will not look sideways again at me for the rest of the flight.

I sail back into economy class with a huge grin plastered all over my face. I could kiss that kid for sending me up to get the jellybeans. Now, where is the brat?

I spot him and he's fast asleep. Drat. I make my way over to his mother.

'Too late,' she snaps.

'I'm very sorry,' I explain, 'but . . . '

'Just FORGET it,' she says rudely and I slink away.

Sugar. What am I going to do with the damn sweets? I want to burst the bag over that spoilt child's head. Or even his mother's. Instead I go down to the back galley but the girls have sealed the duty-free bars. Sugar, sugar, sugar. There's no way on earth I'm going up to first class again. In the end I take five euro out of my handbag and buy them myself, just to save me the hassle of going back up there again.

'Was there any yummy desserts left over in first class?' one of the girls asks me as I stuff the jelly-beans into my little overnight case.

'Well, if there were, Snake-Face wasn't offering them to me,' I grumble.

'Snake-Face, you're hilarious. Snake-Face hahaha.'

Suddenly all is quiet in the back galley. It's deafening actually. I am down on my knees with the jellybeans sticking out of my overnight case as if I bought them for myself. And the dragon herself is standing beside me. I can smell her. That nasty rich stink that I could get up in first class has made its way down to economy courtesy of its owner.

I look up. Her eyes bore into me. If looks could kill, I would now be swinging from the aircraft ceiling, the straps of one of the yellow safety jackets around my neck. She says nothing for a few seconds and then turns on her heel and storms off.

'Oh my God,' the other girl pales. 'Do you think she heard you?'

'I dunno,' I shrug. 'She can't prove I was talking about her, can she?'

'Do you think she'll write a report?'

'I doubt it,' I laugh. 'Some man up in first class said he was going to write a nice comment about me, so if she writes something nasty it'll just look like sour grapes.'

'Was he nice?'

'Who?'

'The guy in first class.'

'Well he was oldish . . . like probably married and that, but very funny. I think his name is Norman something. Devins or . . .'

'Levins?'

'Yeah, that's it.'

'Well then she'll be wasting her time writing anything negative about you. That man is one of our top one hundred customers. His company spends over one hundred thousand euro on flights for him a year.'

'How do you know?' I'm intrigued.

'Everyone knows,' she shrugs, and I wonder for the thousandth time since I started flying, why everyone seems to know everything in this place, except me.

'Good-bye, good-bye, cheerio, take care now, safe home, good-bye, good-bye, take care now, thank you, you're welcome, thank you very much, good-bye, our pleasure, not at all, bye.'

As soon as the last passenger disembarks, I rush up to first class to see has anybody left any goody-bags on board. The goody-bags are nifty little bags that first class passengers receive when they take their seat. They contain earplugs (great if your hotel neighbours happen to be the noisy sort), razor (to do my legs when I soak in a long hot bath with a glass of wine), comb (which fits nicely into my back pocket if I go clubbing), socks (you can never have too many pairs!), perfume spray, lip balm, eye-mask, etc.

Now, most first class passengers could not be bothered taking these little bags home, so they usually just use the eye-mask or say, the socks, and then dump the bag as rubbish. Of course, once a bag is opened, you can't recycle the products, and the cleaners just take the stuff away unless I happen to help myself. This leaves me with an endless supply of earplugs and combs. Whoever said this job didn't have great perks?

We wait for our cases and the porter carries them out for us and loads them into our mini bus. Now that I'm here I'm thrilled to be in Boston. It really is a special city and is beautiful at this time of the year, when the leaves have turned a beautiful warm golden colour. Mind you, it's not warm here though. Not at all. The weather is freezing. That's the thing about Boston and New York. It's either bitterly cold or sweltering hot. They have real winters and summers here not like home, where the weather can never seem to make its mind up.

Snakely is sitting up at the top of the bus chewing the poor captain's ear so I make sure I head down to the back. One of the stewards is already sitting beside Amy, which is really annoying because I have to ask her about Adam, and I really haven't had a chance since my break.

I've got a second wind now that we've arrived in Boston. I think I'll wrap up and go for a walk down Newbury Street, or maybe I'll just go to the mall and wander around. I'm sure some of the crew will be heading out so I'll try and find out what everybody's doing. Of course if Snakely is planning on coming with us, you can count me out.

It doesn't take us long to get into town. The roads from Logan Airport into town are great. Hmm. A far cry from the route from Dublin Airport into town at the moment. Have you tried it recently? One lane of traffic as you approach Drumcondra – welcome to Ireland, how are ya?

Soon we're in the Back Bay area where our hotel is located. Everybody stares as we walk into the hotel. Imagine, this is how famous bands must feel all the time. Like fish in a tank. It's funny the way people always stare at airline crews though, isn't it? I mean, it's not like we're *that* exciting. It must be the pilots and their caps. Women love men in uniform. Sure just look at all the attention Tom Cruise got in *Top Gun*. And then there was Leonardo di Caprio dressed up as a pilot in that film *Catch me if you can*. He looked great. Sadly, the pilots in our airline look about as much like him as I look like Gisele Bundchen.

We're handed our room keys and spending money at the hotel reception. I rip open the envelope to make sure all the cash is there. It is, thank God. Oh, I can't wait to go shopping now.

The first thing I do when I get to my room is light a cigarette. I don't smoke that much usually, but after a long transatlantic flight I'm always gagging for one. I kick off my high heels, and replace them with the furry purple slippers I bring everywhere with me. I wonder whether Adam has arrived in New York yet. I wonder if he's thinking of me or even missing me. Maybe he isn't. After all, most men don't go on with all that sentimental slush, do they?

After finishing my ciggie, I lie on the bed. My eyes close and I'm in danger of falling fast asleep. This is something I absolutely must not do, I remind myself. See, if I go to sleep now I will wake at two or three in the morning, which is definitely something I don't want to do. However, if I manage to stay awake, I could sleep until six or seven American time, which would be great. After all, tomorrow night will be a long old night. Those night flights are a killer. I'm dreading it already.

The phone rings and Amy is wondering what I'm up to.

'Not much,' I tell her. 'I'm thinking of maybe just wandering around the Prudential Centre 'cos it's bitter out there. Then I'll go downstairs for a bit of a sauna and swim and then I dunno . . . are you going out for something to eat?'

'I rang some of the others and they say they're just taking it easy.'

'Taking it easy? The boring sods. I can't understand people who come to America to stay in their room watching telly. You can do that at home.'

'I know,' Amy agrees. 'Well, let's say we meet at seven?'

'Okey dokey.'

Right. First things first. I take off my uniform and fling it on the floor and then head into my huge en-suite and run a hot bubble bath. I had thought of going downstairs to the leisure centre but my stomach feels kind of bloated after the flight and to be honest, I'd feel a bit self-conscious wandering around in my bikini. Suppose I met the captain in the jacuzzi and had to make small talk with him with only a few bubbles between our bare skin and us? Don't laugh – it's happened before!

I lie in the bath soaking my tired feet and almost regret that I've arranged to meet Amy now. The hot water just makes me feel sleepy. What I'd love now is a nice glass of red wine and maybe a video. I could watch a video in my room. I must see what films they're offering and I don't mean the XXX-rated ones. I mean, who watches them anyway?

Speaking of X-rated videos, wait 'til I tell you about one overnight I had in Amsterdam. I couldn't for the life of me get to sleep, so I decided to watch some TV. I couldn't get the TV/video to work and by mistake (I swear to God) I ended up playing a graphic porn film. I was shocked out of my mind by what I saw and believe me; I didn't come down in yesterday's shower. But seriously, how do people really do this yeuch stuff to each other? Anyway once I'd got over my initial shock, I rang reception immediately and asked the porter to come up and help me switch the film off. You see, I wanted to let them know there and then that the porn film was a mistake, because I didn't want to be arguing the matter of payment in the morning in front of my fellow pilots and cabin crew.

The young porter came upstairs and I tried to explain what had happened. I pointed to the TV screen and said 'This is a mistake. I do not want to watch this.' The porter turned to the TV screen and we both looked mortified to see two women and a man er . . . well basically I don't want to go into it too much, but none were wearing clothes and there was no real 'acting' going on if you know what I mean.

The porter didn't bat an eyelid and said he would get someone to fix it straight away, and I asked if it could wait until the morning. Frankly I had seen enough and wanted to see no more thank you very much. There was nothing erotic about the three fat white naked bodies I had just seen, complete with tattoos, body piercings, dodgy haircuts and even dodgier accents. Can you believe businessmen entertain themselves by spending money on that crap?

And wouldn't you feel sorry for the people who make these awful films? I always believe that the, ahem, 'stars', are drugged up to their eyeballs anyway. Speaking of Amsterdam, the last time I was there my friend insisted we go down to the red light district. It was really awful with women sitting in shop windows touting for business. Some were just knitting or reading a book or whatever, and you could see into the room.

It was all a bit horrific really. I know the Amsterdam red light district has become a tourist attraction in Holland but it's depressing to see human beings treated like pieces of meat by lager louts on stag weekends.

I told my friend I couldn't bear it any longer. It was like being in a zoo only worse. In zoos you're not allowed touch the animals. Anyway we went off to a club and had a laugh, and then when it was over at 2.00 am, I remember thinking I knew the way back to the hotel.

'You just follow the canal,' I told my friend.

Two hours later, at 4.00 am, we ended up back outside the door of the nightclub again. We had basically walked around Amsterdam in a circle. My friend was livid and . . .

My hotel phone rings suddenly, and as there's conveniently a second phone in the bathroom, I reach over and pick it up.

'Hey, it's me.'

'Adam!' I'm startled. How the hell did he get my room number?

'You told me the name of your hotel, remember?' he laughs. 'The operator was able to trace it for me.'

I frown. Did I really give Adam the name of my hotel? Oh so I did. I'd forgotten.

'How's your head?'

'Fine, fine.'

'What are you doing?'

'I'm in the bath, daydreaming.'

'Wish I was there.'

'Um it's not really big enough for two.'

'I meant in Boston, you saucy minx.'

'Oh.' I can't help smiling to myself.

'So, are you just taking it easy? Having a nice early night after last night?'

'Well no actually I'm not. I almost wish I was though 'cos I'm pretty wrecked but I'm going to wander around the Prudential Centre and do a bit of window-shopping. Then I'm meeting one of the crew for a drink.'

My words are tripping over each other in a hurry and my voice doesn't really sound like my own. I wish I sounded a little cooler.

'One of the pilots?' he asks immediately.

'Don't be daft. I'm meeting one of the girls.'

'I see.' He sounds relieved. I'm kind of pleased that he wants to know whom I'm going out with. It shows he cares, doesn't it?

'Well don't stay out too late.'

Christ, he sounds a bit like my mum.

'And be good,' he adds, in a much softer voice.

I wonder what he's thinking. Does he think all air hostesses get up to all kinds of wild antics on

our trips away? Good Lord, if only life were that
exciting! It's funny the way a lot of people perceive
cabin crew to be a bit mad, with a man in every
airport. God, nothing could be further from the
truth. But actually I don't want to reassure him too
much. Keep 'em guessing, that's what I always say.
Never be an open book.

'Well goodnight so,' I say because I want to be
the first one to get off the phone. I don't want him
thinking I've no life, and am hanging on to his every
word.

I put down the phone and feel warm inside, even
though the bathwater is getting cold and my skin
is going all wrinkly. As soon as I step out of the
bath, the phone hops again. It's Amy, wanting to
know if I'm ready.

'Just give me ten minutes,' I say, before wrap-
ping myself up in a huge fluffy white towel straight
off the piping hot towel rail.

I meet Amy in the hotel lobby and she looks an
absolute vision with her hair down. As we wander
past reception, men openly turn and stare. They
can't help it. She's typical of most of the cabin crew.
They're mostly tall, very slim and glamorous.

As I've said before, there's a good incentive for
remaining slim in this job. You see when you're
doing the safety demonstration, you have to lift
your arms high in the air as you show passengers
how to buckle their seat belt. The last thing you
want is the passengers staring at your stomach while

you're doing this. Seriously though if you had to stand in front of strangers every day with your hands in the air, you'd also think twice before scoffing that extra muffin.

When we leave the warm hotel, the icy temperature attacks the bare skin on our faces. The air is so freezing it numbs the skin. I wrap my scarf tightly around my face so that all that's showing are my eyes. We head straight for the Prudential Centre. As soon as I get in, I feel a rush of excitement. I have an obsession with American malls.

How do I describe shopping malls in the States? Well, for a start you can't compare them to our own shopping centres. In Ireland the shopping centres always seem to be packed. There are always people smoking despite the 'No Smoking' signs. Young haggard mothers always clip your heels with their trolleys, and young teenage boys in tracksuits stare at you menacingly. In Irish shopping centres, people just seem to hang around. Not so in the States.

The Prudential Centre is so clean you could quite easily eat off the floor. Everybody walking around here is well dressed and the window displays are to die for. The smell of fresh coffee wafts from the various coffee shops and handmade chocolates from the pretty little delicatessens are calling out to me. But I won't succumb. I am being very self-disciplined.

Amy wants to visit the Warner Bros. shop to get

a present for her little nephew's birthday. I oblige 'cos I'm just a big kid anyway. Seriously though, when I went to Disney World I went on the Peter Pan ride no less than five times and I still wanted to go on one more time. My mother and father put their foot down eventually, saying enough was enough. I was twenty-five at the time.

There are so many cute things to buy at the Warner Bros. shop, and clearly Amy has her heart set on buying half the merchandise. There's no point me splashing out here though as I've no kids, and the chances of me having any in the near future look pretty slim at the moment. If I end up marrying Adam however . . . oh stop it Katie. Aren't you just jumping the gun a little bit? You've only gone on one date with the poor lad. I quickly banish any notion of settling down with Mr Kirrane any time soon, and just hang around waiting for Amy to pay for her purchases. Jet lag is setting in now and I'm struggling to keep my eyes open.

Amy comes away from the checkout laden with clothes and toys for her nephew. Lucky little boy. I can't remember ever having had an auntie who went shopping for me. She says she wants to go back to the hotel to leave the stuff in her room, as she doesn't want to be carrying it around all night. She's also forgotten her passport, she tells me.

'Oh God, you'd better get that,' I agree heartily. It's not like Amy looks particularly young or anything but anyone under fifty gets asked for ID in this city.

She runs off and I decide to pop upstairs to have a browse in Banana Republic. I usually pick up something nice in that shop and it's great 'cos you normally won't see anyone back in Ireland wearing something you bought there. I pop into a coffee shop, grab a coffee-to-go and head up the escalator. In the Banana Republic shop, the assistant goes 'How are YOU?' with such a wide smile that for a split second I'm convinced I must know her. But then I remember that most shop assistants in the USA greet you like this so I just answer 'fine thanks' with an equally big smile. I think it's kind of nice that they're so cheerful. In Ireland sometimes the shop assistants look at you like they're doing you a HUGE favour when you ask them to get you your right size.

Mind you I don't like assistants to be too enthusiastic. Like when they follow you around the shop and stuff. That's not really on.

I can't really afford anything here because I only have my overnight allowance with me and I have to have drinking money for tonight and pay for breakfast in the morning. Do you know how expensive breakfast is in the States? Ok, I know they give you huge portions but still.

I can't go home with nothing though so I get myself some cute underwear and wonder if Adam would like it. God, stop it Katie. Get that man out of your head. He's obviously got women who'd kill to share his bed. You gotta be different. See? I'm thinking in an American accent already and I'm not even here three hours. It's just a habit I have. If I'm in London I start talking with an English accent. Hell, if I meet a Cork person on the street I start singing in a Cork accent!

Very pleased with my new purchases, I wander around a bit more. I'd better not go too far though or Amy won't be able to find me. I head into a little newsagent to get some Peppermint Patties. Oh I love them so much I'm addicted.

They used to sell Peppermint Patties in Ireland when I was a kid and I loved them. Therefore I was devastated when they were taken off the market. So you can imagine my absolute delight when I first saw them in the supermarket here. I nearly screamed with delight as I stumbled across my favourite childhood treat. Hence any time I'm Stateside I make sure to stock up.

While I'm in the shop giving into my sweet tooth, I pick up *People* to catch up on all the gossip. I haven't read anything about Julia Roberts and J-Lo and co. in over a week and am in serious need of a fix. The assistant puts the magazine and chocolates in a bag. It's great the way they still give you plastic bags here for free.

A tap on my shoulder. It's Amy. She's changed her clothes. What is it about cabin crew and clothes? They can never make up their mind about what to wear. I blame the fact that we're forced to wear a uniform all week. It gets so boring wearing the same old thing day in day out. But at least our uniform is very nice. It's designer, well-cut and flattering. And at least we don't have to wear a hat like some other airline crews. I must say I'd feel a bit silly wearing a hat or a flowery skirt.

'Ok, where will we go?'

'I'm starving,' Amy pats her washboard stomach.

'Let's go up to the food hall,' I suggest. 'So if you fancy Italian, I can always have Chinese. Food halls are just the best invention, aren't they?'

We make our way to the food hall. Amy really is so thin, I envy her. She's not scrawny or anything but just has a perfect waist, long legs and slim arms. She's like a friend of mine, Kerry, who is always ringing me to go for meals.

Kerry is always dragging me out to restaurants even though all she ever seems to eat is just one or two garlic mushrooms. I, on the other hand, have been trained by my mother to clean my plate so that's what I do. I think Kerry must have an eating disorder. I mean the girl is constantly going on about chocolate and crisps and what she had to eat for breakfast and what she's going to have for dinner. In the meantime she just seems to get thinner and thinner. I, however, am always on some kind of a crazy diet, which usually leads me to putting on more weight because after two days I usually just go 'ah feck this,' and pig out on a whole cake or something.

Do you know what I once did? I went down to
my local Tesco's and bought a huge box of Milk
Tray all for myself. And I felt terribly guilty about
it. So guilty in fact that I started explaining to the
girl at the checkout that the chocolates were for a
friend of mine. As if the woman gave a fig!

'Is that all you're having?' Amy stares at my salad.

I try to refrain myself from glaring at her. Why
do thin people always comment on other people's
food? It's a bit rich, isn't it? It seems that the thinner they are, the more concerned they are about
other people not eating enough.

'I'm not that hungry,' I explain wearily.

Her plate is full of pasta. I bet she won't eat
half of it but I will polish off my salad drenched
in a high calorific dressing. I ask for a large Diet
Coke and Amy asks for a regular Coke. Is she
trying to prove a point? Oh maybe I'm just being
paranoid. It's very late. If I were at home I'd be
in bed.

'I wonder where the rest of the crew are?' Amy
says, as we take a seat.

'I dunno, none of them rang me to see what I
was doing.'

'Nor me.' Amy looks a bit miffed. As if there's
a possibility that the rest of the crew have organised a big night out without us. I couldn't give a
tinker's curse what the others are up to. It's bad
enough being cooped up in a large metal container
with them for hours, without us all organising to

meet up again as soon as we land. I mean we need a bloody break from each other!

'Show us what you bought,' Amy grabs my plastic bag like an excited child. When God was dishing out lessons in subtlety, Amy was obviously off getting her nails done.

'Oh look, you got *People*! I love that magazine,' she pulls it out of the bag. Luckily for me it's just *People* she's waving in the air, and not some saucy erotic magazine.

If there's one thing that drives me absolutely mad it's someone reading a magazine I've bought before I've even had a chance to read it myself. Amy is busy flicking through the magazine and commenting on all the celebrities.

'Would you look at the state of your woman?' She points to a singing diva in a low cut sparkly dress. 'If I'd a figure like that I'd keep it well covered up.'

I stare at her plate of pasta that she has already passed to one side. 'Aren't you finishing your dinner?' I enquire.

'Nah, I'm stuffed.'

See what I mean? She *must* be related to my pal Kerry.

'Oh look, there's your man.'

'What man?'

'The one you were going on about earlier, Adam Kirrane.'

I feel my stomach muscles tense. I crane for a

look at my own magazine but I can only see Adam's picture upside down. I almost want to grab the magazine and clock Amy over the head with it.

'He's looking well,' she comments.

I say nothing. She's staring at him and I suddenly feel very protective of Adam's photo. I mean, anyone on the street can just walk into a shop, buy his photo and keep it and comment on it or slate it or whatever. And there's nothing he can say in his defence. It's the price of fame I suppose, but I'm not sure I like it.

'Here, show it to me,' I pull the magazine towards me. I stare at the image and it's hard for me to imagine I even know the guy, never mind the fact that we dined together last night. Adam is wearing a white tuxedo and he's at some party in LA. He looks relaxed, suntanned, happy and quite at ease with being in the spotlight. I wonder when the photo was taken. I wonder has he seen it yet. After all, it's quite an achievement for an Irish actor to feature in a big American magazine like that.

Suddenly I feel very insecure. After all what would a huge star like that be doing with someone like me? What if he just sees me as another play-thing, like a curious child in a toy department store? The very same guy could quite easily click his fingers and have his pick of the world's female population. Maybe I'm getting in over my head here. Perhaps I should leave while the EXIT sign is still visible.

Oh God, I don't really know what to do. I'd love to see a fortuneteller now. I just want to know where all this is going. My heart is fragile enough without letting somebody else throw it on the ground to stomp on.

I push the magazine away again. I don't want to look at Adam's photo anymore. What's the point of thinking about him and trying to figure out where all this is going? He'd probably freak if he realised how much I was reading into last night's date. God I wish I wasn't such a romantic, I really do. But sometimes I want my life to be just like the movies. I want love at first sight; lights, camera and action.

'Do you want to go around any more of the shops?' Amy asks.

No I don't. I'll go around the shops again when I'm not this tired. Anyway, I'm not keen on shopping with other people. It's a pain. I just want to go to a bar now. And forget that Adam's in America and I'm in America. But we're not together.

God I wish in a way I'd never met Adam. Am I mad I wonder, as I struggle to get up off my seat? Being single is so much simpler. Granted, you don't get the terrible highs you get in a relationship, but there are none of the horrible lows either where you just want to crawl under the duvet and not come out for days.

I often find that my single friends are a lot more career-driven than my 'attached' ones. This isn't because they're bitter or have nothing better to do, but because they don't spend half the week wondering if they're partner is happy or not. They're not constantly concerned about somebody else's welfare, which is good. It isn't healthy. Especially if they are out on a Friday night and you are sitting in. Or they are in New York. And you are in Boston.

You're probably wondering about Tim and where he fits into all of this, but I'm convinced Tim rings me out of boredom, not out of love. I mean it. He sees me as a cinema partner or somebody to keep him company in the passenger seat, as he drives around aimlessly on a Sunday afternoon. Like the hordes of other Irish couples who obviously can't bear to 'rest' on Sundays either. Have you noticed the traffic jams on Sundays recently?

I wonder what people did on Sundays before Sunday shopping was introduced. I suppose they went for walks and that, or just sat and watched telly. I remember Mum and Dad took us for a walk every Sunday to Dun Laoghaire pier. I dreaded it. I remember thinking the pier was the longest, most boring walk on the planet, and my little legs could never keep up. It was always freezing and I was always bumping into other kids from school whom I didn't like but was forced to talk to because our parents knew each other.

The only good thing was that we always got an ice cream afterwards from Teddy's. However I would have happily foregone the ice cream, if it had saved me from walking that never-ending pier.

Now of course, I don't think the pier is long enough. It's too short, I think, to get any real exercise. And it's pretty boring too. If you want a proper walk go to Howth or the Dublin mountains or something.

'Where will we go?' Amy pipes up. 'Where do you think everyone else is going? It'd be great if we knew, wouldn't it?'

'It *would* be great to know,' I agree. 'So we could go somewhere else.'

Amy looks so surprised I have to laugh.

I don't mean to be rude, but people who spend their lives wondering where everybody else is, really annoy me. I'm sure you know those kind of people. They are so afraid that everybody else is somewhere else, with someone else, doing something else that they end up never enjoying themselves. My advice is to start the party yourself and see who turns up.

'Let's go to Kitty's,' I suggest.

'Kitty's?'

'Yeah, Kitty O' Shea's. Nice bar with talent. We need to grab a taxi though.'

Amy follows me outside and we both pull our scarves around our faces to prevent the icy air biting any exposed skin. I notice the Bostonians don't look as cold as we do. Maybe they're just used to the big freezes.

We hail a taxi and hop in.

'I'm dying for a drink,' Amy says.

She's reading my mind.

We tell the taxi driver where we're going and hop out ten minutes later.

We enter the pub, which is Irish, but the only person in it who looks Irish is the guy behind the bar. All the other customers look American. They're tall, well-built 'suits', who look like they've just popped in for a single drink or a bite to eat. By the looks of things, the crowd won't be here all night. Pity. I wish they'd stay and keep me company. If this bar was in Dublin, I'd be here all the time. In fact, you wouldn't be able to get rid of me.

The friendly bartender takes our orders and is back almost immediately with our drinks. I tip generously as I'm never sure how much is acceptable in the States and am always nervous about not tipping enough. One of the air hostesses once didn't tip enough after breakfast in a New York diner and the waitress followed her out onto the street and started shouting at her.

Of course, Kitty's is not the type of place where people shout thankfully. There's a nice atmosphere in here and I feel I thoroughly deserve a drink after all my hard work today. Amy is drinking Malibu and pineapple. It's a drink I used to love when I was about seventeen, as I couldn't stand the strong taste of alcohol. Now I honestly don't know how anybody drinks it.

I have a vodka and orange juice with lots of ice. They never skimp on ice in the States. Irish bartenders take note!

'So what's this big secret about Adam?'

I just blurt it out. I've decided I'm not beating around the bush for another hour.

Amy looks at me blankly.

'Who's Adam?'

Oh for God's sake.

'Adam Kirrane.'

'Oh,' she laughs into her Malibu and pineapple. 'That's hilarious haha. When you asked me about Adam I thought you were asking me about somebody we knew. The way you just said 'Adam', instead of 'Adam Kirrane.'

She laughs again and I laugh too although I don't find anything particularly funny. Mind you, she does have a point. If somebody asked me what I thought of 'Colin', meaning Colin Farrell, I'd probably think it was funny too.

'I've been told not to say,' Amy says in a very irritating voice, as she pulls a mock zip across her mouth. 'You know yourself.'

Actually, no. I do *not* know at all. The one thing I do know however is that I'm sitting in Boston with a girl I barely know who keeps laughing for no reason. The other thing I know is that she claims to have this big secret about Adam. And I will not let her go back to her hotel room until I've got it out of her.

I absolutely will not.

And yes, I know I probably sound like a psycho.

'Oh well,' I shrug, deciding to change tactics. 'It's probably not even that interesting.'

'Oh but it is though,' she tilts her head to one side but still refuses to tell me the secret. What does she want? Money?

My mind is racing. What is this flipping secret? Does Adam like to wear women's clothes? Does he have a love child? Does he have a history of violence? Does he swing both ways? Is he having an affair with Hillary bloody Clinton? God, I can't stand this.

'Mmm, that was lovely,' Amy says dreamily after letting the remains of the Malibu and pineapple trickle down her throat.

'Another one?' I offer and shoot to the bar before she's had a chance to answer. Amy is going to have another drink here whether she likes it or not. If I can't personally get her to talk, a few drinks should do the trick.

I'm back with the round. Amy reaches for her purse.

'Put your money away,' I say firmly.

'But . . . '

'You can get the next round,' I say cheerily and pretend not to notice Amy's rather crestfallen face, as she realises we're in for a far longer night than she thought.

'Okay,' she says in a quiet voice.

I can tell she's pissed off.

'So do you like flying?' I ask completely changing the subject as if I don't care if she's not going to tell me Adam's big secret.

'Mmm, yeah, I love it. It's always been my dream to fly, you know.'

'Have you ever thought of doing anything else?'

Amy stares vacantly. 'No, why?'

'Oh I was just wondering.'

'Would *you* like to do something else?'

'Well I'm writing a script.'

'A what?'

'A script.'

'For the telly?'

'Well, a feature film.'

Amy looks at me like she's trying to figure out if I'm joking or not.

'It's about Ireland during the famine,' I tell her.

She's not impressed. At least if she is, she doesn't show it.

'It's about a family who have no money but whatever money they get the father drinks it and then . . .'

'You could get Liam Neeson to star in it,' Amy suggests brightly, and I notice she's drinking her Malibu and pineapple a little faster now.

'If he's free, yes. I think he'd be good.'

'Will you get to pick the cast?'

'I dunno. Hopefully they'll let me have some say.'

'Who's producing it?'

'Nobody yet, because I haven't finished it to send it around to the studios.'

'Oh.' Amy's eyes begin to glaze over. I can tell

she's had enough of this conversation.

'Maybe Adam Kirrane could star in it,' I say suggestively.

'Maybe.' She looks away.

What on earth is she trying to hide? Why won't she tell me Adam's secret?

'Anyway, I'm hoping to go into films after this job,' I tell her. 'Have you no dreams of doing something else?'

'No.'

We sit side by side, deafening silence hanging between us.

'Are you tired?' Amy asks eventually.

'Not a bit,' l lie. 'Come on, finish your drink and let's check out another bar.'

We leave the bar and she's sulking now, but I'm determined not to go back to the hotel. If I go back I'll only be lying on the big double bed thinking of Adam and torturing myself wondering what this big secret of his is.

'Where to so?' Amy jumps up and down on the pavement, demonstrating how unbearably cold she is.

'Have you been to the Littlest Bar?' I ask.

'Huh?'

'Follow me.' I start to run before the frost bites my toes off.

Amy just loves the Littlest Bar. Not because it's Irish. Not because it's so small it could only fit about thirty-five people. Not because of the jolly atmosphere. But because Amy recognises two of the customers.

They're pilots.

Suddenly Amy is no longer showing any signs of tiredness. A big smile seems to be sellotaped onto her face and her eyes are dancing in her head. My heart sinks as the two lads approach us and she eyes them flirtatiously. My chances of finding out Adam's big secret have plummeted.

'Hi Mike. Hi Derek,' she beams and she looks the happiest I've seen her all day. Mind you, she's had a couple of drinks, which seem to have added some colour to her cheeks. 'Have you met Katie?'

'Hello,' I say politely without being too enthusiastic. I notice there's not much left in their pints. With any luck they might be leaving.

Mike is quite good-looking, I notice. He's got very short dark hair and clear blue eyes. I don't think much of his dress sense though (brown bomber jacket and black jeans). But he's got a nice face. No wonder Amy is all over him. Derek isn't that good-looking, but I noticed his eyes lighting up when he saw Amy so I guess there's no chance of himself and Mike heading off just yet.

'Can we get you girls a drink?' Mike offers.

Well, I must say I'm impressed. Some pilots have a name for keeping their hands firmly in their pockets. Especially if they're considered good-looking.

Mike obviously isn't one of them.

'I'll have a . . .'

'Listen, I'll get them,' Amy shouts. 'It's my round.'

Oh no, I think. They're going to think she's bloody brilliant now. A beautiful bird who's only falling over herself to buy them alcohol.

Derek looks like he's about to accept but Mike won't hear of it and insists on paying the round. Amy flutters her eyelids in thanks. I think I'm going to be ill.

Derek goes to the toilet and Amy whispers to me. 'He's pretty cute, isn't he?'

'Which one?'

'Well both of them are nice, aren't they? But I think Derek likes you,' she says.

'No, I think he likes *you*,' I insist.

If she thinks I'm going to entertain the ugly one while she cops off with handsome Mike, she can feck off.

Mike hands us our drinks. 'So where are the rest of your crew?' he asks.

'Oh they were all going to another bar so we came here instead,' I tell him and he laughs.

Amy looks annoyed. Obviously I'm supposed to back off here but I'm just not getting the message, am I? Well too bad about her. Anyway she's supposed to be going out with another pilot.

Then again, I'm supposed to be with Tim. Tim *and* Adam. Well just Adam really. I just haven't got around to letting Tim down yet. I want to break it to him gently. It's always awful being dumped. I've never quite got used to it anyway. I don't think anyone ever does.

'So did you arrive in this afternoon?' Mike asks me and I wish he wouldn't stare at me like that 'cos he's got this really intense look that I'm sure lots of women find irresistible, but I don't because I don't suffer from pilotitis like Amy obviously does.

'We're just on a one-nighter,' Amy tries to elbow me out of the way but I stand my ground. The Littlest Bar is obviously not the biggest bar on the planet but there's no need to push and shove. 'How long are you here?'

'Well we're actually here on a training course. We'll be in Boston for another three days.'

Derek is back but Amy is still focusing on Mike, hanging on to his every word. She looks fascinated, as if he has just told he once flew a plane home by taking a short cut through space. I notice she's not on Malibu any longer. She's on vodka and orange like myself. Copycat.

'What's the craic?' Derek nudges me in a jovial manner. 'You're not saying much.'

'Oh I'm fine,' I turn around to talk to Derek even though I don't see why Amy gets to talk to the good-looking one. But I try not to let it bother me. I only came out tonight to get Adam out of my mind, not to meet a new man. And it's not like Mike is *that* great anyway. He's very attractive but presumably he thinks he's bloody amazing too.

Derek proceeds to tell me about the last three overnights he's had and how much he had to drink on the last one, and how he is building a house in Howth. He tells me he hired a bicycle a couple of months back and went cycling in Kerry for two weeks with four other pilots.

'Gosh,' I feign interest while struggling to keep my eyes open. 'Why did you go to Kerry when you could have flown standby to anywhere in the world.'

'Oh but I never fly standby,' Derek tells me proudly. 'I always need to know if I'm going to get on the flight. I have to know exactly where I'm going.'

Derek is like a lot of pilots in that respect. Most are not the type just to take off at the drop of a hat. Unless they're getting paid of course. I, on the other hand, will head off anywhere. I once planned to visit Florida but ended up in Los Angeles instead. My standby flight to New York was no good because the flight was full (and the plan had been to fly from New York to Florida). Anyway I really didn't fancy coming home with my packed suitcase once I was all psyched up to go away. So I asked ground hostess to swap my New York ticket for one to LA. An hour later I was heading for Disney Land instead of Disney World.

I was travelling on my own anyway so didn't really care where I ended up. I like to travel alone because it helps me think. There's nothing worse than a travelling companion who signs up for all the rip-off touristy trips and insists on visiting every bloody museum within a hundred miles of the resort. On holidays, I just love to wake up and realise that I've nothing to do and nobody to report to. Also, I'll let you in on a little secret here. If you travel alone, you lose lots of weight. Seriously. Because it's not much fun going out for dinner alone. Especially if you're a woman. Or are staying in a particularly romantic resort like the Whitsunday Islands, surrounded by loving couples.

Every time I head off on my tod, I come home a half stone lighter. Beats any of those fad diet books they try to sell you.

' . . . the roof should be on by March of next year and the plumbers should be finished by . . . '

Derek is droning on about his yet-to-be-built house but I'm not really listening. I'm mentally picturing my next foreign holiday. Thailand would be nice. I haven't really travelled much in the Far East although I did stop off in Singapore for a night on my way back from Oz.

I glance at Mike and Amy. They seem to have run out of things to say to each other, and are now showing a vague interest in the progress of Derek's house, which is great because it takes the pressure off me. I wonder where Mike lives and if he has a house and a girlfriend. He's not married. At least he's not wearing a wedding ring anyway. Anyway why am I even thinking about Mike?

I excuse myself to go to the bathroom. As I wash my hands I look in the mirror and don't care for what's looking back at me. My eyes are bloodshot, my skin looks almost grey and my hair is dull and lank. No wonder Mike has been ignoring me and Derek thinks it's all right to bore me stupid about his future house.

When I come back out, Amy and Mike have disappeared.

'Amy didn't feel that well, so Mike brought her back to the hotel. She said she'd give your room a ring in the morning,' Derek explains.

This takes a second or two to sink in. I'm pretty stunned. I cannot believe Amy waited for me to go to the bathroom so she could sneak off. The pair of them must have been dying to get rid of the pair of us. Derek and myself must have been cramping their style. Jesus, I'm really annoyed. I feel completely used even though *I* was the one who had practically forced Amy into the bar. I'm also annoyed that Mike obviously preferred Amy to me. God, what is wrong with me? Suddenly my head feels like it's being crushed. I feel drowsy and I just want to collapse. I want to be in my bed right now. And don't want to go out and face the cold again. I don't even want to have to fly home again tomorrow. In fact I don't want to fly ever again. I want to be a famous scriptwriter and be the person sitting in first class with my feet up.

'Katie?'

'Mmm.'

'You're a million miles away.'

'Oh sorry,' I say dreamily.

'I bought you another vodka and orange but you don't have to drink . . .'

' . . . thank you,' I lift the glass and knock back the contents.

Chapter Nine

My head. Oh God, my head. It definitely doesn't feel the best. Opening my eyes I try to remember which country I'm in. Oh yes, America. Boston. It's all coming back to me. Yes. Kitty's and The Littlest Bar. I vaguely remember going there but don't remember leaving. I must have come back though. With Derek. Derek the pilot. Not the good-looking one. No. That was Mike. I don't remember saying goodbye to Derek but I must have. It's all a bit of a blur.

I'm parched. I can't believe I forgot to leave some water beside the bed yesterday evening. Very silly thing to do. Not to worry though, there's a soft drinks machine on the corridor outside. And as far as I remember there's also an ice machine.

I'd better slip out and grab a can before I die of dehydration. I pick up my hotel key and sneak outside wearing my pink Dunnes Stores pyjamas with an elephant on the front. They'd be cute on a ten-year-old but I'm not sure they suit me. I pop a dollar into the machine and press the button. A can of Diet Coke crashes to the bottom.

It's nice and chilled but I may as well grab some ice. Sugar. I realise I've nothing to put the ice in. I'd better go back to my room and grab an ice bucket. I dart back inside, leave down the can and re-emerge with the ice bucket. The ice cubes smash into the bucket making the loudest sound. I hear somebody coming out of their room. Sugar, sugar, sugar. I don't like to be caught standing out here in my jammies. Oh well, it's probably just some American whom I'll never see again.

The door slams and I feel somebody approach me and stop behind me. Suddenly I panic. A chill runs along my spine. Suppose it's a rapist or someone who's thinking of dragging me into their room and clobbering me over the head with my own ice bucket?

I swing around. And my eyes meet another pair. They're blue and inquisitive. And they belong to Mike. Mike, the pilot. He looks gorgeous. And I look like shit. I'm furious at him for sneaking up on me like this. I hate him for seeing me in this state.

'Hello,' he says, really casually. As if it's perfectly normal to be chatting to a colleague in her night-clothes. He's wearing denims and a white t-shirt. I bet he's been up for hours. He looks like he got a good night's sleep. Hmm. That's weird. I wonder what happened between himself and Amy. Then I remember how he left me in The Littlest Bar without saying goodbye. The nerve!

'Hello,' I answer back, very coolly. I have no intention of having a conversation with a man who abandoned me in a bar in order to cop off with another airhostess.

'Did you get home all right?' he enquires.

Well, actually, I was mugged, raped and stabbed on the way home but sure I'm grand now.

'Poor Amy wasn't feeling well,' he continues as I try to manoeuvre my way around him. He's standing between the ice machine and me so it isn't that easy. I wish he'd let me pass.

'Really?' I answer dully.

'Yes, but I think she's fine now.'

'Well that's fantastic. Now forgive me for being rude but I need to go back to bed. Last night turned out to be a very long one.'

I ignore Mike's puzzled expression and disappear back into my room.

I shut the door and immediately run to the mirror. Oh Jesus. I knew I wouldn't exactly win a beauty contest this morning but I didn't realise I was looking *this* shit. My mascara has run half way down my face as I forgot to remove it last night and my skin is puffy and blotchy. I am so annoyed with myself for letting one of the pilots see me in this state. I'll be the laughing stock of the airline. Hmm. Bet Mike is glad he picked Amy over me. I'm sure he's thanking his lucky stars he left me in the bar with Derek. Well, good luck to him, I think. I'm not going to worry about what

he thinks. He might be cute enough but I would-
n't go *near* him. Not if he was the last available
man on the planet.

I sit down on the bed and wonder what to do
with the rest of my day. I'm sure as hell not going
to waste it thinking about Mike anyway. God, no.
I'd like to go down to the leisure centre and sweat
off last night's drink fest in the sauna but am afraid
of bumping into Mike in a near-naked state. He's
already seen my very unsexy just-got-out-of-bed
look, but I simply refuse to let him see my cellulite
too!

I think I'll go down to Boston Common for a
walk, that should clear my head. Then I might have
a root around Filenes's basement to see if I can pick
up any bargains. Mind you, with the head I've on
me this morning, maybe a walk in the park is all
I'll have the energy for.

It takes me an hour to get ready. Thank God I've
my heavy coat with me. Walking around Boston
when you're not appropriately dressed can be miserable. Once outside, I immediately feel better. There's
something very claustrophobic about hotel rooms.
Must be the air conditioning. It's nippy though.
Outside the hotel foyer, I hug myself against the icy
morning chill.

When I get to Newbury Street, I wander around
marvelling at the quaint little boutiques that line
the street. If I'd lots of money I'd hang out here all
the time, I think. I love everything about this street,

especially the gorgeous little shops that sell exotic-looking ice cream even in the depth of winter. I walk and walk and walk and I'm soon feeling much better. Walking in Boston is therapeutic. My hangover is rapidly disappearing. Last night seems months ago. I'm wondering how Adam is getting on in New York. I'd half expected him to send me a text or something but there hasn't been a peep from him. He's probably really busy, I tell myself. He'd said something about meeting a powerful film executive. Adam wants to get into movies. He told me that. He doesn't want to be a mere TV star all his life. Doesn't want to be typecast. He has visions.

I love walking alone. It helps me think. I'm sure Amy is still in bed with the remote control watching some mindless soap. I still can't get over her behaviour last night. What did she think she was playing at, abandoning me like that?

After a while I'm in Boston Common and I sit on a bench watching kids skate on a frozen pond. The park looks really Christmassy, like a postcard. I wish I could stay in Boston a while longer. I'm not looking forward to going home. I never am.

I love my job, don't get me wrong. Love the perks and the cities I visit. I just don't like working the actual flights. I did at first because it was a novelty but I get bored easily, and now I just wish there was a bit more to my life. I fly to places and then fly back again but sometimes I just want to fly somewhere and keep flying.

I get up from the park bench because it's too cold. I consider heading to Filenes's but then decide I can't face the crowds. I'll do it another time. Right now, I just want something to eat. I make for the nearest deli.

At the deli I help myself to a little bit of everything. The choice of food is wonderful and everything seems to be low fat so I can fill my plate without feeling guilty. I wish there were delis like this back in Dublin where I could always eat well. It's a struggle to stay slim living in Ireland.

After lunch, I head back to the hotel. Pick-up is in five hours. The coach will collect us outside the hotel. And then it'll be back to Logan Airport where we'll face the long flight home. The flight home is usually a lot shorter than the flight over, especially if we've the wind behind us. But it always feels longer. Yes, coming home always feels a lot longer.

Back in my hotel room I wonder if I should grab a couple of hours kip before my flight. If I can do it, the flight home will be more bearable. Then again, I don't want to lie in bed tossing and turning with one eye on the dreaded clock. That often happens. I'm not one of these people who conks out the minute my head hits the pillow. I wish I was.

Sometimes I see passengers sleeping on the short hop from Dublin to Manchester. As soon as we take off, they're out for the count and wake up as the wheels hit the runway. They must be very peaceful, those people. I can never sleep because my mind is always racing. And I'm always worrying about things. Stupid things. I read somewhere that most things people worry about never happen, and the things that do happen, there's nothing you can do about them anyway. Therefore worrying is completely pointless. But that nevertheless doesn't stop me.

I worry a lot. About people not liking me and not achieving everything I want to. Sometimes I worry about being left on the shelf, but equally worry about marrying somebody I don't really love. I worry about not being able to have children but also worry that having children will take away my freedom. Most of all though, I worry about really small, really insignificant things.

Like my roster.

My roster is something I'm never terribly happy about. In fact I resent the fact that somebody I don't know is organising my life, deciding what time I get up at, what country I'll have lunch in, and who I get to spend the weekend with.

If I were a successful scriptwriter I could write whenever I pleased, in whatever country I chose. I would write my own roster, and not even stick to it if I didn't want to. Now somebody else does that. Somebody else decides if I get Christmas or New Year's Eve off. They decide what time I must set my alarm and God do I hate that.

One day, I'm going to do it *my* way. That's the dream anyway. I want to live my own life. And not have to ask someone for permission for a weekend off. If I go to the doctor it should be own private business. I don't want to get a written note explaining everything to my employer. God, some things should be sacred!

I get undressed. I think I'll have a bath anyway. A nice hot bath where I can relax using the luxurious hotel bath gel. A bath is a luxury I rarely indulge in at home. Mainly because there's somebody always in the bathroom. And if there's not, there's always someone trying to get in.

If I had my way, I'd have a bath every day and then go to the hairdresser too because that's the secret to looking great. No matter how tired you are, if your hair is shiny and blow-dried, you can get away with murder.

I've one toe in the water when the phone rings. Dammit. I bet it's housekeeping wondering can they clean my room. Well no, they bloody can't, I think irritably, retrieving my toe from the bubble bath and reaching for the phone.

'Hi, it's Amy,' says the voice although it doesn't really sound like Amy. It sounds like an impersonator. What does she want anyway?

'Hello.' I don't sound very enthusiastic. Not surprisingly really since Amy is not my favourite person since her surprise party-piece last night.

'How are you?'

'I'm fine. In fact I'm actually about to get into the bath Amy so if you don't mind . . .'

'Oh I'm sorry, I really am. I was just ringing to apologise about last night.'

'What happened last night?' I pretend not to know what she's talking about. I'm not going to give her the satisfaction of knowing that she hurt me.

'I left without saying goodbye.'

'Oh yes. So you did. I'd completely forgotten. You see, Derek and I were having such a laugh, we didn't even notice you'd gone.'

'Oh.' Amy sounds subdued.

'Yes. Well see you later.'

'Katie?'

'Yes?'

My bath is getting cold. Can't we talk later? Like on the plane? Or preferably never?

'I think Donald is cheating on me.'

I don't say anything. My blood has run cold. How much does she know? Did somebody tell her about Debbie? Does she know I know? Suddenly I don't care about my bath any more. I actually feel sorry for Amy. There's nothing more horrible than suspecting someone you love, or even like, is cheating on you.

'I'll come around to you and we can talk properly,' I tell her. 'What room are you in again?'

* * *

Amy looks like I looked this morning when I bumped into Mike, only worse. Her eyes are red and her skin is ropey looking.

'You don't look well at all,' I say grimly.

'Thanks.'

She looks miserable in fact.

'So,' I sit on the end of her bed. 'What makes you think Donald is cheating?'

'Well I'm not one hundred per cent sure,' she leans forward in the bed. 'But I have my suspicions.'

'Oh?' I play dumb.

'Yes. So last night I was quizzing Mike to see if I could get any information out of him.'

Aha. It's all beginning to make sense now. So Amy wasn't trying to lure Mike into the sack last night after all. What a relief! She was merely using him as a means of finding out information. Well that makes me feel a lot better.

'I hope you didn't think I was ignoring you in the bar. Donald's strange behaviour has been on my mind for quite a while now, so last night I just grabbed the opportunity to get some inside information. You know yourself.'

'Mmm.'

'Yes, and I didn't want to let on that I was Donald's girlfriend, so I started asking Mike about lots of other pilots so he'd think I was, you know, just taking a general interest.'

'Very wise.'

'I asked him about Gary Teller and his girlfriend

Shelley. And then about Tony Kent and his fiancée Aileen and then about Donald and . . . I pretended I'd forgotten the name of his girlfriend.'

'Oh my God, I'll have to remember that one.' I chuckle.

'I wasn't happy with the answer I got though.' Amy's face crumples and horror of horrors, a lone tear rolls down her face.

'Who is she?'

I'm starting a slow descent towards panic. I'm absolutely dreading the answer to this one. Does she know Debbie is my friend?

'Rose.'

'Sorry?'

'He said her name was Rose. He'd met her at a wedding they were both at recently.'

What!

'How recent?' I blurt out.

'Last week.'

Oh my God. Shock and double shock. I wonder if Debbie knows anything about this? How dare Donald treat my best friend like this! I'll bloody kill him!

'As soon as I heard that, I wanted to leave the bar straight away,' Amy continues, reaching for a tissue. 'I felt really bad because Mike really didn't want to leave.'

'Did he not?' I ask, suddenly perking up.

Amy shakes her head. 'I got the feeling he was pretty pissed off for being dragged away.'

'Yeah?'

Now, I'm suddenly seeing Mike in a brand new light.

'Not that he said anything,' Amy adds hastily.

'Of course not.'

I feel awful now for being so rude earlier on.

'I just told him I was sick and needed to go back to the hotel.'

'I understand.'

'And then this morning he called to my room with croissants and freshly squeezed orange juice. Said he wanted to make sure I was feeling okay.'

I feel jealous. What happened to my croissants?

'He's cute, isn't he?'

'Hmm?'

'Mike,' Amy says. 'He's pretty cute.'

'Oh I don't know,' I shrug. 'I'm seeing somebody at the moment so I don't really notice other men.'

'Is it serious?'

Is it? I don't know, do I?

'I'm not sure.'

Should I tell her about Adam? Is it safe?

'I hope he treats you well,' Amy says with a self-pitying sniff.

'All men are bastards at the end of the day,' I say, in a feeble attempt to bring a smile to her face.

It doesn't work though. Her face crumples again. She reaches for another tissue.

'Speaking of bastards . . .' I venture, wondering if I'm treading on thin ice here but going ahead and treading on it anyway, '. . . what were you going to tell me yesterday about Adam Kirrane?'

There. I've done it. It wasn't too bad. Now I'm holding my breath, already afraid of the answer.

'Why? Is he a bastard?' Amy asks after she finishes blowing her nose.

'Um, I don't know. He's good looking and all good-looking men are bastards, aren't they? I mean the only men who aren't bastards are ugly, because they can't get away with treating women like shit.'

Amy's tears magically disappear. She looks completely shocked at my outburst. As if I'm a deserted wife who has turned to drink in despair.

'You shouldn't be so bitter,' she says in a voice that implies she actually feels sorry for me.

I'm slightly embarrassed now. God, Amy thinks I'm some kind of man hater with a massive chip wearing down my shoulder. And she couldn't be more wrong. I don't hate men at all. Not at all. I love them in fact. But there's no point backtracking now or else I'll really confuse the poor girl. So I say nothing and silently squirm.

'You must have been badly hurt in the past,' Amy says after a long pause. 'I'm sure people think Adam Kirrane is a bastard but they're wrong.'

'How do you know?' I ask pretending to be casually interested even though my internal organs feel like they've suddenly tied themselves into one gigantic knot. How does Amy know the first thing about Adam Kirrane? Granted, she seems to know a hell of a lot about every pilot working in the company but Adam? My Adam? How does Amy know anything about him?'

'I think people in the public eye have a very difficult time,' Amy insists and I notice the colour has returned to her face.

'How's that?'

'Well, people, as in the public, people like you and me say . . . '

She pauses and I wait for her to continue. I'm not sure I like where this is going.

'Well the public just judge the rich and famous by what they read about in the press.'

I wait for her to continue. I'm intrigued but also slightly scared. Is Amy Adam's secret sister or something?

'I mean you can't blame people. I mean, I've been guilty of it, you know? I've seen pictures of supermodels or whatever and have automatically thought they've been vain or bitchy or whatever . . . '

Jesus, would she ever just get to the point?

'But then I've met them, say, on a flight and they've been very nice.'

'God Amy, just because someone's polite and says 'please' and 'thank you' on a flight doesn't mean they're an extremely nice person. I once had the most charming man on a flight to Paris and when we arrived, the French police were waiting to handcuff him.'

'For what?'

'Murder,' I say morbidly.

'No way! Tell us more,' Amy shrieks.

No way am I telling her more. She can forget it. Pick-up is only a few hours away and I still haven't got Adam's bloody secret out of her. But I'm nearly there. It's just at the tip of her tongue and I'm not giving up now.

'I'll tell you on the way home,' I promise.

She looks disappointed as if I'm just fobbing her off.

'So as you see,' I badger on, not wanting to lose momentum. 'As you can see, there's no telling what someone is like just because you serve them a cup of tea and they thank you for it.'

'Adam Kirrane is *not* somebody I've just served on a flight though,' Amy lowers her voice as if someone might be outside eavesdropping.

I take a deep breath. This conversation is pure torture. In fact I'd like to press the rewind button and then erase.

'Was he on one of your flights?'

'Well no, but . . .'

But WHAT? I want to scream.

'I dunno if I should say.'

My heart sinks. You know I had a horrible niggling feeling that this might happen.

I sit on the bed rigidly. If I give her enough rope and all that . . .

'I promised not to . . .' She says uncertainly.

'You can trust me,' I tell her; aware I'm probably

blushing furiously. I'm sure I look like a cocaine smuggler going through Schipol airport.

'Well you know Sandy Elkinson?

Do I know her? Jesus, of course I do. I mean, who doesn't? She's the best-looking girl in the airline. All the pilots want to marry her and all the airhostesses want to be her. Not only is Sandy Ireland's answer to Claudia Schiffer, she's also a tennis pro who speaks five languages and has a degree in law, but the amazing thing is that Sandy is also very funny and nice. It's impossible not to like her. But what has Sandy got to do with anything?

'She's dating Adam.'

Ouch. I feel I've been slapped in the face. My heart has been sliced with an imaginary knife. I get up from the bed slowly and unsteadily. I feel faint.

'I'd better go and get ready,' I say weakly.

'Sure,' Amy smiles, as if she hasn't noticed my stricken face. 'I feel much better now by the way.'

'Good.'

'And you won't tell anyone?'

'About what?' I ask, dazed.

'About Adam Kirrane and Sandy.'

'I won't,' I promise.

I leave her room quietly, somehow dragging my heavy heart with me.

Chapter Ten

I hate writing. It's really crap, anti-social and headache inducing. No wonder most writers are bonkers. Sure, you couldn't possibly spend so much time by yourself and be normal, could you? I've spent the last two days writing my script. In the process however I've forgotten to sleep or eat. I'm completely engrossed in my script. My parents think I have lost the plot but one day, when I collect my Oscar for best screenplay, they'll realise they had a genius sitting in their midst. And did nothing about it.

Dad is not happy with me. This is due to the fact that in between writing my script I am looking up information on the web to see which production company I should send my masterpiece to. After all, I don't want to send it to just anybody. This script must end up in the right hands. It's my baby and I don't want anybody killing it. No foreign actors with nauseatingly awful Irish accents are going to be allowed snatch the main parts. I'll forbid it. I want strong, well-established, talented actors.

Liam Neeson would be great but I'm not sure who'll play the female lead. That's a tricky one.

My sister and I are not talking. She picked up my script yesterday, skimmed through it and said it was shit. I silently fumed but said nothing. In five year's time when she has achieved nothing but a permanent sneer and general ill will towards everybody, I'll remember her nasty comments.

What makes family members think they've got a God given right to insult each other anyway? If somebody on the street spoke to me the way my family sometimes do, I'd have them arrested. And certainly if any of my friends spoke to me that way, I would never entertain them again. Unfortunately family members are like beetroot stains – it's almost impossible to remove them.

I will not stoop to Ruth's level though. Instead I will simply feel sorry for her because she is marrying somebody the whole family secretly distrust, her husband-to-be is the most unreliable person we've ever met. Ruth ignores our advice though. Her belief is that one man, any man, is better than none.

'Suppose it doesn't work out?' I asked her one day, knowing in my heart of hearts that her marriage probably doesn't stand a chance. Her fiancé is a serious nut.

'I'll get divorced,' she said defiantly.

'But wouldn't that be awful?'

'It's better than remaining single. At least if I'm

divorced, people will know that I was loved once. That can't be said for people who never get married.'

She'll learn, I thought sadly. And she'll learn the hard way. My sister honestly thinks none of us want her to be happy. Anyway she was over yesterday to discuss her wedding dress but I'm not going to bore you stupid with details. It's bad enough that my family are so involved without you having to be part of it too. The only reason I mentioned her was because she was the first person to see my script. And the last. Nobody else will get to see it now. Nobody else will get the chance to ridicule my work.

Dad has just come into the kitchen and needs to check something on the Internet. He says he heard from Mr Foley next door that there are great last minute deals going to Lanzarote. Mr Foley has written down the travel web address for him and says not to leave it too late or all the bargains will be snapped up.

I save my hard work into 'My documents'. I hope my dad *does* get a last minute trip to Lanzarote and takes off with Mum. I wouldn't mind the house to myself for a week so I can write in peace.

I head up to my room and check my phone. No text messages. No. No missed calls either. Not a peep from Adam since my overnight in Boston. But sure who did I think I was kidding? As if he was going to call me when he's dating my 'supermodel' colleague whom I used to think was a lovely girl.

But don't any more.

How can I like somebody who has helped break my heart?

I'm trying not to think about Adam and the fact that I have been discarded like an empty pack of fags. Or at least ignored for the last few days. I don't like thinking I've been dumped as he might still call. I am a strong woman. I have a lot going for me and just because one man hasn't called yet, doesn't mean it's the end of the world. My script is really coming together now and should be finished by the end of the month. New Year's Eve is my deadline. It's a good night to have a deadline because it gives me something to do on the worst night of the year. God, I hate New Year's Eve more than anything. I love Christmas but New Year is the ultimate anticlimax with nobody willing to commit to doing anything just in case something more exciting comes up. And of course nothing ever does. And all those uncommitted people are always left wondering where the party is.

So this year I have a perfectly good excuse for not shelling out a couple of hundred euro for a naff New Year's ball. I have a deadline. My script must be finished before midnight. Being disciplined is the only way forward, I've decided. Successful people are ruthless when it comes to time wasting. And my script will only ever get finished if I place my bum firmly on my seat and keep scribbling.

Sometimes I sit at the computer and wonder

where the whole story is going. Other times I wonder is it just a load of old crap and if I'm completely wasting my time. Perhaps I'm just a talentless git who won't accept it. Then again, suppose Richard Curtis had had that attitude? I'd never have had the pleasure of watching *Notting Hill* a hundred times. I'm not saying that I could be the next Richard Curtis or anything but I do remind myself now and again that he was a young boy once, just like me. I mean . . . well you know what I mean. The thing is, he wasn't born a scriptwriter and Madonna wasn't born a singer. Yes you have to have a shred of talent to start off with. At least it would help anyway, but there are lots of talented people out there licking envelopes and answering phones.

Okay, now that I've convinced myself that anyone can achieve anything, I once again turn my attentions to the computer screen. There's nothing more terrifying than the blank screen but I suppose most writers go through this. If it was easy, then everybody would be doing it.

I'm going to LA tomorrow and intend doing a lot of thinking over there. I'm really looking forward to it. A bit of sunshine in my life. When I'm out in LA I'll do nothing but sit by the pool drinking water and eating fruit. Then when I come back I'll be like a new person: slimmer and slightly more tanned depending on the weather . . .

Oh God, I think I'll just leave the script for now.

I'm bored silly writing it. I suppose I'll have to wait for inspiration to hit me and it's certainly not doing that now.

I've agreed to meet Debbie for a couple of drinks later. I'm not really looking forward to it. Do you think I should tell her about Donald? I mean, seriously, what would you do if you were me? It's a hard call and I wish to God I wasn't in this situation. After all, I don't want to be the bearer of bad news but if I'm supposed to be a good friend, I'll just have to tell her straight, won't I?

The other thing I have to do is tell Tim our relationship is not working out. I'm not looking forward to that either. I don't want to hurt him but it's just got to be done. I'm sure he'll get over me fairly quickly though. I hope he has the strength to move on.

Debbie looks a million dollars. I meet her in the Cock Tavern in Swords, which is her local pub. At least it's become her local ever since she started seeing Donald.

Nowadays, wherever the pilots hang out, Debbie tends to be not too far away. She's meeting him here later. I hope I can try and be civil to him, knowing what I now know but it won't be easy. My mother always told me that my facial expressions leave no doubt to what I'm thinking. I guess I'll never be a poker champion so.

Debbie wants to know all about my trip to

Boston. I tell her about the underwear I picked up in Banana Republic, my run-in with Snakely, The Littlest Bar and about meeting Derek and Mike. I don't mention Amy. For obvious reasons.

'Oh that Mike is very cute,' Debbie's face lights up with interest.

'He's not too bad,' I agree.

'What was he saying?'

'Oh this and that, you know, airline stuff. You know what pilots are like.'

'Tell me about it,' Debbie rolls her eyes to the ceiling as if she finds it all very annoying. But I know she loves it really.

'Who else was with you?' she probes.

Oh God, I'd better tell her. If I don't tell her she'll wonder why.

'Do you know that girl Amy?'

'Yeah, yeah, 'course I do. She lives in this place. Bit of an airhead really, herself and her pal Sandy.'

'Do you know Sandy?' My eyes widen. Perhaps Debbie will have something on her.

'I've flown with her a couple of times. She's pilot mad. I used to think she had a bit of a thing for Donald.'

'But not any more?'

'No, I haven't seen her around for a while. She rarely comes into the Cock Tavern any more even though she's renting in Swords with a couple of the girls. She must be going out with someone.'

'I wonder who,' I say testily.

'Who knows and who cares?' Debbie shrugs. 'I can't keep up with all the airhostesses and their boyfriends.' She raises her Bacardi and Coke. 'Cheers,' she smiles.

The bar fills up but there's no sign of Donald yet. Just as well really. It means we can enjoy our drinks in peace. I wonder is this a good time to tell Debbie about Donald. I've a feeling it isn't. Somehow I don't know if I'll ever be able to bring myself to tell her. She looks so happy. She has a glow about her. I wish I had the same glow.

'So how's Tim?' she asks politely.

'Dunno, I haven't seen him in ages,' I admit. 'I'm seeing him tonight, but probably for the last time.'

'Whaddya mean?' Debbie looks puzzled.

'It's just not working out,' I sigh. 'I mean what's the point in continuing to see someone when you know they're not the One?'

'Tim's not that bad.'

'I know he's not that bad but that bad isn't that good, is it? He's not as nice as you think anyway Debs. I know him a lot better than you do and this is not a decision I made today or yesterday. I've seriously thought it over. And do you know what I've decided? I'd rather be single and alone than attached to the wrong person.'

'How do you think he'll take it?' Debbie frowns and starts playing with her beer mat.

'I wouldn't say he'll take it too well. In fact I'm

dreading telling him.'

'Rather you than me,' Debbie takes a slug from her drink and looks serious. 'I think there's nothing worse than having to break it off with somebody.'

'Tell me about it,' I mutter gloomily. 'It's easier when they do the dirty work. I hate to be the one to make that final decision. I'm never sure if I'm doing the right thing.'

'What are you going to tell him? Are you going to give him the "It's not me, it's you" crap?'

'I'm just going to tell him the truth.'

'Which is?'

'I think we've grown apart.'

'God, that turkey?'

'There's no right way to tell someone it's over. If there is I certainly don't know about it.'

Our conversation is interrupted by Donald who miraculously appears at Debbie's side. He plants a kiss on her head and her face breaks into a smile.

'Hiya Katie,' he goes to give me a kiss too but I turn away quickly. As if I'm going to let that rat give me a kiss!

'Have you met Mike?' he says catching me by surprise.

I turn around and face Mike for the first time since our rather uncomfortable meeting outside my hotel bedroom. I'm mortified. By the looks of things, the feeling's mutual.

'Yes, we've met,' I say hastily feeling my cheeks

burn. In the name of God, what did I do to deserve this? He looks well, very well in fact although for some strange reason I hate admitting this. He smells nice too – Polo, Ralph Lauren, I think.

'How many of you are here?' Debbie asks brightly.

'Five of us. It's Colin's birthday.

Great, I think. Colin is Donald's brother, although he's not half as good looking. What he lacks in the looks department though, he makes up for with his huge ego.

Personally I don't think the Cock Tavern will be big enough for all of us.

As if by magic, the front door swings open and Colin and the rest of the lads crowd into the bar. Jesus, it's like an airline bloody reunion in here. Come to think of it, this might be a good time to leave.

'Oi, where do you think you're going?' Colin bellows as he sees me standing up. He's so tall he makes me feel like a midget. Hmm. So much for my escape plan.

'It's my birthday. You can't leave without buying me a drink. And where's my birthday kiss, haha?'

Mike and I exchange awkward glances.

I go to give Colin a kiss on the cheek but he turns swiftly and our lips collide. Ugh. Should have seen that coming. Why can't it be Mike's birthday instead?

I wipe my mouth as if to make a point.

A couple more pilots arrive. They all look exactly the same: striped shirts and jeans. Mike stands out though. He looks good enough to eat. It's a pity I'm not technically single. Although I will be in about one hour. That reminds me, I'd better get going. I'm meeting Tim in town and I just want to get this over and done with. I'm dreading seeing his face when I tell him. It'd be much easier to do it over the phone. But of course, I'd never ever do anything as cowardly as that. Tim deserves more. We've known each other for almost three years. We've got memories for God's sake. We've even got a song. I just can't remember what it is right now.

'I'd better get going,' I whisper in Debbie's ear.

'Ah stay for just one more,' she pleads. 'It's awful being the only female among a group of lads.'

'Liar.'

'Don't go,' Colin booms in a loud voice. 'Mike. Make her stay.'

All the lads seem to find this very funny. Everybody except of course Mike, whose face has gone a curious crimson colour.

'What's the rush?' Donald raises an eyebrow and I'm amazed at his coolness. Who does he think he is, bloody Casanova?

Debbie leans over and explains in hushed tones.

'Oh,' he nods mysteriously, as if he suddenly understands. I can tell the others are dying to know what Debbie told him. No doubt he'll inform them once I've gone. They'll probably think I'm a callous bitch. That's how I feel anyway as I put on my coat and wrap my big black woollen scarf around my neck. It's awful to end a relationship so near to Christmas too. I do hope Tim hasn't gone and bought my present already.

As I bid the group a farewell wave I catch Mike looking at me and wish he wouldn't. He has a very intense stare. As if he knows more about me than I know about myself. It's unnerving.

I head outside and hail a taxi. I told Tim I'd phone when I was on my way into town. In the back of my taxi I take my mobile phone out of my bag and see a missed call. I didn't hear the phone with the noise in the pub.

My heart gives a little leap as I realise Adam made the call. I'm thrilled. I really am absolutely over the moon. Quickly I ring him back but unfortunately get his answer machine. I'm about to leave a message when I panic and hang up. What'll I say? I'll have to think about this. I don't want to sound like I've been waiting desperately by the phone for the last few days. Anyway I'd better ring Tim first. I can't get through to him either, which is very annoying.

As soon as I press END, the phone rings and Adam's name flashes up. OhmiGod, I can't believe he's ringing back so quickly.

'Hello?' I answer with a big grin on my face, which thankfully Adam can't see.

'Where are you?' he asks. Just like that. As if I was speaking to him five minutes ago instead of five days ago.

'I'm coming into town. I was out in Swords having a drink with a bunch of the lads,' I tell him, thinking that makes me sound rather exciting. I just want him to know I haven't been sitting in all evening twiddling my thumbs.

'What lads?'

'Oh just some of the pilots.' I say casually.

'I see.'

He sounds put out. Good. He probably thinks the pilots all look like Greek Gods and are wildly exciting. And I'm not going to bother correcting him. Let him think I've all these dashing Tom Cruise types chasing me around the planes.

'Where are you now?'

'I'm going into town.'

'What are you doing there?'

God, he isn't half nosy, is he?

'I'm meeting a friend.'

'Male or female?'

'As I said, it's a friend so it doesn't matter whether they're male or female, does it?' I tease.

'So it's a male.'

I don't answer.

'Is it a date?'

Quick Katie. Think of something.

'It's just an old friend.'

An old friend whom I also used to sleep with incidentally.

'Where are *you*?' I want to stop talking about

me now.

'Still in New York.'

'Missing me?' I say boldly.

'Kind of.'

Missing Sandy too? I obviously don't say this but I'm thinking it. Is he going to phone her straight after me or has he just got off the phone to her? Maybe she didn't answer so he dialled my number instead?

'You should come over to New York,' he says and my heart momentarily soars. I cannot believe Adam is on the phone suggesting I come and meet him. Doesn't sound to me like a guy who's in love with somebody else. Someone other than me.

'We'll see.' I'm determined to remain uncommitted. No point jumping the gun too soon. After all, only a few minutes ago I wasn't sure if I'd ever hear from Adam Kirrane again.

'Wish I was there,' he says.

Yeah, right.

'Thank you. Er . . . when do you think you'll be back?' I ask, hoping I don't sound too eager.

'As soon as I can get away Babes. Schedule's pretty hectic at the moment. But I'll talk to you soon, okay?'

'Sure. Talk soon.'

He's gone. Just like that. God, I wish I were in New York instead of Dublin, waiting to give Tim the bad news that we are no longer to be known as 'we'.

I get out of the taxi at The Conrad Hotel. I walk

down to the bar and order myself a glass of white wine. The place is empty except for two couples chatting quietly. I phone Tim again. This time he answers immediately.

'Are you on your way in?' I ask him.

'Um no, I got held up at a meeting. Where are you?'

'In The Conrad waiting for you.'

'Listen, I'm not sure if I can make it in.'

What does he mean he can't make it in? Is he thinking of standing me up?

'I need to talk to you,' I say putting on my most serious voice.

'I need to talk to you too,' he answers just as seriously. He doesn't sound like the Tim I know. He sounds almost hostile. I don't like it.

'Can't we get together and talk face to face?'

'Well actually Katie,' he pauses for what seems like an age, 'I don't think this is going anywhere.'

'What?' I'm all confused. What's he playing at? I'm in no mood for playing games. With Tim or with anybody. I am sitting in a bar on my own, I'm tired and my head is beginning to ache. My warm comfy bed is beckoning.

'You and me. I think we've run our course.'

Hang on. Am I hearing what I think I'm hearing? I can't be. No. There's no way Tim would . . . he'd never . . . God, is this Tim's way of telling me he's finishing it with me?

'Are you still there, Katie?'

'Yes.'

'I know it'd be better if I told you to your face but as I said I've got held up. I'm really sorry. It's never nice to be the one who has to break it off but I'm just being cruel to be kind.'

'I'm shocked.'

That's an understatement. I'm completely stunned. What is Tim doing breaking it off with me when I'm the one supposed to be doing the dumping? How on earth is this happening? Has he met someone else? Is he held up because he's on a date with another woman? Is she sitting there with him as he's having this conversation with me? How humiliating! I don't understand.

'Listen Katie, I'm sure you'll get over me. One day I'm sure you'll meet somebody a bit more deserving. You're a wonderful person, Katie. This isn't about you, it's about . . .'

'. . . don't even say it,' I warn. 'Please do not insult me.'

The walls of the bar are beginning to spin. I feel like this is a dream and I'm not really having this conversation. Why has Tim had a sudden change of heart? Instead of feeling elated that Tim wants to end our relationship, I feel kind of ill. Did somebody tell him something about me? Oh my God. I know what it is. His bloody sister must have gone and said something to him. She must have told him about bumping into Adam and myself.

'Are you still there Katie?'

'Yes,' I say in a small voice. I'm feeling very subdued.

'We can be friends.'

'Sure.'

'Not straight away of course. We probably need a "cooling off" period. It won't be easy for either of us at the beginning.'

'I know.'

'But let's just remember the good times.'

Were there good times? I can't think of any right now. Then again, I can't think of anything. Only that Tim is breaking it off and it's a complete shock.

'You're still welcome to call me any time you need to chat.'

'Thank you,' I say, although what I'm thanking him for, I really have no idea.

'And Katie?'

'Yes?'

'Take care of yourself.'

'Mmm.'

Bastard.

Chapter Eleven

'God Katie, you're so immature. Here rub some of this on my back will you?'

Debbie rolls over on her tummy as I squirt the vile smelling suntan lotion onto the palm of my hand. I slap it on her sallow-skinned back.

'I still can't believe he broke it off though,' I whine.

'But it's what you wanted, isn't it? He was actually doing you a favour when you think about it.'

I know she's right. Tim actually saved me from doing the dirty deed but for some reason that doesn't make me feel better. I'm still reeling from being dumped. I want to know why he did it. And so callously over the phone too. I feel hurt. Almost as hurt as if I had really loved Tim. I'm thinking that if he didn't think I was worth going out with, then what hope do I have of holding on to Adam? What will Adam see in me that Tim obviously didn't? The more I think about it, the more I sink into a horrible depression. Not even the sunny skies of LA can lift my spirits.

'I'll get over it,' I tell Debbie even though I'm really talking to myself. Trying to convince myself I am strong.

'Of course you will,' Debbie agrees. 'It's never nice splitting up with anybody. I just hate the finality of it all, don't you? You begin to wonder what the wasted years were for. What have you got to show for your investment? However,' she adds with a sympathetic smile, 'we all get dumped at some stage in our lives and just get on with it. I'd like to feel that if Donald and I ever parted company that we could be mature about it and still remain friends.'

I say nothing. First of all, I know she's kidding herself. If I told Debbie right now what Donald has been up to, she would never speak to him again, never mind want him as a friend. It's easy to say we should all be friends, blah, blah, blah, but it's just wishful thinking. In an ideal world we'd all be friends, but we don't live in such a world. And human beings do not, to my knowledge, stay friends with people who have hurt them.

The sun is beaming down forcing me to head for the small, heated pool. I lower myself into it thinking that there's something quite wonderful about being able to swim outdoors in winter. I think of Tim walking around Dublin in his Parka jacket trying to keep warm and I secretly hope it's lashing rain back in Ireland.

I'm on my second lap of the pool when a

thought strikes me like a slap in the face. God, it's so bloody obvious. Tim must be dating somebody else. He *must* be. Of *course*. That's the reason for his bizarre behaviour. Why else would he have got rid of me like that? I know Tim's not the type of man to give something up unless he has something better lined up. I feel nauseous. The idea of Tim calling to some other girl's house with a plant for her delighted mother makes me feel ill. I'll never forgive him for treating me like this.

After my swim I feel marginally better and lie down to dry off in the sun. After a while Debbie says she's sick of the pool. She suggests heading to Venice Beach instead. I like the idea. Sitting by a small pool all day can become monotonous and Venice Beach is always so full of crazies, it's bound to cheer me up.

Half an hour later I wait for her in the hotel lobby. It doesn't take us long to reach Venice Beach with all it's weird and wonderful patrons and sidewalk vendors. Body builders literally work out on the prom, roller bladers with enormous rigid breasts zoom past and a zillion fortune-tellers wait to tell passer bys about their future. We stroll along looking out at the Pacific. It looks deceptively inviting but given the time of year, the water's probably freezing.

We head to a little café and order black coffees and salads with no dressing because after a walk on wacky Venice Beach, one is not exactly inclined to stuff one's face. LA is a very strange place. Everyone seems to be either very thin or very fat. There's no in between really. Also, nobody really seems to belong either. They come from all over the world to search for something here. Something, which I'm sure, most never find. I don't know if I could live here full time but God, it's a incredibly interesting place to visit.

The girl who serves is us a stunning brunette with a flawless face and a foreign accent. Russian maybe. She's so thin she looks like she might break. She completely understands when we refuse the dressing. I'm sure the only dressing she ever does, is for auditions.

Of course, I'm sure she's not really a waitress. She's probably just one of thousands of gorgeous-looking women standing on their feet in this town. Feeding and watering ordinary people like myself and Debbie. I'm sure she could tell you about the stars who've popped in here. Maybe Nicole Kidman has also enjoyed a dressing-free salad in here too. Or somebody who looks like her. Or wants to be her. The possibilities are endless . . .

I'm so glad I never just arrived out here armed with my script and a prayer. I wonder what drives people to come out? What makes them stay and why are they so afraid to go home? Maybe they never go home and just hide out on Venice Beach forever withering their skin in the relentless sun.

Maybe all the street performers who hang out there once had dreams of making it big.

Thankfully I never wanted to be an actress. At least not since I was a child. After auditioning for Dorothy in the *Wizard of Oz* and ending up being one of the munchkins, I hung up my acting hat. I often think it must be one of the hardest professions. I suppose that's why I admire Adam so much. Imagine putting yourself up for rejection after rejection day after day. Adam must have gone through all the hell before he hit the big time. And he's still going through it in a way. He doesn't find TV challenging enough apparently. He wants to be a big movie star.

The Russian waitress arrives with two glasses of iced water and I can tell by her eyes that she's on the verge of giving up. If she landed a two-bit role in a TV series or a commercial, she might just hold out a bit longer. Turning up for auditions has to be the hardest work ever. And it's unpaid.

'You know, most of the actors living here, work for free to get experience,' says Debbie, obviously reading my thoughts.

'I know,' I nod.

'The film companies get away with it because there are so many wannabes just desperate to put anything on their CVs. Have you seen all the ads in the acting magazines?

'Mmm. That's just what I was thinking. I was flicking through a magazine for actors and the only jobs offered were unpaid.'

'Yeah, it's a disgrace.'

'Or you can sell your eggs I suppose.'

'What?' I throw Debbie a surprised look.

'Oh you know, those magazines are full of ads looking for women to sell their eggs. I suppose they're aimed at wannabe actors living on the breadline.'

I shudder. Once again I'm just so glad I abandoned any acting ambitions when *Fame* came to an end. But still, I would really, really love to have my script accepted.

And have other people act out the parts I've created.

Debbie wants to visit the mall in Santa Monica so we head there after lunch. She hits the clothes shops while I stop off at the bookshop to browse. I always treat myself when in LA by buying a screenplay or two. I'll browse through them later in bed with a nice glass of wine.

Not much happens in LA at night around the Marina Del Ray area. Everybody's in bed by ten. At least that's how it feels. If New York is the city that never sleeps, LA is the city that seems to shut down at sunset.

An hour later I meet Debbie, laden with bags. I show her the books I've bought and she rolls her eyes to heaven. She thinks the whole scriptwriting dream is daft. As do most people.

Debbie doesn't want to carry her bags home so we get a taxi. When I get to my hotel room, the little red light is flashing on my answer phone. My heart gives a little leap. Could it be . . . oh could it be that Adam has found out my hotel room number and left a little love message? My excitement is short lived however. I've three messages but they're all from the same person. Wendy, one of the air hostesses, is wondering what I'm doing for dinner later on. Dinner? God help us, but how is anybody expected to lose weight around here? I ring her back and ask what the plan is. She suggests The Cheesecake Factory, which I have to admit is the most fab restaurant around here. They serve over forty types of cheesecake, so how can I resist? Forget the diet – there's always tomorrow.

Wendy, Debbie and myself head over to The Cheesecake Factory at around seven. Both girls have made a huge effort to dress up and look pretty glam. Debbie always makes an effort anyway, even if it's only to run down to the hotel gym. But Wendy looks like a young Cindy Crawford in her figure-hugging black trousers and delicate white backless top. I wish I'd made more of an effort.

The restaurant is jammed and there's a terrific buzz about the place. Heavenly aromas waft from the kitchen area. My mouth is watering. My tummy is grumbling. Out of the side of my eye I catch sight of the display of desserts. The cheesecakes are out of this world. I'm going to die deciding which one to go for.

We sit down and scan the menus. There's so much to choose from that it's almost impossible to make a decision. Determined to be good, I opt for a salad. This time I pour a delicious, calorie-ridden dressing over it. I don't care. I've been dumped. Adam hasn't called and I deserve a treat. We order a bottle of house wine and Debbie is asked to produce ID, much to the chagrin of Wendy and myself. Why the hell didn't he ask us? Not to worry though, the waiter looks like a film star so I'll forgive him just this once.

After dinner, my jeans are fit to bust but still I order a chocolate and raspberry cheesecake. It's so sinfully delicious and large I just eat a sliver and ask for the rest to be put in a bag. I'll have it later, I tell the waiter. He doesn't bat an eyelid. People do this kind of thing all the time in the States.

I wouldn't mind hitting a bar now, any bar, but the others are yawning and Debbie wants to go back to the hotel and call Donald. I don't think it's a great idea.

'But he's my boyfriend,' Debbie answers crossly as we split the bill. I try to figure out how much of a tip to leave.

'Who rings who the most?' I suddenly question her. What I'm really trying to do is point out the obvious. I just feel she's doing all the chasing. And I'm afraid she'll get hurt.

'Well . . . it's about fifty fifty,' she answers back. 'Why?'

'He should be ringing you more than you ring him,' I tell her.

'Says who?'

'They were the rules the last time I checked.'

We walk back to the hotel in silence. Debbie seems clearly annoyed with me for pointing out the obvious. Deep down though, she must know Donald is playing games. I wish I could come straight out and tell her about himself and Amy but I can't bring myself to. I'm just hoping she'll find out soon. If there's one thing I can't bear to see a man getting away with, it's infidelity. It's just unforgivable.

I'd hate to think of Adam physically being with anybody else besides me. He's probably so busy filming he wouldn't have time anyway. But I'd hate him, you know, to even think about being with another woman. I don't sound obsessed, do I? After all I don't think I've fallen for him completely. And I know we've only been on one date. But I can't stop thinking about him.

Back in the hotel Wendy asks me to join her for a drink in the hotel bar. Unsurprisingly Debbie has gone to her room to ring Donald. I'm amazed Wendy wants to stay up drinking. The girl has hardly said two words all night. Maybe she's one of those people who miraculously comes to life after a couple of drinks though. I'm pleased to oblige however. I'll have a drink with basically anyone. No need to twist my arm or anything. Besides I don't

want to be alone in my hotel room. Being alone
gives me time to think and I don't particularly want
to think right now. About anything.

'Debbie seems mad about that guy,' Wendy
observes once our drinks have been ordered.

Her big chocolate-brown eyes look full of
concern for poor Debbie and I can't help thinking
what a nice girl she is.

'Well, you don't have to be a genius to figure
that one out,' I point out.

We're sitting in the magnificent white lobby
admiring the enormous silver and white Christmas
tree. Yes, I know it's only November and we're in
LA but the Christmas tree is up and it feels funny.
It's funny because we've been sunbathing all day so
I don't feel Christmassy. In fact I'm not really looking forward to Christmas this year because once
again I have nothing organised. Every year I swear
I'm going to be one of those people who do their
Christmas shopping in the January sales. But every
January the thought of me heading into town
battling for bargains is just too much to bear so I
avoid town. Of course the fear of my credit card
being declined in front of a long queue of sneering
women doesn't encourage me either.

Anyway I'm not even going to think about
Christmas. Because it comes around so early every
year now it's ridiculous.

'It's a lovely tree isn't it?' Wendy suddenly
comments.

'Fabulous, but you know I feel silly thinking about the festive season so early,' I explain.

'Are you spending it with your family?' she asks regardless.

'I suppose so,' I mutter, secretly swearing to myself that if my Dad insists on hammering *Silent Night* on the piano again this year, he can forget me joining in. I used to sing it to please my grand-parents but I'm much too old for all that kind of carry on now.

I wonder if my sister, Ruth, will join us this Christmas. She threatens not to turn up every year and leaves me to peel all the Brussels sprouts, untangle the Christmas lights, and hoover the entire house. By the time she usually arrives in there's no more work to be done, I'm barely speaking to my folks and she swans in looking a million dollars while my mother nearly falls over with gratitude over the fact that she has honoured us with her presence. Then she sits for the meal like the bloody guest of honour, guzzles the champagne and then heads off before the piano playing kicks off and the washing up needs to be done.

God, this Christmas I think I'll go on strike. I really do. If I were rich I would book a month in a five star luxury hotel in Barbados and escape it all. The way things are, however, I couldn't even afford a night in a Mullingar B&B.

'What are you getting this year?' Wendy wants to know.

Jesus, does this girl not want to talk about anything besides bloody Christmas? I don't mean to be mean but her life must be pretty boring if she's already planning her Christmas stocking. 'I'm hoping for some socks and bubble bath.'

'Seriously?'

'Of course not. I haven't even thought about Christmas. Why are you so obsessed with it?'

'Well . . . it's just that . . . I want to get something brilliant for my boyfriend this year,' she confides. 'So I was thinking about getting him something in the States 'cos everything's so much cheaper out here, isn't it?'

'It is if you're thinking of getting clothes, I suppose.'

'Well, I was thinking I might go into Beverly Hills tomorrow and have a look around to see if I can get him anything on Rodeo Drive.'

'Rodeo Drive?' I almost laugh out loud. 'Who is your boyfriend – a TV star?'

Wendy suddenly looks very uncomfortable. Her sallow skin flushes a deeper shade and she lowers her thick black eye lashes.

'Well, yes,' she says. 'As a matter of fact he is.'

It takes a few seconds to make a connection. This is followed by a flicker of panic. Immediately thousands of worrying thoughts cross my mind. But then I tell myself not to worry. This is ridiculous. I'm just jumping to conclusions here. My imagination is running away with me. Surely . . .

surely Adam wouldn't have asked out another
. . . I mean somebody else working in the same
company as me?

I open my mouth to speak but no words escape.
Instead I take a deep breath and wait for Wendy
to continue. But she doesn't. An uncomfortable
silence hangs. The seconds tick by. I have a horrible feeling that maybe . . . but surely Adam
wouldn't . . . couldn't . . .

'Who is he?' I force the question even though I
don't really want to hear the answer. Just in case.
Not if it's what I think it might be.

'I shouldn't really say,' Wendy takes a strand of
her chestnut-coloured hair and starts plaiting it
slowly.

'I won't tell anyone,' I promise. I'm beginning to
feel numb.

'Will you not?' she looks at me trustingly.

I shake my head. And brace myself for the bad
news.

'His name is Adam,' she says as my heart plummets. 'Adam Kirrane.'

I want to throw up. Or cry. Or laugh or something. Instead I remain remarkably calm and start
talking. It's weird but it's a well-known fact that
people act unpredictably when in shock. I tell
Wendy I heard he was actually going out with
another airhostess. A girl called Sandy.

'Not any more,' Wendy refutes this suggestion.
'I heard that rumour too but then I spoke to Sandy

the other day and she told me there was nothing going on.'

'Indeed. He must be very, very busy.'

'Yes.'

'But not too busy to see you?'

'No,' she says, looking slightly uncomfortable. 'So anyway I want to buy Adam something special. To show how much I care. He's a very special guy. He's not a bit like the way you see him on TV. But I'm in a dilemma. What on earth do you get the man who has everything?'

'I have absolutely no idea,' I answer.

I mean it. After all what do you get a guy like Adam?

More to the point, what does he deserve?

Chapter Twelve

I'm standing outside Debbie's room knocking on her door. Not too loudly though in case I wake everyone else up. Then again they've probably already been woken by the Hispanic maids who shout to each other in Spanish over the noise of their vacuum cleaners. It drives me mad. What is the point in hanging a 'Do not disturb' sign on your door when nobody takes a blind bit of notice?

Anyway, here I am, about to do something I really don't want to do but have to do. It's my duty. Debbie is my friend. And I'm not going to let her get hurt.

I didn't sleep well last night. No. I tossed and turned thinking about Adam and then berated myself for getting my hopes up about him. I thought about Tim too and how he doesn't want to have anything to do with me either. And then eventually I got thinking about every man who'd ever dumped me and ended up pretty depressed. I hadn't ever thought about it too much before but during the night I must have totted up at least twenty or thirty men. I never realised the figure was so high. Jesus!

Then I sat up in bed, switched on the light and lit a cigarette. As I sat there, clouding the air with smoke I suddenly had a vision of clarity. Yes and I began to feel a lot better. I decided that from now on I'm not going to revolve my life around men but will let them revolve about me instead. I'm not going to phone them, visit them or even meet them half way. No. In fact I am going to spend quality time with family and friends, doing fun things. Like not wasting time thinking about members of the opposite sex.

I'm also going to get involved with some kind of a charity group, which will make me feel a lot better off. And maybe take up a sport. I'm also going to throw myself into my script when I go home, in order to make my mark on this world. Definitely. I am not leaving this planet with nobody knowing who I was and why on earth I was here.

And then I fell asleep.

This morning when I woke up I remembered all my promises. Then I thought there was no point trying to be a good person when my friend was in another hotel room down the corridor being deceived by a dirty old scoundrel. So I got dressed and headed off on my mission. I have turned over a new leaf. I am a good person who will not let my friends be trampled on by men.

Debbie opens the door slowly. Though still in her pyjamas, she looks remarkably well rested. It's obvious she spent no part of the night tossing and turning and fretting about the world, like I did.

I enter her room. It's dark because the heavy curtains are pulled over.

'What time is it?' she asks groggily before pulling back the curtains and peeping outside. Rays of sunlight flood the room.

'Oh I do love LA,' she continues happily and I feel even more dreadful. I'm about to burst her happy bubble, but what can I do?

'Debbie,' I say in what I hope is a kind, sincere voice. 'I've something to tell you but don't know how I'm going to do it.'

I sit down on her bed and try to look sad because obviously my face should not look at all happy when I deliver the bad news.

'Oh my God, are you okay?' Debbie looks extremely concerned and she lowers her eyes from my face to my stomach as if I might be . . . oh God this is ridiculous.

'Now don't worry I'm not pregnant or anything,' I try to put her mind at ease. 'In fact this has absolutely nothing to do with me. It's er . . . about you.'

Debbie looks slightly amused but then again, she doesn't know the horrible thing I'm about to tell her. There's no easy way to do this.

'Debbie,' I take a deep breath. 'Donald is seeing somebody else.'

I can hardly bear to look at her face, which remains surprisingly expressionless. The poor girl has obviously gone into shock. I know exactly how she's feeling. In fact I'm sure I looked the same way the night Tim broke up with me on the phone. And maybe I looked like that last night when I found out Adam had also asked Wendy and God knows how many other airhostesses on a date.

I wait for a reaction, hoping madly that Debbie doesn't burst into tears or even worse, accuse me of being a liar. Some girls do that you know. They're so blinded by men that they won't accept that they're being cheated on.

'I'm really sorry,' I tell Debbie. And I mean it. I can't bear the fact that I'm hurting her. I wish there was something I could say to make her feel better. I wish Donald wasn't cheating on her. I feel like I'm part of a sick joke.

Debbie suddenly bursts out laughing and I try my best not to be alarmed. After all, it's a well-known fact that people react to shock in different ways. So the fact that Debbie is laughing is okay. It's just a normal reaction. I'm glad she's not crying anyway. That would be hard to deal with.

Debbie is still giggling away. I refuse to join in. That would be highly inappropriate. Instead I just sit there waiting patiently for her to stop. At last she does but still looks amused nevertheless.

'Katie, you silly moo,' she leans over and gives my shoulder a friendly punch.

I'm lost for words. Seriously. Does she think this

is a joke? Can you believe it? As if my sense of humour could be this awful! I'm also trying to ignore the pain in my shoulder, the result of her not-so-light punch.

'Debbie, I am NOT joking,' I say very, very slowly as if I am talking to a tiny child.

'I know you're not pet, I know. And I do appreciate you telling me but the thing is . . . Donald is in fact dating a couple of women but he told me about them so it's fine.'

'Them?' I just stare at Debbie as if she's totally lost her reason.

'Listen Katie,' she sighs, 'Donald was in a seven-year relationship until this summer. The last thing he needs right now is to get heavily involved. We're just casually dating but we're not sleeping together because I've explained that I won't go to bed with somebody I'm not serious about.'

This all takes a while to sink in, but eventually I find my tongue.

'So that's why you were annoyed last night when I was trying to give you advice?'

'Yeah, basically. I'm old enough to make up my own mind. I'm not going to put pressure on Donald to commit to me or anything in case he goes running in the opposite direction. Men run a mile from women who seem too keen so I've no intention of doing that.'

'Do you not think he's having his cake and eating it though?' I ask bluntly.

'Who's to say I'm not having my *own* cake? She grins and there's a twinkle in her eye.

'You're NOT!'

'Am so.'

'Who?'

'You know Tim's friend Shane?'

My jaw falls. Debbie has been seeing Shane? Why hasn't she said anything? Why am I always the last person to know what's going on?

'Oh I haven't been seeing him properly or anything. I met him in Lillies the other night and we shared a taxi home and had a bit of a snog in the back.'

'Was er . . . Tim with him?'

'Not in the back of the taxi, no.'

'But he was in Lillies?'

'Yeah, just for a while though.'

Funny, when I was going out with Tim he absolutely refused to go to nightclubs.

'Was he with any . . . actually no, don't tell me. I don't want to know.'

Debbie says nothing, which of course confirms that he was indeed with somebody. I don't care though. Tim wasn't right for me so good luck to him. Anyway I've enough on my plate without worrying about somebody who didn't even have the decency to finish our relationship properly.

'Are you not worried though that Donald will fall in love with one of those other girls?'

'It's a chance I have to take,' Debbie shrugs. 'Who

knows what'll happen? I'm hoping he'll just get tired of the others.'

I admire the girl. I really do. This is a very mature attitude to have. I wonder if she's right though. Maybe I'm being completely unrealistic trying to keep Adam all to myself. Should I just adopt Debbie's attitude and date him casually?

'A penny for your thoughts,' Debbie says suddenly.

'I'm thinking about Adam Kirrane,' I tell her, deciding it's time to come clean with Debbie. 'I went on a date with him.'

'No way,' Debbie screeches and nearly falls off the side of the bed. 'I can't believe it. Here I am going on about Donald and Tim's bloody friend Shane and you're dating a flipping superstar!'

'Well, that's the thing,' I tell her, twiddling the tassels on the bedspread. 'I get the feeling he's dating other people too.'

'He probably is,' Debbie answers matter-of-factly. 'But you're in with a good chance, aren't you? He asked for your telephone number. Hey I was there so nobody can ever say you ever chased him. So um . . . what's he like? Where did he take you? God, this is pretty exciting.'

I'm not sure I think it's as exciting as Debbie is making out. I mean if this is exciting, then why am I not excited? I suppose I've forgotten what a big star Adam is and how I should be *honoured* that he chose to take me on a date. I wonder what Debbie would do in my position.

'I'd just enjoy it,' she advises. 'I'd have a great time and not think too seriously about it all. After all, a guy like Adam Kirrane is not going to be settling down any time soon and he probably has a lot of Hollywood twigs chasing him anyway. Just be different. Be yourself and see what happens.'

'But suppose nothing happens?'

Debbie makes a face. 'Don't read into it too much. I mean at the end of the day we'd all like men to declare undying love for us but most don't. Anyway men like independent women. I mean some men do seem to like doormats but would you like someone who likes doormats?'

'Definitely not.'

I feel better already. I am so, so glad I spoke to Debbie and got everything out in the open. From now on I'm going to be more like her and not think too much about the future. I'm going to concentrate on the present. And on me.

The new me.

God, I should be on *Oprah!*

Chapter Thirteen

The taxi drops me outside my house. I somehow manage to drag my heavy suitcase all the way up the garden path to the front door. When I try to push the door open, I can't because something is blocking it.

'Hang on there Katie,' I hear my mother yelling. 'I'll just move the flowers.'

What flowers?

A few seconds later I'm able to gain access into the hall. A massive bouquet of fresh white lilies with their pretty heads dancing in all directions is now not blocking the hall door, but the kitchen door.

'They're for you,' Mum says. She's just standing there as if she's waiting for an explanation. Then Dad arrives into the hall and nobody seems to know what's going on.

Least of all me.

'They're from someone called Adam,' Mum says before I have time to check the accompanying tag. 'Who on earth is Adam?'

I'm so shattered I could sleep for a month, but I have to admit I'm also thrilled. The flowers are magnificent. Wow. I bet Wendy didn't get a bouquet like that. Or any of those other girls who are claiming to be seeing my Adam.

My mother and father are still looking at me expectantly.

'He's just a friend,' I say feebly. 'God you know I'm so wrecked. If I don't lie down now I think I'll die. Talk to you in a couple of hours.'

I head upstairs and my mum yells after me. 'You're not leaving that suitcase in the hall Madam and what about the flowers? Who's going to put them in water?'

'Will you do it Mum?' I plead. 'You're great at that kind of thing.'

I honestly don't have the energy to do anything besides haul my exhausted body straight to my bed.

My mother has changed the sheets on my bed in an extraordinary act of kindness and has switched on the heat in my room. I am so grateful because my tiny room has three outside walls which makes it about as warm as fridge. I usually spend my time shivering because my mum won't let me have an electric blanket ever since the last one went on fire when I forgot to switch it off after one particularly heavy drinking session.

Thankfully Ruth had barged into my room to see if I'd worn one of her tops out that night and she got the smell of burning wire immediately. To this day she still claims she saved my life. Anyway my electric blanket was confiscated and although I have a hot water bottle I really couldn't be bothered filling it up every night. I also really hate waking up to a cold water bottle in the morning.

I throw my uniform on the floor, avoid the mirror, step on the scales to see if I've lost any weight (I haven't) and crawl into bed.

Within seconds I'm out for the count.

When I wake again I feel happy and relaxed. The few days in the sun have made the world of difference. And of course Adam has sent flowers, which means he likes me a lot obviously, although I am trying desperately not to read into it too much, just in case. Oh and Christmas is coming, which is nice. I love Christmas 'cos I get to meet all my school friends who return home from all over the world for the week. Christmas day however is not as much fun as somebody, usually Ruth, picks a fight over nothing and ruins the day.

Anyway maybe this year we'll hopefully all remember to be civilised. Thinking of Christmas, I'd better get myself organised. I am not, definitely not, going to waste Christmas Eve this year running around Grafton Street like a blue-arsed fly buying scented candles and pot-pouri holders for people who won't appreciate it. In fact maybe I'll venture into town later today and have a browse. If I buy my Christmas cards now I can

post them off to America and the UK before the
deadline. And that's another thing. This year I will
not just scribble the usual 'Happy Christmas and
New Year' greeting. No. I will try and write a
personal message to everyone. And anybody who
dares send me a Christmas email in return is so
dead.

Before I leave the house I text Adam a quick
thanks for the flowers. He doesn't text back but
he's probably in work. Rehearsing a passionate love
scene or something with some sex bomb. Oh God,
I always presume the worst don't I?

I pop into the little shop beside the bus so I've
something to flick through on the journey in. If I've
nothing to read I'll end up unintentionally catching
people's eyes on the bus, which I hate.

When the bus comes along I sit on one of those
single seats so nobody will sit beside me trying to
read my newspaper. I glance at the headlines but
that's about it. There's nothing but doom and gloom
in the world at the moment. If there isn't a bloody
war, there's an earthquake or somebody blowing
themselves up in the name of religion. Then I flick
to the social pages to cheer myself. I love to see
photos of people out and about having fun.

But as I turn the page, my heart sinks. I feel dizzy.
There he is. Adam. A huge photo dominates the
page. He's in New York. He's dressed to kill. And
there's a supermodel on his arm.

I feel I'm about to throw up. They look perfect

together. She is everything I'm not: tall, wealthy, skinny, famous and tanned. I couldn't compete in a million years. I wouldn't even try.

Distraught I turn the page again. I don't want to see any more pictures of Adam. Does the world really think he's that amazing? Then what on earth is he doing with me? Is he just playing games?

I look out the window at the people walking up and down Baggot Street, heads bent against the freezing wind. I wonder what makes them happy? What are they looking for from life? Are they happy with their lot or do they just plod along, taking every day as it comes without even thinking about it?

Maybe I'm mad to hanker after a mad exciting life, which might not even exist. I mean I'm not even sure what I'm looking for! Suppose my script got accepted? Would that make me happy or would I still want more? What do I really want from Adam? Do I want him to love me exclusively, marry me and love me forever until the end of time? Or would there always be supermodels and actresses hanging out of him, never mind the fans and the groupies? How could I handle that? I turn back to the page Adam's photo is on. According to the caption, the picture was taken yesterday. After he sent the flowers. He still hasn't replied to my text. Maybe he's with her. At this very moment. Maybe he thinks all his Christmases have come at once. Suppose they're in bed right now? Enjoying a marathon love-making session. Perhaps Adam even showed her my pathetic text?

I need to snap out of this negative mood. It's not doing me any good. What would Debbie say to me now? She'd probably tell me the photo was a publicity shot and not to read anything into it. I wish I were as strong as Debbie. And I wish I wasn't so bloody fragile.

Just as I'm getting off the bus I receive Adam's text. It's short and simple. IN DUBLIN THIS WEEKEND. R U AROUND?

I'm so thrilled I could shout for joy. All is forgiven. He could have his photo taken with Cindy Crawford, Kate Moss and Naomi Campbell altogether now for all I care. The girl in the photo obviously meant nothing. She was probably just paid by the TV company to show up for an hour and smile with the cast. Models do that the whole time. And because Adam is so good-looking they made a decent photo opportunity. Everything makes sense now, I think happily as I make my way to the Jervis Street Centre to buy some nice new cosmetics in Boots.

What a difference text makes!

Chapter Fourteen

When I was very young I was dying to go to school. After a while I was dying to leave. When I was in college I was dying to get my exams finished so I could get an office job. Then I was dying to leave that and work in an airline so I could see the world. Now I'm dying to finish my script. But I've never been dying to meet a man or settle down. Not before now anyway.

Meeting Adam has definitely been one of the highlights of the year. Of course if my script was accepted that would be the icing and the candles. I'm working furiously on it at the moment because Adam's back in town in three days and I want to be free when he's around. The annoying thing is that I can't judge if it's any good or not. I'm too involved. Sometimes I'm in the middle of writing it and I think it's really crap. The next minute I'm wondering if Hollywood will come knocking on my door. Jesus, who'd be a scriptwriter?

Anyway I'm supposed to go to be going to Zurich

tonight but I rang in sick because I'm meeting Adam. Oh I know that sounds terrible but I've been flying for four years and have only taken two sick days in my life so I'm kind of entitled to it. Funnily enough though, ever since I rang in sick this evening, I haven't felt great. I hope I'm not coming down with something.

I'm out in Dun Laoghaire getting my hair done. I wasn't going to chance going into town in case I bumped into someone from the airline. It's a pain really because I won't be able to be seen gallivanting all around town tonight either. As much as I love Adam, I still don't fancy losing my job over our secret date.

After I get my hair done I wander around the shops desperately trying to find something nice to wear. Of course, because I'm looking so hard and happen to have money in my bag, I can't find a damn thing. I suppose I'll just wear something I already own or rob something from Ruth. When she left home, she left a whole wardrobe full of stuff. Mum keeps threatening to give it all to the St Vincent de Paul's so it doesn't matter if I borrow something for the night, does it?

God, I've never spent so much time fretting over a date as I have today. You see, I know this might sound incredibly silly but I keep thinking about that supermodel Adam was pictured with. And I know I shouldn't be comparing myself with her but I can't help it. A body to rival Elle McPherson, she also had a thick mane of glossy hair and wore a tiny gold, sequinned skirt, which could have passed as a belt.

I'm worried. If I turn up in a comfy pair of jeans and a black polo neck, Adam isn't going to be impressed is he? Oh God, sometimes I just remember how much simpler it was with Tim. If I'd worn a nightie out with Tim, he wouldn't have noticed. In fact he'd probably have thought I'd made a huge effort.

Adam phones at about six. Will I be ready for seven? Considering I've been getting ready for the last few days, I shouldn't think it'll be a problem. I tell him I don't want to go to town because I'm being a bad girl and skipping work.

'Oh I love bad girls,' Adam purrs down the phone.

Yes, well . . . oh God I hope he doesn't think I'm leading him a merry dance here. Skipping work is about as naughty as I get. Except for smoking of course and getting twisted out of my head every now and then and insulting anyone who crosses my path as I do so. Anyway I'm giving up drink in the New Year. I don't enjoy it that much anyway and enjoy it even less the following day when I have to ring everybody to apologise for things I don't even remember doing and swearing not to do it again. Anyway, getting hammered may be fun as a teenager but once you get past a certain age there's something pretty awful about it, isn't there? I mean have you ever seen a woman staggering about the place and thought she looked great? So that's it. My New Year's resolution is to give up getting drunk. In public anyway.

Speaking of drink, don't you just hate the way you always lose things when under the influence? Over the last few years I have lost among other things, handbags, jackets, make-up, keys, new lipsticks, money, friends, self-respect, prospective boyfriends and a mobile phone or two. In fact now that I think about it, I should save quite a bit of money by cutting out drink. It's not cheap replacing make up on a weekly basis as well as having to get extra keys cut all the time.

But tonight I'm going to have just a glass of wine and be civilised. Adam has booked dinner in a lovely little hotel in Co. Wicklow. I've never been before. I believe it's lovely and very exclusive.

When the doorbell rings at seven o'clock, my nerves are in bits. I hear Dad open the kitchen door downstairs and make his way to the front door. I have a minor panic attack. Of course Dad wouldn't watch *DreamBoat* in a million years but he might just recognise Adam from the papers and say something really embarrassing. I open my bedroom door slightly and I hear Dad telling Adam to step in out of the cold. Phew! It's obvious Dad doesn't know him from Adam haha.

I take one last look in the mirror. I look okay. Just okay though. My hair is a bit flat because the bored-looking girl who washed my hair today obviously didn't rinse out all the conditioner. I'll never go back to that salon. And for some reason I think my face is a bit redder than usual. Maybe I shouldn't have had the full twenty minutes on the sun bed this morning. Hopefully this lovely hotel in Wicklow will not have bright fluorescent lights on the ceiling. Anyway if Adam comments, I'll just tell him it was hot in LA. Very bloody hot.

My dad has left Adam in the sitting room flicking through a book on Irish castles, which my mum leaves around to impress random visitors. When I enter the room, he stands up and tells me I look beautiful. His whole face is smiling; even his eyes, and his teeth look even whiter and straighter than I remember. His hair is slightly damp as if he's just got out of the shower but maybe he's just wearing hair gel or something. He looks like a TV star but then again that's what he is, so I shouldn't be too surprised.

Adam kisses me fully on the lips. The kiss is warm but strong. It makes me feel loved if only momentarily. We head out into the night and into Adam's car. I slip into the passenger seat of his shiny black BMW. The moon is clear and the night is full of promise. I'm high on excitement. Soon we're on the motorway heading out of Dublin. Neither of us says very much but it doesn't feel awkward. There's no point talking just for the sake of it. And anyway, I read somewhere once that men don't like women who yap on about nothing. I don't blame them. The sound of silence is golden.

As we drive past Foxrock church Adam asks me how I've been. I tell him about my script and he seems suitably impressed. He admits he's still looking for the perfect script but that everything his agent sends him is crap. Strangely that gives me hope. Maybe people won't think mine is rubbish. After all, with all that crap circulating around Hollywood, maybe my script will be snapped up.

Adam tells me he's desperate to move from telly to big budget movies. He says people like Colin Farrell have opened the door for young Irish actors trying to break into the game. I tell him I hope he's not going to take up swearing and womanising in order to get noticed. He laughs and gives my thigh a squeeze.

I wonder if he's going to mention the woman I saw him photographed with during the week. I know I shouldn't really ask in case it annoys him. In case he thinks I'm paranoid or something.

'What kind of part are you looking for?' I ask.

'A strong lead. In a comedy maybe. I'm not sure what part I'm looking for exactly but I know I'll know it when I see it.'

I tell him my script is as far from a comedy as can be. He tells me writing a comedy is the hardest thing to do. It's much easier to write tragedy, he says.

'How do you know?'

'Because everything that's sent to my agent is tragic,' he explains. 'Everyone's got a sad tale to tell. I mean it. Everyone.'

I wonder why he's being so negative about it all. Maybe he thinks he is doing me a favour. Letting me down gently before I even get the chance to put my script out there. Does he think I haven't a chance in hell of being accepted? I don't blame him really. Most people are sceptics. My mother never fails to tell me I'll never be anything. And all the teachers in my old school used to write 'Katie is an idler' on my numerous report cards.

'Who do you hang out with when you're in New York?' I ask Adam suddenly, because I don't want to talk about my script any more.

He seems slightly surprised at the question.

'I'm usually working all the time so I don't get to hang out that much.'

'But don't you have any friends over there?'

'I'm friendly with the cast but I don't socialise with them after work or anything. I just tend to chill in my apartment or go to see a movie or something.'

'Have you a nice apartment over there?'

'It's great,' he tells me. 'You should come over and see it sometime.'

My heart soars. Oh my God, did you hear that? Adam has just invited me to come and see his apartment. Wow. He's obviously pretty serious about us.

After all, you don't invite people you don't really care about to visit you, do you? Especially not when they live on the other side of the world. No. Nonetheless I can't believe how fast things seem to be progressing between us. It's almost scary. But I don't want to slow down though. No. This might be the real thing, so why not just go with the flow?

'You could write your script in my spare room,' he continues. 'I have a lovely big desk and a computer in my place in Soho. It's really peaceful there and a lot of writers live in the area, so you'd probably find it quite inspirational.

I'm listening but not saying anything. I can't. My mouth has gone dry. My heart is palpitating. Has Adam Kirrane, *the* Adam Kirrane just suggested that I move in with him? I mean, if he were just inviting me over for the weekend, he wouldn't expect me to be working, would he? God, he must really, really like me. After all, he isn't inviting Wendy over to New York, or Sandy or the girl in the photo, is he? I'm so thrilled I can barely keep the smile off my face. Of course, moving in with him would be too much at this stage, and anyway I can't just pack in my job and head off blindly. But it's terribly flattering to know he's thinking so far ahead. Just wait 'til I tell Debbie. She won't believe it.

'I don't believe it!'

'I swear to God Debbie. What do you make of it all? He must seriously be interested.'

'Just be very careful though,' she warns.

I'm locked in a bathroom cubicle of the quaint Wicklow hotel where Adam has brought me. Adam is in the dining room checking out the wine list. I've just checked my reflection in the mirror and I look different. I look so happy I almost didn't recognise myself. Maybe this is the way people look when they realise they've finally met Mr Right after years and years of meeting Mr Wrongs. I wish Debbie wouldn't put a dampener on things though. I thought she'd be happier for me.

'I *will* be careful,' I retort. 'I just wanted you to be the first to know.'

'The first to know what?'

'That he's asked me to move over,' I say, sounding more than a little exasperated. I almost wish I hadn't rung her now.

'But has he actually *asked* you to move over?' Debbie sounds suspicious. 'I mean, are you sure you didn't take him up the wrong way?'

'No, I didn't. He even told me I could write in his apartment.'

'Mmm. Don't get carried away though, do you hear me?'

'Yeah okay, talk to you tomorrow Debbie.'

Huh! I wonder what's eating *her*? She didn't sound too excited for me, I think, as I wash my hands and dry them on the soft fluffy white towel. Maybe Donald hasn't rung in a while and she's feeling a bit down. Or maybe it's just that time of the month and her hormones are at her. Oh well, I'm not going to let Debbie's negativity ruin my night. Adam is waiting for me in the dining room and that's the most important thing.

There are only six other tables in the hotel restaurant apart from our own. It's very small, but homely and luxurious. According to Adam, this place used to be owned by an English aristocrat. It was his country home and he actually kept a mistress here, and nobody ever found out about her until the old man kicked the bucket. Then she refused to leave and the whole thing caused quite a scandal.

I hadn't realised Adam took such an avid interest in Irish history. It's refreshing to have dinner with such an educated person. God, when I think of what I put up with all those years I was seeing Tim. He used to go on about the bank, and all the people he disliked in his office, and how so and so didn't deserve a promotion, and how such and such a female manager was so bitchy in order to hide her inferiority complex. God, he hadn't a good word to say about anyone. Unfortunately, *I* was the one who had to listen to him ranting and raving on our twice weekly drives to the cinema multiplex.

It's only when you look back on a relationship that you realise how unhappy you were in it. At the time, I suppose you just go along with it not questioning it. It just becomes routine and you get used to it. When I think about it now, I had quite a lucky escape when Tim finally dumped me, didn't I? Can you imagine what a boring married life we might have had?

Anyway I'm not going to waste any more time thinking about Tim. Especially not tonight. The idea of it! Adam has ordered champagne and the waiter is pouring two glasses. I'm impressed. He asks me what I'm going to order and I pick up the menu. Unfortunately there's only one vegetarian option, which I always think is a bit ignorant to see on a menu. As if vegetarians don't deserve a choice or anything! But the pasta dish sounds tempting so I don't complain.

Adam orders smoked salmon as a starter. I'm very surprised 'cos I distinctly remember him being a veggie.

'But I eat fish,' he explains.

'But they have eyes.'

'Sorry?'

'Fish have eyes. You can't be a veggie and eat things with eyes.'

Adam looks slightly uncomfortable as if he'd never actually realised that fish in fact have eyes. But I certainly don't want to get into a heated debate about vegetarianism now, so I quickly raise my glass and say 'cheers' and then lean over and kiss him seductively on the lips.

'Very nice,' he smiles at me. 'I hope there's more from where that came from.

'Well if you're a good boy, you never know what might happen,' I give him a seductive wink.

I'm getting quite good at this, I think. Considering I was with Tim for so many years and got no practice at seduction at all. Tim's idea of foreplay was asking me if I was 'on for it' before rummaging through his wardrobe for a condom. That would usually take a while because his room was so messy. I would start reading a magazine or flicking through the TV channels or something while I was waiting. Sometimes I'd even ring someone for a quick chat on my mobile.

Anyway, what in the name of God am I still thinking about Tim again for? Didn't he waste enough of my time when I was with him? He really shouldn't be granted any more quality thinking time.

I notice Adam is knocking back the champagne. I hope he realises he has to drive me home later and can't be drinking and driving. You wouldn't believe how many of my friends still do that. They always think they're fine to drive and then the next day they're all remorseful and thankful they weren't caught and are swearing never to do it again. Funny how they're more pleased about not getting caught then not having knocked down some innocent passer by.

Adam refills my glass. He's staring into my eyes seductively and I have to admit he is probably the sexiest man I have ever seen in my life. Of course he looks genuinely scrummy in photos and on the

TV screen. But up close he's even better. His skin is sallow and flawless yet his jaw line is strong and defined. But it's his eyes, which have captivated me. They're the type of eyes that undress you with a glance. No wonder women find Adam Kirrane totally irresistible.

Our starters arrive. I can't wait to tuck into my pear and walnut salad with blue cheese – yum! Adam plays around with his starter. I bet he watches his weight. How else could he maintain his perfectly toned body? It's great though. So many men have grey, unhealthy skin, shocking receding hairlines and schoolteacher glasses. They wear woolly nondescript jumpers and own large, soft bellies. I must say it's very disappointing doing pub-crawls these days. You leave one pub hoping that the next one will offer something more exciting, but it never does. That's why when you meet a guy like Adam you realise what a rarity he is. Oh I know I said earlier that I didn't like good-looking men any more but a girl's got to be able to change her mind along the way.

I wish I'd a camera with me right now so you could see for yourself. Picture perfect. And he doesn't even seem to realise it. At least if he does, he doesn't let on. Right now Adam's wearing a white short-sleeved shirt, which shows off his toned tanned arms perfectly. The candle in the middle of the table is flickering uncertainly between us and the champagne bubbles seem to have shot straight to my head. I reach out my hand and bravely rest it on Adam's strong arm.

'You feeling tipsy already?' he laughs.

'No.'

'Well then you definitely need some more,' he refills my glass.

When my main course, linguine with three cheeses and black olives, arrives, I devour it. It tastes even better than it looks. The portions are small which suits me fine. That's what I love about gourmet food. It's so good for the figure. Although sometimes I'm so hungry after gourmet meals, I feel like stopping off at McDonald's on the way home.

Our conversation flows easily. Adam explains how he got into acting after studying drama in Trinity. He says so many drama students waste time talking about dreams rather than pursuing them. He says it's easier to sit in someone's flat smoking pot and wallowing in the injustice of the world of entertainment than to get out there and put your ass on the line. He tells me about the bitching and the backstabbing that goes on behind the scenes of *Dreamboat* and how you never know when the studio bigwigs are going to scrap the entire show, leaving most of the actors where they started out. On the dung heap.

I ask Adam if he feels under pressure to stay single in order to maintain fans. He looks fairly surprised and says he doesn't really care what anyone else thinks because at the end of the day it's his life and he's got to live it.

I barely notice Adam ordering another bottle of champagne. I'm fascinated by his conversation, by his life, his ambitions and his dogged determination to succeed. I ask him if women throw themselves at him just because he's on TV.

'Not as many as people think,' he insists.

I ask him if he has dated any other air hostess.

'A couple,' he answers. And I'm relieved he's not lying to me.

He's not very keen to discuss the other air hostesses he's dated. He tells me about Soho in New York and how he really likes hanging out there. Some really big names live in Soho, he says. And they just walk around without being hassled. I promise to visit him there soon and he looks pleased. After a while I realise that we've spent most of the night talking about Adam and hardly any time talking about me. But that's okay because Adam's life is a hell of a lot more interesting and anyway in the past I've given out far too many details about myself, far too soon.

When the waiter comes round with the dessert menus, we agree to share a chocolate hazelnut torte. Adam also orders two Irish coffees. I don't know how the hell we're going to get home now, but I'm too happy and drunk to care.

All my life I've waited for someone like Adam. In fact I'd almost given up. Venturing out for a night on the tiles is a chore sometimes. I'm tired of being verbally attacked by men who seem intent on taking women down a peg or two. Thankfully I didn't settle for any of *them*. I don't know what I'd have done if Adam hadn't come along to rescue me.

After a while I notice we're the last customers in the room. Everybody else has quietly disappeared. I check my watch and am stunned to discover it's almost midnight. It seems like we just got here five minutes ago. Where did the time fly? Hesitantly I show Adam the face of my watch. His fingers reach out and intertwine mine. He holds my gaze and suddenly it's obvious we won't be going home.

Adam, it turns out, has already booked a room. When I ask why he didn't mention it earlier he says he wanted it to be a surprise. I'm so touched. It's a gorgeous Victorian type room with a chandelier and a huge four-poster bed. Like something straight out of an interiors magazine. Another champagne bottle is chilling on the bedside table.

'I'm not drinking that,' I insist drunkenly.

'You don't have to,' Adam smiles and removes his dinner jacket. 'But you don't mind if I have a glass, do you?'

He pours himself another glass and sips it slowly. As far as I remember I pretty much drank the rest.

Chapter Fifteen

I am NEVER EVER drinking again. No really, I mean it. God I feel my head has got caught in a cement mixer. I'm leaning over the toilet in the pretty little bathroom next to the gorgeous bedroom where Adam and I made love for the first time last night. But instead of being wrapped in his arms in post-coital bliss I feel wretched.

Oh, and by the way, you're not getting any sordid details about last night because to be honest, even if I *wanted* to tell you, I couldn't because I remember very little about anything after that third bottle of champagne.

The bath is running because I don't want Adam to hear me getting sick. The sweat beads gather on my face and neck and tears are streaming down my face. My stomach retches and I feel totally miserable. Why am I being punished for this? Why did I let myself get so plastered? Adam's going to think I'm a drunken twit with no morals. He'll think I'm the type of woman to jump into bed with anyone. I stand up unsteadily and give the mirror a fright.

I look a holy show. Should I have a shower? I look at the tiny hotel standard bottle of hair and body shampoo and don't think it'll do my hair any favours. Then again, if I go back out and climb into the bed with bits of vomit stuck to my hair, it'll be even worse won't it? Oh Katie, why do you never learn?

As I'm in the shower washing the remnants of last night's meal from my hair I hear a knock on the door. Adam's wondering if he can join me. Suddenly I become all shy. I mean I know he saw my body last night but it was dark then so it was completely different. However, I don't want him to think I'm a prude so I wrap myself in a bath towel and open the door. Adam is standing there naked, like a Greek God, looking ridiculously sexy. I'm mortified and don't know where to look.

'Get back into the shower missus,' he orders and I obey.

He takes the soap and lathers it all over me and we make love again but I refuse to kiss him. God, do you know how much I'd pay for a toothbrush and toothpaste right now?

At breakfast the dining room looks completely different. Fresh flowers have replaced last night's candles. The room looks more homely than romantic. I don't have any appetite though. Black coffee will suffice.

Adam orders a fry. I order toast because if I eat anything else I'll probably throw up again. I feel more normal once I've tasted the coffee. I'll feel even better when I hit the fresh air.

'Listen I was probably talking a load of shite last night so forgive me,' I tell Adam as he drives us home.

'You were funny,' Adam laughs. 'Anyway *I* should be apologising for letting *you* get so drunk.'

'You can bring the horse to the well . . . but nobody forced it to drink champagne. I bet I made a fool of myself though. Alcohol has a weird effect on me. I always either get really abusive or else I become all lovey dovey.'

Adam places a hand on my thigh and squeezes it. 'You're a refreshing girl, do you know that? So many of the actresses I work with won't drink. I dunno why. Maybe they're afraid of putting on weight or don't like to lose control. Women are different in the States. They don't let themselves go.'

'Wise women,' I comment.

Adam slows down the car and then stops it. 'Listen,' he turns to me. 'You're not to go beating yourself up about last night. I thought you were fantastic.'

'You did?'

'Hey, let's do it all over again later.'

'Oh em . . .'

'No excuses. Hey my folks are away at the moment. Why don't you come and stay in my place tonight?'

'Do you not have a place of your own?'

'Well no actually, my home is in New York now so I tend to stay with my parents when I'm in Ireland. They don't mind. I'm an only child so they adore me.'

'Really? I don't know any only children. Aren't they supposed to be spoilt?'

'Spoilt rotten,' he grins. 'But you don't see me complaining.'

I never told you that Adam's parents live in a palatial mansion complete with indoor swimming pool and outdoor tennis court. Nor did I tell you about their mini-cinema, private bar and snooker room. No. And the reason I didn't tell you any of this was because I had absolutely no idea. Of course, you can imagine my shock as Adam's BMW pulled into the drive of his family home in Foxrock.

If I felt intimidated before, I'm absolutely stunned into silence as the imposing electric gates open and his car sweeps into the drive.

'Wow, you have a lovely home,' I say because although I'm stunned, I feel it'd be terribly rude not to say anything at all.

'It's a house,' he contradicts me. 'Just a house. And it's not mine, it's my parents.'

He parks the car and I follow him up the steps to the huge Georgian front door.

Before he finds his keys, the door opens. A small

suspicious woman wearing thick glasses and flat, brown shoes looks me up and down.

'Hi, I'm Katie.' I give her my best air hostess smile and shake her hand. It feels like a dead fish in mine. She doesn't tell me who she is or what she's doing here. Nor does she ask who I am.

'Hi ya Rosie, looking well.' Adam greets her as he grabs my hands and leads me up the big sweeping stairway.

As I ascend the stairs I can almost feel that strange woman's eyes in my back.

'Who the hell was that?' I ask in a whisper, once we're safely in his bedroom. As if she might be lurking outside, her ear pressed to the doorway.

'She's the housekeeper,' Adam sits down on the side of the bed and kicks off his shoes. 'She's a bit wary of me bringing back strangers to the house.'

'Does it happen a lot?' I ask, sitting down on his knee and ruffling his hair playfully.

'Nah, but she doesn't like it all the same. Give her a while. She'll get used to you.'

I like that way he says that. I love it, in fact. It makes me feel secure. Adam obviously expects me to stay in his life for quite some time. Suddenly I think of my parents and feel guilty. They must be wondering where the hell I am. I tell Adam I'm going to ring them to let them know I'm okay.

'What time do you have to be back at?' he teases, toying with the top of my bra strap.

'Uh . . .'

'Is tomorrow morning too late?' he asks.

I ring my house but thankfully there's no answer so I just leave a message. I tell them I'm in Debbie's and feel really awful for lying. But the guilt soon passes.

'Right then,' Adam says, unbuttoning the front of my shirt. 'What are our plans for this evening? Are you still supposed to be off sick from work?'

'Yep,' I laugh. 'I'm sick.'

'So we can't go out?'

I shake my head.

'Okay. What's plan B? We'd better order some food in. What do you fancy?'

I shrug. 'I don't mind.'

'Can you swim?'

I nod. I saw the swimming pool on our way in but I don't have a swimsuit. I tell him this.

'Who needs a swimsuit?' he murmurs as his fingers reach the last button on my shirt.

Chapter Sixteen

Okay, so what's the catch? That's what you're thinking, isn't it? Let's face it, the guy's gorgeous, rich, famous, confident, generous, hard working and nice. He doesn't hate me for getting drunk and doesn't think I'm easy for hopping into bed with him on the second date. But men like that don't exist, do they? Well, that's what *I* thought. Until now.

Adam is everything I've ever dreamed of. At this very moment there are no other men left on my planet. They've faded into oblivion. The only man standing is Adam Kirrane.

I am utterly hopelessly addictively in love. And I'm almost sure Adam feels the same way. He's asked me to come out to New York (again) so a future together looks highly likely. In fact, right now it seems to stretch ahead of us like an airport runway on a clear night. No air traffic controllers are telling us we can't take off. I'm just waiting for clearance.

'You expect too much,' my mother always said to me.

'You're standards are way too high,' my sister used to agree.

'There are plenty of nice guys out there. You just don't notice them,' my friends would advise.

Well I held out. Against all the odds. I held out. I refused to settle. And look what happened. Nobody, and I really mean *nobody* could be as happy as I am now.

I've just emerged from my bed now after a much-needed snooze. For the last forty-eight hours I've hardly slept a wink but Adam has just gone back to the States and I'm back in my parents' house.

When I dragged myself through the front door this morning I got an earful from my mum. She was yelling at me for treating her house like a hotel, blah de blah de blah.

God when that woman gets going she's pretty unbearable.

'You'll have to get out,' she screamed at me as I slunk up the stairs.

Now, where have I heard that before?

I don't take much notice any more really. I've been threatened with eviction since I was about eighteen. Actually long before that, come to think of it. As a child I was being threatened with the orphanage almost on a daily basis.

'You're nearly twenty-eight,' is the last thing I hear as I close my bedroom door behind me. Jesus, I think, what the hell's got into her now?

My mother is always reminding me that she got

married at twenty-two. I'm not sure why she keeps telling me this as if it's some kind of huge achievement. I mean back then everyone got married young. Careers for women weren't really an option and everyone got married by twenty-five. Now everyone waits till they're thirty.

It's such a coincidence isn't it? All these people falling in love and marrying at the same time. Personally I think most get hitched just because everyone else is doing it. Just like they used to go to a certain school disco when they were young. Not wanting to be left out.

Some people are terrified of being different. So they jostle along with the crowd, getting married when their peers do. Killing themselves paying high mortgages to live in the same suburban area as everybody else. Bankrupting themselves to send their kids to the same schools as everybody else's kids. Fretting over being left out of dinner parties thrown by the 'right' people.

I, on the other hand, am terrified of simply fitting in.

Of being just one of a million ants pushing along until somebody's foot squashes me, bringing my dull, meaningless life to an abrupt end.

As I've said before my biggest fear in life is to exist without living. I'm not quite sure what I mean by that but I'd rather die than just plod along without out a map. Don't get me wrong, it's not like I've got everything worked out. Admittedly I'm not sure where I'm going, but I'm determined to get there all the same.

As a kid, when I was feeling down, I used to think about my funeral all the time. I would imagine my mum sobbing her eyes out and being remorseful for all the nasty things she'd said to me. I would also imagine my sister, overcome with grief and begging God to forgive her for bullying me and putting me down constantly.

I tried to imagine my dad being in tears as he remembered the time he locked me in my room for an afternoon with no food or water, but couldn't. I could never see him crying.

Especially over somebody as insignificant as me.

Like many angst-ridden teenagers, I couldn't stand being overweight, friendless and facing my Leaving Certificate. I thought about killing myself now and again, if only there'd been an easy way. But I didn't fancy any of the options. Jumping under a train didn't appeal. And the Liffey was a big no no. Someone once told me about a man who jumped in and didn't drown but got bitten by a rat. It took him three weeks to die. How horrific! There was no way I was taking that chance. And not having access to a gun, shooting myself wasn't an option either.

Of course I didn't think about killing myself *all* the time. Only a handful of times really. I decided against it in the end because I was afraid of all the attention Ruth would get. Left as an only child,

I imagined everyone would end up feeling really sorry for her. Losing her only sister. What a tragedy, people would say. I didn't like to think of Ruth becoming something of a local hero. No. That thought was enough to keep me alive and kicking.

They say what doesn't kill you makes you stronger. And life has done that for me at least. I think I'm strong anyway. My mother always called me self-destructive. But I was just a very sensitive child. Misunderstood. Badly bullied as a child by my classmates in school and my sister at home, I completely lacked confidence, and used to walk around with my head down most of the time. I thought if I kept my head down, people wouldn't see me and just forget I was there.

It didn't work. I was basically a punch bag for a certain school bully called Celeste who'd threaten to do my head in if I didn't steal cigarettes from my mother's bag to give to her. Celeste, the pest, I really hated her. She made life hell for me. Then to top it all, my mother would hit me when she realised her cigarettes were missing.

They say that your school days are the happiest days of your life. I wonder who actually said that incidentally. Could it have been someone called 'anon'? Happy is a word that could describe few moments of my teenage life.

I remember the day I left school. The sun shone very brightly and the birds seemed to be singing a bit more cheerfully than usual. I walked out of the building and didn't look back. Not once.

That was the first day of the rest of my life. I literally ran home from school, lit a big fire in the back garden, threw my petrol-coloured uniform on it and watched it go up in flames. It was the same uniform Ruth had worn before me. She had wanted to burn it the year she left, but Mum warned her if she did, she'd have to work all summer to get the money to buy me a new one. So that was the end of that.

I'm glad I was the one to burn the damn thing in the end.

Chapter Seventeen

Hello again. You haven't heard from me in a while 'cos I've been holed up in my room finishing my damn script. I'm off to Milan later this afternoon, so I'm busy printing out copies of my script before I go. I'm posting them to ten agents that I got out of the *Writers and Artists' Handbook*. Don't ask me if they're any good 'cos I don't know but hopefully all ten won't get back to me at once. How on earth could I choose?

Funnily enough, I'm looking forward to my trip to Italy. I mean it's just a day trip. Over and back. But the flight is long enough to do the service quickly and then sit in an empty seat at the back, looking out at the clouds. I love doing that. There's something so peaceful about it. Gazing out the plane window, I often pretend to myself that this is heaven up here. I adore flying over the Alps and staring down at the snow-capped mountains. Miles and miles of snow, clear blue skies, and best of all, miles and miles of no people, no houses, no nothing. Just lifeless beauty and possibly one of God's most extraordinary pieces of art.

The plane is only half-full, which is a nice change. Mostly skiers, a handful of Italian students, a couple of businessmen and a fairly large American family, doing Europe, I suppose.

Luckily I'm working down the back so apart from doing the routine service, I don't have much else to do. No 'hellos' or 'goodbyes' from me today thank God.

I've brought a couple of magazines to help pass the time once the service is done. However it appears that Lydia, the other air hostess flying with me down the back today, has no intention of letting me relax. She only started flying about two months ago and this is her dream, she tells me. I know how she feels. I used to feel the same way.

'Have you seen the first officer on this flight?' she asks, as I pretend to read my magazine. I look up at her. She's a pretty young thing, wearing far too much foundation and red lipstick. Her dyed jet-black hair frames slightly gaunt features. But I can see how men would find her attractive.

'No,' I admit, 'I haven't'. And I've no wish to. The pilots all look the same to me anyway. But sure why should I care who's flying the plane? The only man I find attractive at the moment is Adam Kirrane. I don't blame Lydia for getting excited though. She's young and new so that's why she's so naïve about the pilots. She'll learn though, I think to myself. Oh God yes, I imagine she'll learn.

I suddenly remember I've a letter in my bag. It was left in my pigeonhole and I'd just stuffed it in my bag. Now, I suppose is as good a time to read it. I fish the crumpled envelope out of my bag.

It's handwritten. I wonder if it's from a fan. I know it might sound weird but now and again, we air hostesses get letters from passengers who happen to take a mental note of our name-badges, and write to us care of Dublin Airport. Not that we take much notice of the fan mail. At least *I* don't anyway; I'm afraid I can't vouch for my colleagues. What these passengers don't realise is that, when we give them that extra big smile, it's not because we find them extraordinarily attractive. No. It's just part of our job.

Mind you, I sound like a bit hypocritical, don't I? After all, *I'm* dating a passenger myself. Still, he's Adam Kirrane the TV star and not some random nut on a flight. But I'd probably never have met him if I hadn't been on the New York flight that day. It must have been fate.

I open up the envelope and read the note. It's from my supervisor. She mentions a thank-you letter that was sent into head office about me from a certain Mr Charles Daviston. I'm very pleased that someone has gone to the trouble of writing such a complimentary letter. Passengers often promise to write but then rarely do unless it's to complain. It's heart-warming to know there are still genuinely nice people left in the world. I'm very, very pleased. The letter has almost made my day. Out of pride I show it to Lydia.

'Do you get many letters?' she asks almost accusingly.

'Well it's probably my third or fourth,' I tell her. 'So no. But it was nice of him to write in, wasn't it? I mean he didn't have to.'

'Are you sure he's not a relative of yours?'

'Definitely not,' I laugh.

She reads the letter. 'Levins,' she says frowning. 'I know that name.'

'Yes, well, he's a frequent flyer.'

'I see,' she says, fairly dismissively. 'Anyway I'm going up to the cockpit to see if the lads need anything.'

She disappears. God, she's a bit of a goer, isn't she? What on earth does she think the 'lads' *need* for God's sake? Sure isn't there a senior hostess in the front galley to make sure the pilots are fed and watered? Honestly these young hosties can be clueless!

A young Italian man interrupts me for a glass of wine. I hand him a quarter bottle with a smile and my compliments. I ask if he's going home and we have a little chat about his life and I tell him that yes, I love flying, and no, I will *not* be staying in Milan tonight.

'Oh. Is a peety.'

'Yes, indeed, a real pity. Well do enjoy the rest of your flight and if there is anything I can do, please don't hesitate to ask myself or any of the others.'

Oh and nice try buddy!

I hear the intercom coming on. The pilot's announcement. Yippee! I'm *dying* to know how many feet we are above sea level, what country we're presently flying over, and when we'll be landing at Linate Airport. Not.

Oh God, why am I being so giddy? This is ridiculous. Then again, being in love makes you silly, doesn't it? I'd almost forgotten that feeling.

'Good afternoon Ladies and Gentleman, this is your captain Mike Hanron speaking. I'd like to welcome you all on . . .'

What the f . . . ? I nearly fall of my seat. Am I hearing things? What the hell is Mike Hanron doing on a 737? When did he get off the airbus? And when did he get promoted? Why does nobody ever tell me anything?

I take a deep breath. God, this is unbelievable. How can I face him? No wonder Lydia has been hopping up and down to the cockpit like a bloody yoyo all afternoon. She must be mad into him. Still I don't blame her. He's pretty cute.

I can't believe Mike's already got his stripes though. He's so bloody young looking. He can't be more than thirty-four. Thirty-five max. Jesus all the girls will be after him now. A hunky single co-pilot is rare in this airline as it is, but a good-looking charming captain is practically unheard of.

Thank God, I'm taken now, or else I might make a beeline for him myself. Then again, I probably wouldn't have the nerve. I still haven't forgotten the time I met him in Boston wearing my pyjamas and no make-up. Christ that was embarrassing wasn't it? And I was in such a huff 'cos I'd thought himself and Amy had, you know, got together. Not that that should have bothered me. No. It shouldn't have had the slightest impact. I wonder why it did? Hmm.

Anyway I've got a boyfriend now, so Lydia and all the other girls can fight over Mike. I wouldn't waste my time chasing him. God no. As if! His head is probably big enough.

I try concentrating on my magazine but can't. Mike's voice is still banging on about all the countries we've passed over. Now he's describing the weather blah, blah, blah. He's got a nice voice though, I've got to admit. Funny I never noticed before.

Oh God, she's back. Lydia, that is. Well that was quick.

'How are the lads?' I ask somewhat sarcastically. 'Still alive I hope.'

Lydia's face is flying off her. She looks fit to kill someone. Her determined blue eyes are flashing. What's her problem now? Jesus, they say the best thing about flying is that you get to work with so many different, interesting people. Right now though, I'm thinking it might be kind of nice to work with the *same* people every day.

'He said you're to go up and say hello,' Lydia leans defiantly against the toilet door. I hope to God she realises somebody has just gone in there 'cos if they open the door suddenly, she's going to fall in.

'Who?' I try my best to look complacent.

'Mike, as in Mike the captain.'

'What does he want?'

'I asked him but he said it was personal.'

She *what*? She asked him what he wanted with *me*? God, she's a bit of a cheeky brat isn't she? I mean she can't be more than twenty-two years of age. Children should be seen, not heard and certainly not heard quizzing the captain about his attentions. Well I'm glad Mike put her in her place anyway.

'I'll go up in a minute,' I say, looking back down at my magazine, terrified that my face will give something away. Fuck, this is so annoying. If I *don't* go up to the cockpit Mike'll think I'm exceptionally rude. And if I *do* go in, I won't have a clue what to say to him. You see, I still feel kind of awkward around Mike ever since that morning in the hotel.

Ok Katie. Get up. You can do it. Go on. Get it over with. He's just a guy you work with. He's just being friendly. Grow up and start acting your age.

'I'll be back in a sec,' I tell Lydia who is staring at the view out the porthole of the back door. At least I'll get a much better view from the cockpit!

I walk up the aisle and thankfully nobody stops me for anything. Passengers often think if you're walking around, you're just dying for something to do. Like getting them another cup of tea or a tissue or something.

I push open the cockpit door and Mike turns around with a friendly smile. I get a shock seeing him in his uniform because I've never seen him in it before. He looks unbelievably hot, the crisp white shirt showing off his tan. I wonder if he's just back from holidays.

The co-pilot is a shy spotty thing who looks like he's just out of school. God, I'd thought the guards were getting younger looking recently but the pilots seem to be hot on their heels!

'How are you Katie?' Mike enquires mildly.

The blood flows to my face. The temperature is rising in the cockpit. I feel like a teenager again. But I like the way he says my name. He has a sexy voice. God, you know, if I weren't so in love with Adam, I could definitely go for this guy, which is weird. Because I've never fancied any of the other airplane drivers.

It's always the way though, isn't it? You could g~ 'or months – years even – and not meet anyone Then you meet one, and suddenly all these nen come creeping out of the woodwork.

'Come closer,' Mike orders and nods out towards the cockpit windows. I move a little forward so that I'm standing very close to Mike now. He smells divine. Armani aftershave. I'd almost bet on it.

The clouds part suddenly and the view that emerges stuns me into complete silence. It's captivating. The majestic mountains are so still, elegantly draped in blankets of thick, thick snow. Wouldn't it be so amazing to ski on some of those mountains and have the world to yourself? Then again, the fact that there's no life up here, makes it so perfect. Skiers would probably only ruin everything.

Mike turns to look at me. 'Beautiful isn't it?'

I nod quietly and can't help thinking how the sky is the exact colour of his eyes. Jesus, I sound mental! I wish Mike wasn't this good-looking. It's very distracting. He doesn't look like a film star in the same way that Adam does but then again he's not as intimidating. I could imagine him being great with kids on a beach, building sandcastles and . . .

Right. I should get out of this cockpit this minute before my overworking imagination gets me into trouble.

'Well I'd better get back out to all those demanding passengers,' I say.

'Lydia was saying they're actually very quiet today,' Mike sounds surprised.

'Yes, well . . . oh by the way, congratulations on

your promotion. When did you get your stripes?'

Mike's face breaks into an even wider smile. 'A while back now.'

'But when did you come off the A-330?'

'Oh ages ago. That time we met you in Boston we were just on a training course. I wasn't flying that time.'

'Oh right.' Actually, come to think of it, I *do* remember him explaining something about a course that night in Boston, but I wasn't really taking it in. I find all those flying details a bit boring to be honest. Aerosexuality doesn't do it for me. And anyway I was probably too busy thinking about Adam to take any notice.

'So gentlemen,' I add a note of false gaiety to my voice, 'can I get you anything while I'm up here?'

'I'm fine,' Mike smiles. 'What about you Alan?'

Alan speaks for the first time. 'I'm fine too.'

'Well then, I'll love you and leave you,' I say breezily. 'See you in Milan.'

I close the cockpit door and take a deep breath. I then pause to have a chat with Tania and Tara, the two girls working in the front galley. They're both senior hostesses and a couple of years older than me. And they're also both engaged so I'm sure they've spent most of the flight nattering on about wedding dresses, fiancés, honeymoons etc. Would-be-brides, I find, like to talk about nothing other than weddings. Personally, I'd rather talk about teeth extractions.

The two girls smile at me blankly as I ramble on about nothing in particular.

I try on their rings and make two wishes. One is that my script gets accepted, the other is that Adam and I live happily ever after.

'You're looking pretty pleased with yourself for some reason,' Tania says teasingly as she pours me a glass of orange juice. 'Any men on the scene?'

'Well, sort of,' I say, blushing slightly.

'No names?' Tara chimes in.

'No names just at the moment. It's all a bit hush-hush.'

'Hmm,' says Tara, twisting her diamond sparkler around her finger. 'Don't like the sound of that somehow.'

'Are you having an affair?' Tania asks wide-eyed, tugging at her sleeves excitedly. 'Is it someone at work?'

'Of course,' I decide to play along. 'And you all know him too. I'll tell you his name at the end of the flight, if you haven't guessed by then. I'm sure you know his wife. She's cabin crew too. God, I hope she's not a friend of yours!'

The two girls exchange uncomfortable glances. My joke has fallen like a dead balloon. I suddenly remember both these girls are engaged to pilots. And Tara's man is on his second marriage. His former wife was also a hosty. Oh shit.

My ass is saved by Mike's announcement. We're landing in fifteen minutes.

'I was only messing by the way,' I tell the girls lamely as I shoot down the cabin, making sure everybody's strapped in for landing.

Lydia is in a huff down the back.

'You were *ages*,' she moans, lathering her hands in foul smelling hand-cream. 'Want some?' She points the tube threateningly in my direction.

'Oh no thanks, I was just catching up with the girls,' I say breezily, ignoring her pouting face. 'They're both engaged, isn't it marvellous?'

Lydia ignores me, yawns and puts the hand cream back in her bag. 'I hope the flight isn't delayed on the way home, I'm going to tell Mike to put the boot down.'

Tell Mike? Do you hear her? Cheeky so-and-so.

I wonder if there's a *Coronation Street* omnibus on tonight. Why else would Lydia be in such a hurry to get home?

'I've a date,' she positively preens.

'Really?'

'Yep.' She squashes in beside me and straps herself into the crew seat for landing. I dim the galley lights as the wheels go down.

'Is it a first date?'

'Yep', she says again. God, she's not giving much away, is she? Well, she can sod off if she thinks I'm going to keep probing for information. I couldn't give a tinker's curse who she's going out with.

'Don't you want to know who he is?' Lydia then asks, as I make a mental reminder to carefully check future rosters to make sure this annoying girl isn't on any more of my flights.

'I'm sure I wouldn't know him,' I say closing my eyes. If I stay quiet hopefully she'll shut up.

'I'm sure you would.'

I don't answer.

'Have you ever seen *DreamBoat*?'

Thump!

The wheels hit the runway with a bang.

The plane thunders down the runway with a roar.

'Jesus, that was rough!' Lydia exclaims. 'I'm going to ask Mike what the hell he was thinking?'

'That wasn't Mike who landed,' I say in a sort of dull voice. 'It was the co-pilot. Lydia, I wonder can you excuse me for a minute? Just make sure the passengers stay in their seats until the "fasten seatbelt" sign has been switched off, ok?'

I stand up shakily as the plane zooms along.

Then I lock myself in the toilet cubicle.

And reach for a sick bag.

Chapter Eighteen

'Do you want to go into the airport to get some wine?' Mike asks pleasantly.

I'm sitting down in the middle of the cabin, pretending to eat my crew meal and read the newspaper.

'No thanks, I'm fine,' I manage a weak smile.

'I'll go in with you,' Lydia jumps up. 'I can never have enough wine in my apartment. You never know who's going to drop in,' she chuckles. 'Do you?'

Mike smiles politely and heads off. Alan the co-pilot tags along. I'm sure he doesn't even drink but would rather wander around the airport than be stuck here gossiping with the girls.

'Is that one wrecking your head?' Tara asks me sympathetically, once they've gone.

'Who Lydia? No, she's fine,' I lie.

'I noticed she was drawn to the cockpit like a moth to a flame,' Tania says. 'I'd say she was driving the lads mad.'

'Oh maybe they enjoy her company. I'm sure it

gets a bit monotonous looking at the clouds all day and trying to get the last clue in the *Irish Times* crossword.'

The girls laugh in unison.

'Anyway she's just young,' I say quietly. 'And she's going on a date tonight,' I add. I don't know why I'm telling them this because I actually feel numb. I think I've gone in to shock actually. My heart feels like it has been pierced with a sword, and my head is still reeling. I don't think everything has quite sunk in yet.

'Lucky guy,' Tania says, her voice heavy with irony.

'He's the guy from *DreamBoat* apparently.'

'Who?'

'Adam Kirrane.'

'No way!' Tara almost drops her knife and fork.

'Jesus, how did she get *him*?' Tania is equally astounded.

'I dunno. He probably just asked her out on a flight.'

I'm on a roll here. I can't stop talking but I sound like a tape. I don't even know where the words are coming from.

'I wouldn't say it'll lead to anything though,' Tania says eventually. 'I mean, does she not know that that guy will eventually move onto bigger and better things?'

'How do you mean?' I look at her blankly.

'Well he's a big star, you know. He'll probably

end up with another star. Most of them do. I mean their lives are one big publicity stunt. They're not like normal people.'

'It's true,' Tara agrees. 'I mean he's hardly going to settle down with someone like Lydia. She's a good-looking girl but sure what could she offer him?'

'Yeah, it'll just be a one night-stand,' Tania adds.

'By tomorrow he'll be with someone else.' Tara stands up and offers to pour me a cup of tea. I gratefully accept.

A cup of tea might help calm my nerves.

But realistically I could do with something stronger.

A lot stronger.

'Apparently he has a bit of a reputation,' I add milk to my tea, and lift my feet to let the cleaners hoover under my seat.

'Who has?'

'Adam Kirrane.'

'Really? Are you serious? I never heard that.' Tania looks at me quizzically.

'Well, he wouldn't ask *us* out because we're engaged,' Tara laughs. 'I wouldn't have said no though. I mean if I was still single, haha.'

'So . . . you haven't heard of him asking out any of the other girls?'

They both shake their heads and in a weird kind of way, I'm somewhat relieved. I mean for a minute there I just presumed that Adam asked out every single air hostess he spoke to. Well, come on, you've got to admit; there's been a fair few of us. Sandy, Wendy, myself and now Lydia. Busy man eh?

The pilots and Lydia arrive back on board just as we're clearing away our trays. Lydia is laughing hysterically at something Mike said. I doubt it was remotely funny.

I honestly don't know how I'm going to work the flight home with Lydia without strangling her by her neat little navy and white scarf. I just want to curl up in a corner and cry myself to sleep.

'Mike is an angel, isn't he?' Lydia preens into the mirror in the back galley, as she colours in her full lips with cherry-red lipstick.

'I don't know,' I say quietly, 'I don't really know him.'

I wander up the aisle leaving Lydia to make the baggage announcement down the back. In a plumy over-the-top voice she warns passengers not to block the aisles while placing their luggage in the overhead lockers. I turn around to glare at her. There are only nine passengers on board so far and they are all sitting down. In fact the only person standing in the aisle is me!

I keep myself busy by searching for a baby belt for a tiny tot. I then, in pidgeon Italian explain to the mother how it works. To my delight she seems to understand me. Either that, or she's just exceptionally polite.

Watching the baby with its huge brown innocent eyes, and his gorgeous adoring parents, I feel a little sad. Will I ever have this, I wonder? Will anyone ever love me enough to marry me? And will I ever get some little person to snuggle into me one day and call me Mummy?

Just as I think everybody is on board, Mike announces that we are waiting on two more passengers. Unfortunately they have checked their bags in, so for security reasons we can't go anywhere until the bags are offloaded. Planes can't fly with strange bags. Everyone knows that.

Hmm. Try telling that to passengers who arrive in Florida only to find out their bags have gone to Sydney instead!

I check my watch discreetly but don't make a big fuss. No. It's the passengers' job to complain when we're delayed, not ours. Of course we regularly get attacked when the plane is delayed for whatever reason. But *we* don't mind. Hell, no. We have no lives ourselves of course. And find nothing more fun than being stuck on a plane with a lot of disgruntled passengers. Especially at three in the morning, in some foreign hellhole when the passengers, having had one or two too many, go completely ballistic. At times like that I start to seriously think about my life and think a nice nine-to-five office job mightn't be so bad after all.

Oh here we go. Our late passengers stroll on cool as a breeze. Apologetic? You must be joking. They're Irish too.

Laden with shopping bags (isn't it well for some?) they look annoyed because they can't find any space in the overhead lockers. You'd think that people who've just delayed a plane and its passengers would have the common decency to look mortified and take their seats as quickly as possible. Not this pair.

'Excuse me?' the woman beckons to me, using a condescending, overbearing accent.

I take a deep breath. Right. Okay. I am not a puppy at anybody's beck and call and I'm going to tell these passengers to sit down immediately and strap themselves in.

As I approach mutual recognition sets in. Oh Jesus. My mouth goes suddenly dry. I *thought* I was having a bad day, but this is definitely taking the biscuit. The woman in question is Celeste-Jane Leddy, who was the biggest bitch in my school. Christ I haven't seen her . . . well for years. Not since she got expelled for trying to set someone's ponytail alight with a match. I never knew what became of her in the end.

She's lost weight, I notice unhappily. A hell of a lot of weight. She's very thin. But her features are sharp. And her eyes are a steely grey. Without a trace of warmth.

'Well . . . hello,' she says with a barely concealed sneer. 'Is this what you're doing now?'

'Hello Celeste,' I say calmly, not failing to notice the enormous rock on her left hand. She's married. Jesus, even *that* cow managed to get someone. And he's not even ugly, dammit. At least if he were ugly I could console myself.

'Yes, I am, it's great. Now Celeste, I wonder if you could take your seat as quickly as possible, because we're badly delayed as it is.'

She's furious. Two bright pink spots appear on her razor-sharp cheekbones. She nevertheless obeys me. As she sits down she glances at my name badge. 'Still Redden, I see' she smiles icily.

'Yes, too busy for love.'

'Dear me, that's what they *all* say. God, you career women, I just don't get it at all. Now can you do something with all these shopping bags?'

I take them and strap them into an empty seat. I'd love to open them up and see what she's bought. Just to see how the other half lives but I don't. Because I'm miserable enough as it is.

Instead I go back to my seat. We're ready for take-off.

'Well, did they apologise?' Lydia wants to know. She's furious that the flight has been delayed. At this stage we've missed our slot time for take-off.

'Who?' I ask absently 'cos I'm barely listening to her.

'Posh 'n' Becks'

'Huh?'

'The two with all the bags.'

'Oh *them*? No of course they didn't apologise. In fact it didn't even occur to them that they'd put everyone out. At least it didn't occur to *her*. I know her actually. Well *knew* her. She was in school with me.'

'God, well she's a lucky thing with your man. He's a ride isn't he? And obviously not short of a few bob. Mind you, she's very good-looking as well, isn't she?'

'I don't think she's that great,' I say and then regret sounding so spiteful. But when you dislike someone you never think they're *that* good-looking, do you? At least you wouldn't admit it. No. Not in a million years.

'I'd love to marry a rich man,' Lydia says suddenly. 'A handsome rich man. The problem is though, that most handsome men aren't rich and most rich men aren't handsome.'

'Well, maybe you'll marry Adam Kirrane, and that'll be the solution to all your problems.'

Lydia looks like someone's just punched her in the gob. She turns to me with an astonished look on her face.

'How do you know about me and him?' she practically shrieks.

'It's easy,' I say in a deadpan voice. 'I'm psychic.'

Chapter Nineteen

'And then he'll bring you to his house,' I say, staring at the palm of her hand. 'And he'll ask you do you want to go for a swim.'

'Has he *really* got a swimming pool? How do you know all of this?' Lydia asks suspiciously.

'I told you, I'm psychic.'

'Oh my God, this is so amazing. Can you tell if we'll end up, you know, being serious?'

'I can't tell you that,' I say sombrely.

'Why not?'

'Well, I only ever tell people good things.'

'Oh.' Lydia clearly doesn't like the sound of that. But no doubt she'll just erase that bit from the reading. Most people only ever believe good things about their future anyway. You know yourself, when you read your horoscope and it's bad you just convince yourself it's a load of rubbish. Then you read a good one, and convince yourself it's true.

In the middle of the reading a call bell sounds. I offer to attend to it. Lydia is devastated when I drop her hand. As I walk down the aisle, I notice that the call bell is above Celeste's head. Shit. What does that weapon want now?

'Hey sweetie,' she practically coos at me. 'I was wondering if you could do me a huge favour? Alistair and myself have just celebrated our first anniversary and we were just wondering if there were any seats free in first class? It'd be *such* a treat for us both.'

I open my mouth to say something but am rendered speechless. I'm stunned by her cheek. I seriously am. Over the years, I have met many, many people I know on flights, and not one of them has ever asked for an upgrade. And *this* girl thinks I'm stupid enough to bring her up to first class just because she calls me sweetie. Well elephants may have superb memories but few can recall their schooldays quite as much as me. So I kneel down and say quietly, 'Sweetie, you know I would have *no* problem upgrading you but Tania, the senior air hostess today is very strict, and I know she wouldn't allow it. So I'm sorry about that. Really I'm very sorry.'

I give her my biggest smile as I stand up again and then walk away. The best things in life are free, they say, and luckily a smile costs nothing at all. And that's all Celeste whatserface will be getting from me today. Sweetie, my arse.

Down in the back galley Lydia is having a panic attack. She explains that while pulling out the cart, one of the bread rolls fell off the tray and rolled onto the toilet floor. Somebody had left the door open. She's horrified because normally there are lots of spare bread rolls provided. Today there aren't. We have fifty-three bread rolls. And the same amount of passengers.

'Which bread roll fell on the ground?' I ask matter-of-factly.

'I threw it in the bin.'

I walk to the bin and yank it out of its socket. I retrieve the bread roll, give it a quick wipe on my apron and place it back on the tray.

Lydia just stares in disbelief.

'I'm just repaying an old friend,' I say, placing the tray on top of the cart, lest I forget to give it to Celeste specifically.

I'm actually doing this for Emily. Emily was a rather fat girl I knew in school. She was even larger than I was. I haven't seen her since I was a teenager so I don't know what became of her. We struck up an odd sort of a friendship while queuing daily for the school tuck shop. Two unconfident, unhappy, lost schoolgirls looking for love in a secret world of Mars Bars and Twixes.

Celeste used to make Emily's life hell. She once spat on a chair and made Emily sit down on it. Another time she whacked her across the back legs in a hockey game, claiming it to be an accident. I was too afraid to stand up for Emily because I thought if I did, my turn would be next. And when Emily had a nervous breakdown and then eventually changed schools, I lost contact with her. It haunted me for years afterwards that I'd never done anything to help.

'Bon appetite,' I hand the tray to Celeste.

She's smiling less now. And I'm smiling more. In fact my jaw is beginning to ache from all the grinning I've done on this flight. But it's better than crying. Yes. If I started crying now I know I'd never stop.

'I'll have a red wine for me and one for my *husband*.' She stresses the word 'husband'. 'Is that what you want darling?'

Hubby, at least, has the good grace to look suitably mortified. I give him a sympathetic kind of smile. God, for one who's practically crying inside, I'm certainly doing a lot of smiling today.

When the service is over, I'm fit to collapse. I bring an *Irish Independent* down to the back galley to read. Hopefully it will help take my mind off things. And with any luck Adam's photo won't be in it again. I couldn't bear to look at him now. Really I couldn't.

I flick through my paper with Lydia hovering over me, trying to read it too. I'd like to roll it up and swat her with it. Like a fly.

'Can you see anything about my childhood?' she asks.

'What, in the paper?'

'No, silly, in my hand.'

'But I'm not looking at your hand Lydia.'

'Oh please, can you just tell me a bit more?'

God, I'll be plagued for the rest of my life over this.

I grab her hand. 'You were very spoilt as a child, weren't you?'

'Wow, that's so true,' she says excitedly. 'You are so talented. It's a gift, isn't it?'

'Er . . . yes.'

Quite.

Tania arrives down for a chat.

Lydia tells her I tell fortunes.

Tania looks thrilled and offers me her hand too.

Jesus, what have I got myself into now?

'This is a very happy time for you right now,' I pretend to concentrate on her palm.

How the hell do I think I'm going to get away with this?

'You've definitely met the right man. But . . . there was a stage in your life when you wondered if you were ever going to meet that special person.'

'You've got that right,' Tania sighs.

Well, come on, what woman doesn't wonder?

'And there has been heartbreak,' I say in a suitably sad voice.

She nods silently.

'But the other men in your life just weren't meant to be, even though at the time you didn't know it.'

Tania isn't speaking now. She's gone very quiet. God, I hope she's not going to cry or anything. That would be so embarrassing.

'Your wedding will be a very happy occasion though. It will be a wonderful day for everybody. Don't worry about it. Everything will sort itself out.'

'Oh that's a relief,' Tania takes a deep breadth. 'I *have* been worried about it.'

'I see some interference from your in-laws,' I offer.

'Yes indeed.' Tania grimaces.

'But as I said any problems will just iron themselves out.'

'*Have* you been having problems with your in-laws?' Lydia suddenly butts in. She's still very young so probably has no experience of nightmare wedding plans. I, on the other hand, know exactly how stressful they can be. I've gone through this crap with practically all of my friends.

'There's a slight problem with the guest list. You've people on it that you don't particularly want at your wedding.'

Tania nods vigorously.

'And others that you'd like to invite but can't because of numbers.'

'Oh yes.'

'It will all work out though,' I repeat sagely. I pause for a minute wondering if I should perhaps quit now while I'm ahead.

Then, I think, I'll just say *one* more thing. I'm quite enjoying this actually, despite my broken heart and the fact that Celeste – my childhood enemy from hell – is sitting just a few feet away.

'I see a foreign holiday; white beaches and a clear blue sea. An island, maybe.'

'Oh, that'll be the honeymoon,' Tania beams. 'We're going to the Maldives.'

Phew!

Tania then sends Tara down to get her fortune told. Jesus, I'm beginning to regret starting my silly little game. But there's no point backtracking now so I tell her much the same thing I told Tania. But since Tara's engagement ring holds the biggest, heaviest diamond I've ever seen in my life, I add that I can see she's marrying a wealthy man.

'Well my fiancé *does* earn a lot of money,' she admits candidly.

'And somehow I can't see you being in this job in a few years time,' I continue, frowning slightly for extra effect.

'Neither do I!' she exclaims. 'Can you really see that?'

'Yes.'

Of *course* I can. If he's that bloody wealthy she's not going to be getting up at four every morning to do red eye flights for the rest of her life now, is she?

'And I see the pitter patter of tiny feet. Sooner rather than later.'

I put Tara's age at around thirty-five so I reckon I'm on fairly safe ground here. The old biological clock must be ticking away nicely.

She's happy. I'm happy. We're all happy. Well . . . I'm not *really* happy. My heart is breaking as you can imagine. But you know, under the circumstances I'm not doing too badly and at least I've survived the return flight without wallowing in self-pity.

I glance at my watch. We're nearly home, thanks be to God. I can't wait for today to be over. I want it to be tomorrow already. Tomorrow things might make a bit more sense.

It's funny but I don't actually feel jealous of Lydia or anything. No. In fact I feel almost sorry for her. She's probably dreaming of romance and fairytale weddings. But to Adam, she'll probably be just another shag. I can't believe I'm going to let her walk into this. I wonder should I say anything. After all, annoying as Lydia is, I don't want to let Adam hurt her.

'Lydia?' I say suddenly.

She looks at me expectantly.

'Where is Adam taking you?'

'Can't you see that?' she asks innocently.

'Let me guess. Probably a little hotel in Wicklow,' I say heavily.

'He says it's a surprise.'

'I'll bet.'

Lydia chews her nails pensively. I wonder what's going on in that head of hers.

'I was thinking,' she says awkwardly. 'I was thinking I might tell him about you.'

'What?' I ask, stricken. My heart does a couple of bungee-jumps. Why in God's name would she want to mention me?

'About what you said. I mean I've never met a real fortune-teller before. I'm sure Adam would think it's fascinating.'

'I'm sure he would, as a matter of fact.'

'Of course, I won't mention your name,' she assures me.

Suddenly a little light bulb pops up in my head. Ping! Then a slow smile spreads across my face.

'Actually Lydia I think you *should*,' I insist. 'My aunt is a famous psychic in New York. Psychic to the stars in fact. He'll probably recognise the name.'

'Really?'

'Yes, but don't tell him straight away, of course,' I advise. 'Wait until you've both enjoyed your meal.'

Lydia looks delighted to be armed with this piece of useful information. And although I feel slightly guilty for lying, at least I've managed to cheer myself up.

Chapter Twenty

I'm on my way home. In Mike's car. Dublin speeds past as I sit back, close my eyes and relax. Yes, I know what you're thinking. You're wondering how the hell I ended up in the captain's car. Don't worry though, I'm not going to suddenly hop on Mike as a means of getting over Adam. No. I never do the rebound thing. It doesn't work.

So how did I end up here? Well, I'll just tell you quickly. I was walking across the ramp and it had begun to rain so I stopped to put up my umbrella. Then Mike came up behind me, picked up my bag and insisted on carrying it across the ramp. Of course I was pretty impressed as you can imagine. I mean, the bag was so light but Mike wouldn't let me carry it myself. Lydia, Tara and Tania had long since disappeared, as had the co-pilot. They were all rushing home. Lydia, of course, had a date. And the others also had things going on. I, on the other hand seemed to be the only one with no plans. So I offered to wait behind with a wheelchair passenger until the ambulance came to help her down the aircraft steps. She was such a lovely good-natured woman who didn't complain once that the ambulance was late. Instead she chatted about life and told me she'd just gone over to Italy to see her first grandchild. Talking to her, and seeing how much she appreciated life, made me realise that there was more to this world than Adam Kirrane and that, in fact, he had done me a favour by asking Lydia out. He could have wasted more of my time, like Tim had done. But at least he didn't get to do that. And besides I don't have another three years to spare on someone who's not worth it.

After the ambulance came and took the woman into Arrivals, I headed down the aircraft steps, not realising that Mike had stayed behind in the cockpit to finish off some paperwork.

I wandered across the ramp, wearing my high-visibility luminous-yellow jacket, so an incoming plane or service truck wouldn't knock me down. And I'm sure a tear or two slid down my cheek as I wondered what on earth I was going to do with myself for the rest of the evening. But luckily, Mike came along before any more tears appeared. If he hadn't, my make-up would have been ruined by the time I reached the car park!

Mike offered me a lift home, which I gladly accepted. I don't think I could have faced taking public transport home with people on the bus staring. You have no idea how much people gawk at air hostesses in uniform. So in case you were wondering how I ended up in Mike's car, now you know.

'I believe you tell fortunes?' Mike asks me as we whiz along Griffith Avenue. U2's *It's a Beautiful Day* blasts from the car radio. I can't help feeling how ironic it sounds.

'Well, I try,' I give a weary smile. Hopefully he's not going to give me his palm or anything while he's driving. The roads are slippery enough and God, forbid, if anything happened to us, and we ended up crashing, I could just imagine the rumours flying around the airport.

'They were having an affair.'

'Apparently she was two-timing him with a famous TV star.'

'And that star was *also* dating another air hostess.'

'And would you believe, the two girls had actually done a flight together on that tragic day.'

'But thanks be to God, she didn't leave anyone behind.'

'No husband or kids or anything.'

'Her parents must be upset though.'

'Yes. And she had a sister who gave an interview to the *Sunday World* about the tragedy. A very pretty girl. Ruth, I think her name is. She looked distraught, poor thing.'

Jesus, Katie, would you stop it!

'You're not even listening to me,' Mike prods my knee as we stop at the traffic lights.

'Sorry.' I snap straight back into the land of the living. 'I get carried away sometimes.'

'I was just asking if you see anything in my future.'

I look at his profile carefully. He has a perfect face, even features, sallow skin, thick dark eyelashes and jet-black hair. One day, I thought, he's going to make some woman very, very happy. And if he ever has kids, he'll probably dote on them. He'd be a great father. At least that's the impression I get. But I can't tell him this. No way, I'd be mortified. Don't ask me why but suddenly I feel myself getting very hot.

'If it's that bad, I don't want to know,' he laughs good-naturedly. Phew! Thank God he's not going to force me to tell his fortune. I just couldn't face that right now.

I'm trying to act normally but I can't help wondering what'll happen when Lydia meets Adam later. Will she tell him she was working with me today? And will he just laugh it off or at least have the decency to feel bad. Somehow, I've a feeling it'll be the former. Sure, why would he care about me? After all, he doesn't even try to be discreet? He could have any girl in the world but he decides to date my airline colleagues instead. Sicko!

'What are you thinking?' Mike gently interrupts my internal monologue. He fishes in his pocket for loose change for the toll bridge.

I'm thinking about Lydia and Adam. I'm wondering if they'll end up having sex tonight. Will he ply her with champagne like he did with me? Is that his party trick? I feel ill just thinking about it.

'Nothing,' I sigh as a sharp pain sweeps through my body. 'Nothing at all.'

'You're in world of your own,' he observes.

'Yes . . . I suppose I am.'

'Where exactly do you live in Stillorgan?' Mike enquires as he drives along the Strand Road and I stare out at sea but see nothing because darkness is falling. And it's raining again now.

I tell him the name of my road.

'Would you like to go for a drink before I take you home?' Mike offers.

I swallow hard. Can Mike read my mind or what? Yes, I would *love* a drink. In fact I'd kill for one just now. Or two. Or three. But I can't go into a pub in my uniform and neither can he. It's against company rules. Surely he's aware of this.

'You mean . . . in your house?' I turn to him. My voice is a whisper.

'Yes . . . if that's okay with you, if that er . . . suits . . . '

'I'd love to,' I smile, putting him out of his misery. Maybe I'm mad, I think. I mean, why am I going to Mike's house when I should be consoling myself with a big box of chocolates in my room singing *All by myself?*

'Great,' he answers back cheerfully. As if I have just simply told him the time or something.

We say nothing else till we arrive at his house.

He lives in Blackrock. In a lovely four bed semi-detached house. It's not out of this world or anything. I mean it doesn't have a swimming pool, or a majestic sweeping drive. And it certainly doesn't have a member of staff to answer the door. But that's a relief to be honest. I felt like a gatecrasher in Adam's parents' house.

The house screams 'bachelor'. But I like it. It's neat, tidy and compact, although, if I'm to be completely honest, I think it could do with a female touch.

I hover a little in the doorway before taking off my uniform coat and sitting down on the chocolate-coloured leather sofa. For the first time since I met him, I wonder why Mike never got married. After all, he's a handsome guy. Very handsome. And he's kind. He's got a good job too . . . but somehow I don't want to probe. It's really none of my business, after all.

'I moved in here just a year ago,' Mike explains as though reading my mind.

'Where did you live before this?'

'In Portmarnack.'

'Alone?'

Our eyes meet and avert just as quickly.

'Would you like a drink?' he asks, ignoring the question. Serves me right.

'Sure'.

'Will I open a bottle of wine?'

'I'd prefer something stronger. You got any Bacardi?'

'You name it, I have it.'

'I'll go for some rum then. With Coke please.'

Mike disappears into the kitchen.

When he's gone I look around the cream carpeted

sitting room. It's bare except for one rather unusual painting, depicting a Connemara setting. I think I recognise the beach. From a family holiday years and years ago. Back when life was a little less complicated. And a little more fun.

A wide screen TV/DVD player dominates the far corner and hundreds of CDs are stacked neatly in a row. There's a plant on the windowsill but it looks like its days are numbered. It was probably a present from his mother.

This all seems very bizarre. I feel like I'm going to wake up in a minute and realise this was all a dream. If you had told me last night that I'd be sitting in another man's house tonight, drinking alcohol in my airline uniform I'd never have believed you. But life is weird. God, yes.

Mike returns with my drink, and he's thoughtfully filled a crystal bowl with peanuts, which he hands to me.

He sits down beside me and opens a bottle of wine.

'From Milan,' he smiles. And I smile back. I feel strangely at home here. I don't know why. And I certainly don't feel like I slept with another man last night. That particular . . . er, incident, seems like a million miles away. I'm glad now I didn't go home. My pillow won't miss the tears.

'There's something on your mind, isn't there?' Mike's eyes penetrate mine. They're so intense. He slips off his jacket and places it on top of my coat. The gesture unnerves me slightly. I feel like an awkward teenager at my first school disco. What's this all about? I wonder. Mike had better not think I'm here to be seduced or anything.

The last thing I need to do now is get involved with another man. Even if it's just a meaningless kiss. I've got to get my head together before I think about doing anything I might regret later. I've made a mistake already this week. A huge one. I won't be doing that again in a hurry.

'Yes, there is,' I take a sip of my drink. It's strong. Good.

'But you don't want to talk about it?'

'That's right I don't.'

'Are you hungry?'

'No.'

God, I'm not making this easy for him, am I? I'm sure he's beginning to regret inviting me to his home. But I don't care. I'm tired of trying to impress men. In fact suddenly I just feel tired, period.

'I was delighted when I heard you were on board today,' Mike leans back on the sofa and opens his shirt collar. I hate to admit it, but he looks sexy as hell and is becoming sexier by the minute. I almost dislike him for it. It would be so much easier if he wasn't so attractive, wouldn't it?

Then I could tell him all about Adam and how my heart has been smashed. But there's no point in that. Anyway I don't even know if I could explain it all properly.

'How did you know I was on the flight?'

'Tania handed me the list of crew names. I couldn't believe it when I saw yours. I suppose I've wanted to apologise to you for a long time. You know, for leaving you in the bar in Boston that night.'

'You already did.'

'I wanted to apologise again. Properly.' He touches my arm gently, sending an excited shiver through me. I don't know if I trust myself sitting in such close proximity to Mike. Not when I'm feeling this vulnerable. Suddenly, I feel like curling up, crying into his shoulder, and letting everything out. But I can't do that. Mike wouldn't understand. Not really.

'Have you ever been cheated on?' I suddenly blurt out, astonishing myself as well as Mike.

He stands up and for a minute I think he's going to throw me out for being so impertinent. He walks over to his CD player, hovers for a moment and then puts on some classical music. I watch carefully, not fully understanding my emotions, which happen to be all over the place at the minute. What's the story with the romantic music? Then it dawns on me. I know what's going on now. Yes, I get it. He thinks I'm just another airhead, who's going to hop into bed with him because of some music and a bit of alcohol. Well, I'm not that cheap a date. And anyway, I'm finished with men. I decided that on the flight today. I should have done it a long time ago. It would have saved me a lot of trouble. Men, they're all the same, all of them. Only the names change.

I get to my feet and make a show of looking at my watch.

'Are you going somewhere?' Mike looks surprised and even a little hurt. I'm not sure why. Maybe he's just disappointed he won't be getting his wicked way with me.

'I'd like to go home now.'

Mike looks so taken aback, I feel terrible. Of course deep down, I know why I'm doing this. I'm just telling him what I wish I'd told Adam last night. Mike is in effect paying for Adam's crime.

'Please don't go,' he says quietly. 'Hey, if you don't like the music I'll change the CD. What do you like? Jazz, R&B, Country and Western?'

I laugh in spite of myself. What else can I do?

'It's not the music,' I say awkwardly. 'I just . . . well, I'm just not sure what I'm doing here.'

'Well neither am I,' he shrugs, 'so that makes two of us. I mean, I know I'm here because I live here. But . . .' he trails off.

'But what . . . ?'

'Well, I haven't invited anyone to my home since . . .'

Mike's face suddenly looks very serious. Pained, almost. I wonder why. And I wonder why he has stopped talking. He turns away from me. Instinctively I walk towards him.

'What's the matter?' I put my hand on his shoulder.

He still doesn't turn around.

'My wife left me two years ago,' he says in a very, very quiet voice.

I say nothing. I'm too shocked to speak.

'She left me for my sister's husband,' he continues.

'No.'

'Yes, it's hard to believe isn't it?'

'So you're married?' I say slowly, letting the news sink in.

'Separated. Legally separated. Soon to be divorced actually.'

My God, this is a shock. I'm truly stunned.

Eventually he turns around and looks straight at me. Our faces are very close to each other and for a moment I'm convinced he's going to try and kiss me. I'm filled with panic and anticipation. What am I going to do? But then Mike doesn't try anything and I'm almost sorry.

We sit in silence. My breathing is heavy. I really need to let all this sink in. My mind is a pool of confusion. Why am I here and how long exactly have I been attracted to Mike? It slowly occurs to me that I've probably seriously fancied him since that first night in Boston. And that I was madly hurt over the fact that he left me alone with Derek. And that I was jealous of Amy because I thought Mike preferred her. In fact, all of a sudden it dawns on me that I was far more jealous of Amy and Mike in Boston, than I was this afternoon when I heard about Adam and Lydia.

Suddenly my mobile beeps. I check it to see who's sent me a text. Funnily enough, I'm not that surprised to see Adam's name.

NOT FEELIN GR8. CN WE MEET 2MORO INSTD?

I simply erase the text. Then I erase Adam's name altogether from my phone. I won't be needing it from now on. No. I won't be needing it any more.

'Sit down.' My eyes meet Mike's. 'You can tell me everything. That's if you want to, of course.'

Mike wipes his brow in mild frustration. 'Jesus,' he sighs. 'I didn't invite you in so I could tell you all about my failed married. God, that's the last thing I wanted to do. How did I even get talking about it?'

'It's my fault. I asked you did anyone ever cheat on you?'

'So you did,' Mike looks at me oddly. 'What a strange thing to ask somebody on a first date.'

'Is this a date?' I can't help smiling.

'Well, I agree it's not the most romantic date I've ever been on but . . .'

We both laugh.

And then we stop laughing at the same time. As our heads draw closer together, Mike's arms creep around my waist and our lips find one another's. And for some strange reason, once again, I feel at home. As if I've been with Mike all my life.

Chapter Twenty one

Of course I didn't sleep with him! Well, we *did* sleep in the same bed but *nothing* happened last night. And to be honest, Mike didn't even try anything. In fact he gave me an old pair of pyjamas to wear and we just lay in each other's arms for hours, talking, kissing and then talking a little more. Incidentally Mike's a pretty good kisser.

Anyway, I ended up telling him all about Adam except I left out the part about us having sex in case Mike thought I was a bit of a loser. Besides, I don't think it's right to discuss having sex with someone other than the person you're planning on having it with. I mean, Mike told me all about meeting his wife, and their wedding and their eventual split. But he certainly didn't tell me what they got up to in bed. God no. Could you imagine!

I think we were still talking at around six in the morning because I've vague memories of hearing birds singing, but maybe it was just my heart singing. Oh God, I know I sound naff but when I woke up this morning I was seriously happier than I've been in a long time.

We didn't discuss 'us' or the future or anything, and after coffee and heated croissants in bed, Mike drove me home. But I know there'll be no sinister mind games this time, which is great. I'm sick of playing games. They're horrible. And besides my heart doesn't want to play any more.

Mike's a fairly straightforward kind of guy. What you see is what you get. He's not a TV star or anything but he's certainly welcome to be the star of my show. He flies planes instead of sitting in them. And his life doesn't revolve around drinking champagne and chatting up every air hostess like he's God's gift to women. More importantly he's a genuine, down-to-earth guy. And I wouldn't trade his toenail for Adam and all his fame and money. Adam will never be happy. I know that now. No one woman will ever be enough for him. Unfortunately he'll always be searching for something he'll never find. Looking for love with all the wrong women in all the wrong places. One day he'll end up one hell of a lonely guy. I just hope he realises it before it's too late.

When Mike drops me home, I see the curtains in my mother's bedroom twitch. Unfortunately that means I can't indulge in one last lengthy snog with Mike. Oh well, hopefully there'll be plenty of time for that in the future. Mike gives me a peck on the cheek and says he'll call later. I practically skip from his car to the front door.

I push open the door and wander into the kitchen. I'm wearing an old tracksuit belonging to Mike. Well, I was *hardly* going to wear my uniform on my day off, was I? I amble into the kitchen and see a huge bunch of flowers on the kitchen table. Instinctively I know they're from Adam.

Straight into the bin they go.

I don't feel too guilty. Knowing my mother, she'll fish them out again later and put them in a vase.

There's also three brown envelopes on the table, addressed to me. Brown and boring. I tentatively open them. One by one. I've an uneasy feeling about the contents. And I'm right. Three rejections from three film companies. My heart plummets. I read the cold standard 'thanks but no thanks' messages over and over again and then tear the letters up. They follow the same fate as my flowers. Into the bin. Along with my shattered dreams.

Epilogue

One year later.

Welcome back folks. Nice to see you. Sorry you haven't heard from me in over a year but to be honest, life has been completely hectic. Still, that's no excuse for ignoring you so please forgive me, sit back, relax and I'll fill you in. This is my last flight by the way. Yes. You see I'm pregnant now so I can't fly for a while . . .

Oh God, don't look at me like that. Yes, I know, I know, I can hardly believe it either. I mean I always thought I'd remain childless forever. And would live alone, surrounded by a hundred cats, with all my married friends whispering about me in hushed pitying tones. But God obviously had other plans. It was quite a shock actually, a huge shock. But Mike and I got used to the idea very quickly. We're also engaged and planning to move in with each other straight away. Oh I know people usually get married first, then move in and eventually get pregnant but we did it arseways, according to Mum. Never mind, she'll get over it. In fact I kind of think she's looking forward to being a gran.

So anyway, I'd better fill you in on everything. Where was I when I left you? Oh, yes I remember now. I'd spent the night with Mike but nothing had happened. Absolutely nothing. In fact not a thing happened between us, in the physical sense at least, for about a month. Because I wanted to be absolutely sure I was in the right frame of mind for passion and romance. My heart was locked up in a box marked 'FRAGILE'. And I wasn't about to let it be manhandled again.

Mike was happy to go along with my wishes until, on one overnight in Paris, I sneaked into his room while the rest of the crew slept, and we made mad, passionate love until the sun rose and it was time to fly back to Dublin again. I knew then, that our relationship would probably last forever. We couldn't keep our hands off each other. Still can't. But it's not just about lust. No. We connect on a much deeper level. It's hard to explain but sometimes I can't really remember my life before Mike came into it.

Once my mother got over the absolute shock of my pregnancy (as far as she was concerned I was still single at the time!), she started tearing her hair out at the thought of yet another wedding. Ruth got married a couple of months ago of course, but there were tears and tantrums right up until the big day. Mum still swears it'll never work out, but Ruth seems very happy for the moment, so we'll just have to hope for the best.

Not wanting to put my mother through any more unnecessary stress though, myself and Mike have decided to get married in a registry office next year, with a quiet meal afterwards in a small, exclusive restaurant. Just immediate family and friends. No hassle. No unwanted relatives. No bickering about the guest list. I'm relieved to be honest. I don't fancy spending my wedding day being introduced to strange relatives. Also, because it's Mike's second wedding, he doesn't particularly want to go through the whole lavish ceremony bit again. You know, having to say 'I do' for the second time. In front of the same friends and family members.

We're going to wait until after Kiera is born of course. Yes, we're having a girl. Oh, you know, I *had* to find out. I was the type of child who couldn't even resist opening my presents before Christmas Day! How could I possibly not know whether I was expecting a boy or girl? I'm delighted about having a girl 'cos I was always a little worried about having a boy in case he wanted to be out kicking a ball all the time or something. Or pretending to be a soldier and wanting to punch me continuously. You see I just had one sister so I never really knew any boys. But to be honest, as long as the child is healthy, that's all that matters.

Mike reckons we're going to have at least two

or three more kids after Kiera. I'm saying nothing. But I have my reservations. It's all very well for him to want a large brood. But while he's still jetting around the world, I'm spending most of my days with my head stuck in the loo. Pregnancy is definitely not all it's cracked up to be. It's funny, they say you're supposed to look your sexiest while pregnant. But Jesus, I have to disagree. My face keeps breaking out in spots, and doing anything strenuous like applying fake tan or shaving my legs, leaves me exhausted. Most days I just want to collapse into bed. I wonder how those pop stars do it. You know the ones who perform in belly tops on stage right up to the week they give birth. God, I wish they'd let me in on their secret.

So what else is new? Well Debbie's fine, you'll be pleased to know. She's going out with a gorgeous toy-boy called Josh. Yes, sadly herself and Donald parted company in the end. The whole 'open relationship' thing they had going on didn't work out. And I can't say I was surprised when they finally called it a day. At least *she* called it a day after Josh gave her a final ultimatum.

As for Lydia, I never *did* find out what happened between herself and Adam on that date. But she started seeing a much older multimillionaire shortly after our flight to Milan. And she's been hounding me ever since to read her palm. She wants to know whether the new man will ever leave his wife for her.

Amy, would you believe, resigned from the company a while ago, and went to New Zealand to 'find herself'. She must still be looking because I haven't heard from her since. I hope she's having a nice time anyway. God, sometimes, when the Irish rain turns to sleet and the wind doesn't stop howling, I think I'd love to go and join her in a nice sunny climate. But obviously, I won't be going anywhere too far just at the moment.

Tim got engaged. To his next-door neighbour, would you believe? Apparently he'd been seeing her behind my back for ages. But I've absolutely no hard feelings towards him because life's too short. He's happy and I'm happy. With separate people. We'd never have made each other happy anyway so it's only right that we've both moved on. He's even sent me an invitation to 'the afters' of his wedding!

Incidentally, his sister Elaine spilt up from her husband and has moved in with a work colleague. So no surprises there really. Hmm. I wonder did Adam ever pop into her shop in the end?

Speaking of Adam, I'm sure you're wondering what on earth ever happened to him. Well I never did bump into him again, although I've bumped into many air hostesses who have, so to speak. But I did get my revenge. Sort of.

Remember that script I was writing? 'How could I forget?' says you. Well, let me tell you what happened there. OK, I got about another twenty

'Please-Fuck-Off' letters and then I kind of lost heart as well as my confidence. The script is now under my bed somewhere gathering dust. For a while I was so deflated I thought about giving up writing altogether. And then one day something extraordinary happened. Something that genuinely turned my life around.

You see, I met Sandy Elkinson at the airport. If you remember she was the babe that Adam was supposed to have gone out with. The Claudia Schiffer look-alike. Well one day, we were both hanging around the cabin crew rest room waiting for a delayed flight to come in. Naturally we got talking.

I felt I had to ask her about Adam. I still had so many unanswered questions floating about in my head. Had the pair of them *really* been going out together? How had it ended? Was it true that she was once the love of his life?

There was no harm in asking, was there?

Sandy, as it turned out, looked anything but pleased at the sound of Adam Kirrane's name. 'Oh I *never* went out with him,' she said hotly as she painted her nails a blood-red colour. 'And I sincerely hope that people don't think I did. Adam Kirrane used to ring me all the time but to be honest, I don't even know how he got hold of my number.'

'So it's not true?' I asked, trying not to pass out from the fumes of her nail polish. 'But why wouldn't you go on a date with him?'

'Why not?' Sandy threw back her blonde curls and laughed loudly. 'Good God girl, haven't you heard about that man's reputation?'

'Is he *that* bad?'

'Worse,' Sandy laughed even louder. 'Much worse. Do you know,' she lowered her voice, 'that they call Adam Kirrane the mile high guy?'

I was completely flabbergasted. Oh my God. Had Adam ever like, *done* it . . . I mean really . . . how *could* he? How could anyone? I mean there's barely room in those toilets for *one* person, never mind . . .

'It's an obsession of his apparently,' Sandy whispered in my ear. 'That's the reason why he's always chasing air hostesses.'

'Good God.'

'You just never know, do you?'

'And you're sure that's not just a rumour?' I raised an eyebrow. 'I mean rumours do tend to fly around this place, pardon the pun.'

'A friend of mine *saw* him. So I got it from the horse's mouth so to speak. She works for another airline and she spotted him following one of the cabin crew into the toilet. Your woman had a bit of a reputation too apparently, so they were well met. Anyway, they were caught coming out of the cubicle in the dead of the night when they thought nobody could see.'

'Jesus, she could have got sacked for that. How shocking!'

'Yes, I know. Honestly some people have no shame. Well my friend confronted the girl but she denied everything. She said she'd gone into the toilet to help him with some medication.'

'Medication?' I echoed incredulously.

'Hmm. Exactly.'

'So if he ever asks you out, I'd advise you to say no,' Sandy said. 'Forearmed is forewarned if you know what I mean.'

'Yes, er, thanks.'

Well it was bit late for me now, wasn't it?

'Some men!' Sandy shook her beautiful head. 'Honestly you could write a book about them. Someone *should* write a book about Adam Kirrane anyway.'

And then it suddenly struck me. A book! Oh my God. What a *fantastic* idea. A book about Adam and his antics. I could write such a book. I *would* write it. An entire book based on that cad. I'd call it *The Mile High Guy*, hahaha. It made so much sense, didn't it?

I'd never thought about writing a book before. Until now I just thought it was something other people did. And anyway I wouldn't have even known what to write about. Most books I read are about women whose husbands have affairs and leave. But being single, I don't think I could have written such a book. And of course when my script was so savagely rejected, I thought I'd never put pen to paper again. But this was different. They say you should write about what you know, and I knew about flying and I sure as hell knew about Adam. So why not write the story? Why not indeed?

So when I got home from my London flight that evening, all fired up, I sat down and wrote CHAPTER ONE. And the words just started to flow. Once I got into the story I could hardly stop. The book seemed to take on a life of its own and I got so involved that I'd dream about the characters at night, and talk about them as if they were real people. My parents grew more and more anxious. My mother said my behaviour wasn't normal and that all writers were obviously mad.

Mike, however, was very encouraging during the four months of endless writing. Sometimes I'd stay up the whole night at the computer, completely forgetting to go to bed. And I'd be so exhausted the next day I wouldn't be able to meet him. But he never complained. Not once. And he patiently read the manuscript as I wrote. And thankfully never asked who Adam was.

I wasn't sure if the novel was any good but was determined to keep writing until I reached THE END. I just had to see if I could do it. Once finished, I posted the script to several publishers. That was followed by a nerve-wracking fortnight peeping out at the postman through the crack of the bedroom curtains.

Nothing happened for ages, and I kind of gave up hope as the weeks passed but then one day the phone rang. An editor asked to see the rest of the manuscript. I'll never forget that moment. I suppose I never actually dreamed that anybody would ever take my writing seriously after the 'depressing script' disaster. But this time it wasn't a dream. And the woman at the other end of the phone wasn't joking.

Yes, the novel was finished, I told her. So she recommended I get myself an agent. Fast. Within one week I had a publishing contract.

Of course, as I said, I never did see Adam Kirrane again but his face continued to pop up regularly in the papers. It doesn't so much anymore. You see, they decided to scrap *DreamBoat* a few months ago, and the last I heard of him, he was on a TV morning show explaining how he was looking for his big movie break. Still waiting. For the right part to come along . . . mmm . . . the right part . . .

Funny that he should mention that.

Because I happen to know of a very big part coming up soon.

Yes. Let me explain. You're probably not even going to believe this 'cos I can hardly believe it myself, but about six weeks ago my new agent phoned out of the blue. Some Hollywood bigwigs had expressed an interest in making *The Mile High Guy* into a movie. Was I interested?

Interested? I nearly dropped the phone! Was I what?

It's hard to believe that just a year ago I was plodding along merrily on the road to nowhere. Now I'm engaged to a man I love. I'm expecting a baby, and my first book, which was published last week, hopped into the top five, which isn't bad going for a newcomer.

Yesterday my agent sold the film rights to *The Mile High Guy*. Not for millions or anything like that but for the same amount of money I'd get for almost two years working as an air hostess. It's not enough for me to retire for the rest of my life, but it isn't half bad either. Anyway I couldn't possibly retire now. A writer can't hide away and just write forever. Writers must write about real life. If you just hid away, then what on earth would you write about? But at least I've the option of working part-time.

But back to the script for a minute. I ended up selling the rights of *The Mile High Guy* under one condition. I wanted a say in who played the male lead. The film company thought it was a weird request, but I insisted. Take it or leave it, I told my agent to tell them. And I meant it.

They took it. Thanks be to God! I mean I was *very* worried that they'd just tell me to hump off. Like who was I to be making such diva-like requests? A first-time novelist should be punching the air with joy to have her book even considered, not making demands. But they obviously liked my story enough to comply. And filming starts some time next year in the States, apparently.

It hasn't quite sunk in yet of course. Everything's been happening so fast. But I'm dying to see who gets to play the lead. Maybe Matt Damon will consider. That'd be great, wouldn't it? I've always had a thing for Matt. I wouldn't mind Brad either, or Ed Burns. Johnny Depp might like to try out for the part too. Hell, why not cast them all!

But seriously though, I'm not that fussy. I suppose I'm just grateful that somebody liked the story enough to do something with it. So they can cast Popeye if they wish. Or Mr Bean. Or Ronald the Rat.

You see, I don't particularly care who plays it.

I couldn't give a hoot actually.

Just as long as it's not Adam Kirrane.

That's right.

Just as long as it's not him.

His time seems to be up unfortunately. I hope he enjoyed the ride. I know I did, although it was turbulent at times. Very turbulent. But the skies are clear now and the winds have eased. So listen up folks, the 'fasten seatbelt' sign has come on. We're heading towards the runway. Thank you for your company. And do please let me take this opportunity to wish you a safe onwards journey. We'll meet again soon . . .